FAMOUSLY
IN
L♥VE

EMILY EMMERSON

FAMOUSLY IN LOVE

PENGUIN BOOKS

PENGUIN BOOKS

UK | USA | Canada | Ireland | Australia
India | New Zealand | South Africa

Penguin Books is part of the Penguin Random House group of companies whose addresses can be found at global.penguinrandomhouse.com.

www.penguin.co.uk www.puffin.co.uk www.ladybird.co.uk

First published 2026

001

Text copyright © Emily Emmerson, 2026
Cover artwork copyright © Sofia Miller Salazar 2026

The moral right of the author and illustrator has been asserted

Penguin Random House values and supports copyright. Copyright fuels creativity, encourages diverse voices, promotes freedom of expression and supports a vibrant culture. Thank you for purchasing an authorized edition of this book and for respecting intellectual property laws by not reproducing, scanning or distributing any part of it by any means without permission. You are supporting authors and enabling Penguin Random House to continue to publish books for everyone. No part of this book may be used or reproduced in any manner for the purpose of training artificial intelligence technologies or systems. In accordance with Article 4(3) of the DSM Directive 2019/790, Penguin Random House expressly reserves this work from the text and data mining exception.

Set in 11/14.5pt Baskerville MT Pro
Typeset by Six Red Marbles UK, Thetford, Norfolk
Printed and bound in Great Britain by Clays Ltd, Elcograf S.p.A.

The authorized representative in the EEA is Penguin Random House Ireland, Morrison Chambers, 32 Nassau Street, Dublin D02 YH68

A CIP catalogue record for this book is available from the British Library

ISBN: 978-0-241-77753-4

All correspondence to:
Penguin Books
Penguin Random House Children's
One Embassy Gardens, 8 Viaduct Gardens, London SW11 7BW

Penguin Random House is committed to a sustainable future for our business, our readers and our planet. This book is made from Forest Stewardship Council® certified paper.

For Stephanie.
Without your musical recommendations,
this book would not exist.
Thank you.

And to JP, PB, PB, BB and BB (and S&S).

ONE

*They say a change is as good as a rest, well arrest me,
then, because I'm not ready for the changes you bring . . .*
– from 'Change It Up', by These Exiles

'JESSY, ALL YOU HAVE to do is message some guys,' begged my sister, hands clasped before her. 'I just need you to –'

'Yeaaaah, no!'

But my older twin wasn't one to take no for an answer –

'Ouch!' I rubbed my ear, the music that had been playing there suddenly absent.

Laura tossed my earbud on to her kitchen table. Her glasses had a few smudge marks in the corners, but it didn't stop the determination in her gaze coming through, flicking away only to look at our best friend. 'Anna's going to help, aren't you, Anna? Ann–'

But Anna was already on the move, her laptop bag, notes and her phone all balanced impossibly in one hand.

'Sorry, babe, I'd love to – but I've got to get going. My caseload at work has doubled since they fired Julian,' she said with a grimace, gold eyeliner making her dark eyes pop even as she rolled them. 'I just came by to grab the notes I left here last night.' The three of us had spent the evening working on various projects, before giving up and bingeing the latest season of *Temptation Hotel*.

'Anna, I am begging you –' started my sister.

'And your begging is noted.' Anna poured coffee into the flask Laura had just handed her. 'I'm sorry, really, but I have to go.'

I called after her. 'You're going to leave me here with her?'

'Duty calls!' our best friend said with a wry smile, grabbing her jacket, throwing it around her shoulders and pulling her box braids free. Her hair tumbled down to her waist, bouncing as she shot back, 'Besides, if I stay much longer, I'll get roped in too. Not a risk I'm willing to take.'

I laughed as Anna hugged my sister and threw me a wink as she shut the front door to the flat behind her.

'Escaping before you bully her into this nonsense too. She's got the right idea,' I teased.

'I'll get her in the end,' Laura said with a grin that was honestly a little frightening. Laura had a tendency to go a little crazy with her projects. 'I always do.'

She wasn't wrong. Laura, Anna and Jessy. Friends for practically forever – and Laura had been talking us into all sorts of things for just as long. She was the one who convinced us to get our noses pierced at fourteen. She was the one who'd found fake IDs to sneak us into the clubs. And now –

'Look, are you going to help me or not?' Laura narrowed her eyes as she placed the coffee she'd made for me on to the kitchen table.

I smiled sweetly. 'Absolutely not.'

I had to stand firm. Unlike the time we got our noses pierced, and the time we got fake IDs, I was not going to give in. She was just going to have to learn to take no for an answer.

Laura turned away from me, but only to grab a cloth and immediately wipe up the offending coffee ring on the table. 'What I don't understand, Jessy,' my delightful sister forced out through gritted teeth, pushing her glasses up her nose, 'is why you even bothered to come over here if all you're going to do is –'

The cheeky – 'You said it was an emergency!' I picked up my phone and thrust our chat into her face. 'The house burning down is an emergency! You're pregnant is an emergency. Wanting me to join your dating app? *Not* an emergency. Matter of fact, it's the exact opposite of an emergency. Can't believe I left a guy in my bed for –'

Laura's eyes widened as she threw the cloth down. 'A guy – a guy? I thought you'd sworn off dating?'

'Screwing is *not* dating, Laura.' I rolled my eyes. Trust her to focus on the least important part of my impassioned speech. 'The point is, I wouldn't have come over if I'd known you were just trying to stick your nose into my love life.'

We may not have been identical twins, and we were distinctly lacking in telepathic skills, but Laura knew me better than anyone. She knew I wasn't ready to start dating again. Casual hook-ups, sure – a girl has needs, after all. But anything more serious than that?

No chance.

I knew Laura's business venture, Butterflies, was important to her. I'd spent the last few years watching her put herself through coding classes by waiting tables, cycling takeaways across London's potholed streets, and working some shitty retail job – how she'd managed all three, I don't know. She'd finally quit all her jobs a few months ago and started her own company from this very kitchen table.

Coffee rings and all.

I was ridiculously proud of her, and ridiculously certain that she was going to become a billionaire before we were thirty – Laura was amazing like that. She'd inherited all the go-getter genes and left none for me.

I put my earbud back in, tapped my phone and pulled up my playlist again. The little nub of tension between my shoulder blades started to melt away as the latest track by These Exiles soared into my ears. I took another sip of my coffee and started to scroll the timeline. Now I knew Laura's emergency was just her meddling, I could go back to doomscrolling through reactions to yesterday's episode of *Temptation Hotel* – the only romance in my near future.

Or at least, I would have, if Laura hadn't chosen that moment to interrupt my scrolling with, 'Considering I'm facing bankruptcy, the least you could do right now is actually listen to me.'

I almost spat out my coffee.

'What? You said you wanted me to chat with random guys on your app – you didn't say anything about money troubles.' Panic raced through me, the taste of coffee bitter on my tongue.

Laura bit her lip, guilt written across her face. 'Fine, not exactly bankruptcy – but it could happen if the investors pull out and the app dies. This is serious, Jessy. This is real life – adult life. If things don't go well . . . they go badly.'

A few minutes' difference, that was all it was – but the gap between our births had always been big enough for Laura to act like we were years apart.

She sighed, her top riding up a little at the sides and her suit trousers bunching around her hips as she pulled a vape out of her pocket. She took a long look at it and regretfully stuffed it away again. 'God, I could really do with a smoke right now.'

That was when I knew something was really wrong. Laura had quit smoking last year, and, damn, hadn't Anna and I heard about it. She didn't turn to it unless she was really stressed, and I couldn't remember the last time she'd had to resort to a nicotine hit.

Shit.

I paused the music and pulled my earbuds out. My stomach twisted as I pointed at her to sit. 'Talk to me. Now.'

'These investors, they're great, but ... but that review meeting I practised with you for? It didn't go well.' She pushed her glasses up her nose again. 'Like, at all. They're going to pull out by the end of the summer. I'll have nothing, Jessy. Butterflies will just ... die.' Laura's voice cracked. Heartbreak was written all over her face.

I hadn't seen Laura this vulnerable in years.

It didn't seem possible. Laura had dedicated everything she had to Butterflies. Hell, she was still living in this dump – mould on the walls, holey carpet, creepy landlord and all – because she'd found the cheapest, dingiest place to live and put every other penny into her app.

'I don't get it,' I said, managing to find my voice in the silence as I pulled at my cardigan, tugging it closer around me. 'I thought the app had thousands of downloads. Loads of people are using it.' She'd told me so herself when we'd practised her review pitch – I'd colour-coded the pie chart.

'Loads of *guys* are using it,' my twin said with a sigh, worry flickering over her face. 'Tons of men are on there, and they're all waiting around because . . . Look, research shows that, on average, there's a seventy–thirty men-to-women split on dating apps –'

I loved my sister, but it was difficult for my eyes not to glaze over when she started quoting figures. Hyper-fixating on numbers was her thing, not mine – and I was the one in finance. 'Can we skip the statistics?' I pleaded. 'I spend all week looking at spreadsheets that I barely understand.'

But Laura was already on a roll: '– need an eleven per cent increase in female-instigated –'

'Sis. Seriously?' I could feel a headache building.

'I'm just saying: men have a seventy-five per cent chance of meeting someone on a dating app, while women only do so sixty-six per cent of the time –'

'Laura!' I finally snapped. It couldn't be healthy having all these stats running through her head.

My twin glared at the interruption, but took a deep breath before admitting, 'There aren't enough women on the app.'

Well, I couldn't say I was surprised. Dating wasn't exactly a picnic, no matter how you went about it. Who *wasn't* sick of being chatted up by men with commitment issues, mummy issues, or – my personal fave – daddy issues?

'I just need you to use this profile –'

'Will me joining even make a difference?!' I asked desperately, pushing aside the nausea that rose at the mere thought of dating again. 'It sounds like you need a lot more than one or two extra women to –'

'I've put the word out: asked all my old work friends, everyone I can find from back home. I even dropped a message in the old school group chat,' Laura rushed, words pouring from her mouth like she'd anticipated my every argument.

'There's literally no one I've ever known that I haven't reached out to at this point. If Mum was still – I'd be begging her too. Please, Jessy. I wouldn't be asking if it wasn't important. You know I never ask much from you!'

I hesitated as I pushed a curl of hair behind my ear.

It was true. Laura was always so self-sufficient, never needing anything from me. In fact, it was usually the opposite; she always gave to me. Gave up those expensive piano lessons so I could keep going. Gave up hockey because our mum couldn't afford equipment for both of us. Looking at her now brought back memories of everything she had given up for me.

Sometimes, looking at Laura in distress was like staring into a cracked mirror. I had the darker hair, she wore glasses – but it was the same eyes, the same chin.

'You know I'm not dating. Not after . . .' It cost me, to even begin to say those words. I'd needed time to process the colossal fuckup that was my last relationship, and, truthfully, I'd probably been ignoring it more than actually trying to move on.

Who doesn't want to just stuff down all their emotions and pretend the bad shit never happened?

A shadow flickered across Laura's face. 'You don't talk about him. I . . . I haven't known how to ask.'

Pain roared through my chest as though it had happened just yesterday. The bags packed by the door. The note I was supposed to find, not read with him standing there.

For a moment I was dizzy, my head spinning, the nausea that had roiled in my stomach returning in a flash. As though I could never think of dating without thinking of Ross and all the promises he broke.

I tried to reassure her with a smile. 'I don't want to talk about him, anyway. I know you'd listen if I wanted to.' I really was trying.

Laura was staring at me, concern painted across her face.

'I'm *fine*.' Even I wasn't convinced – but I was not going to be unpacking my relationship trauma this morning.

'You're better than fine. You were too good for that –'

'Laura, I said I don't want to talk about it,' I repeated more forcefully, pulling a hairband from my wrist and tying up my hair.

'I'm not asking you to date these men, Jessy,' Laura said quietly, after a pause. 'I just need you to talk to them a little. I've already created your profile; all you have to do –' She broke off.

Rain was starting to patter against the cracked windowpanes of Laura's kitchen, and in the growing gloom – honestly, London in summer was so grey sometimes – my twin looked at me before starting again. 'I . . . I really need Butterflies to work.'

I took a long, deep breath.

I was going to regret this. I knew it deep down, and I was going to be mad about it. Future Jessy was standing on the window ledge, banging on the glass, shouting, 'Don't do it!'

But it was too late. She wasn't here, and Present Jessy could see that her sister needed her – for once.

'How much replying are we talking about exactly? Because I am *not – ouch –* shit, my coffee!'

Laura had launched herself at me, pulling me into a firm hug. 'Thank you.'

I hugged her back, tightly.

'Don't thank me. Just tell your investors to give you

more time,' I said, as Laura finally loosened her grip and sat back down.

'Thank you,' repeated my twin. 'Seriously, Jessy. You only have to message each guy once a day. That'll count as engagement. There are even conversation starters on there that you can use; you don't have to think about it.' She looked at me with a hesitant smile. 'But you never know . . . you might meet someone you actually like.'

Right. I very much doubted that.

TWO

*It's a trap and I know it, but I step right in,
knowing that a trap with you could become a
home if you would only stay . . .*
– from 'Stay', by These Exiles

'LOOK, PATRICK,' DEREK BEGAN.

'No,' I said firmly.

I sounded calm – far calmer than I felt, anyway. In reality my head was pounding, and this conversation was not helping.

Derek fixed a strained smile on his face. 'All I'm saying,' he went on, in that tone that he *thinks* is really patient, but which I know means he's at the absolute end of his tether, 'is that you have to pick a celebrity to date. Anyone you want, Patrick. But we need some goodwill right now.'

'Come on, Derek,' Wes said lazily. My bandmate and childhood best friend was playing a scale on the electric keyboard as he leaned against the recording studio wall. His messy blond hair fell over his eyes, and he flicked it back with a twitch of his head. 'We've just got back from tour. Surely the powers that be can give us a bit of a break before trotting us back out again –'

'The problem, boys, is that no one is talking about the completely sold-out international tour – or the fact you broke records with merch sales. The only thing anyone is talking about is how the North American leg ended in disaster.' Derek's eyes were wide as he passed around the coffees he'd just grabbed us from the place opposite the studio. The canteen here was awful, and if there was one thing our publicist was good at it was supplying us with coffee. Especially when he wanted something from us.

Which was every time we saw him.

I had only seen Derek this stressed a handful of times – and I couldn't help but feel guilty as I spotted his tika was smudged. He'd only been to temple for puja that morning. We might be a rowdy bunch, but we weren't divas. Normally we had no problem doing all the shit the label asked us to do. Even when it seemed completely pointless.

Like right now.

'You really think Patrick dating a celebrity again is a good idea?' Wes shot a look over at me. 'The first time didn't exactly go . . . well.'

'Didn't go well' was an understatement. Derek had given me a similar spiel about needing to date someone in the public eye last year and, like an idiot, I'd gone along with it. He'd introduced me to Celine Dellacorte, an up-and-coming actress. Young, hot and talented – she was perfect. And she just happened to be signed to the same PR agency . . .

But that had ended in disaster, and I wasn't about to get burned again.

I sighed and leaned back against the wall. The plan had been to come in and sort through the kit. Too many cables, mixing boards and mics had been dumped into random boxes at the end of our sell-out performance in New York. Wes had agreed to come in and help, along with Ben and Matt – our other bandmates. Only Matt had never turned up, and now Derek had found out the rest of us were here and derailed us with his latest scheme.

'Listen, after *someone's* little mistake,' Derek said, in what he clearly thought was a delicate tone, 'the whole band needs to pull their weight!'

I tried not to wince. Someone's *little mistake*.

If you could call a DUI that.

We'd been celebrating the end of the North American leg of the tour, still in New York, and Ben had insisted on driving us to some 'exclusive' club that he'd been raving about when he slammed into the back of a car. Thankfully the elderly woman driving the other vehicle was fine, but with three points already on his licence Ben would have been well and truly screwed once the police arrived. Which is why I'd offered to pretend I'd been the one behind the wheel. Ben and I often got told we looked like brothers; it had seemed like an easy fix.

Only, I'd done a bit of celebrating of my own that night already.

It was just a drink. Just one. But it always was, wasn't it? That was what people said when they were caught drink-driving. Just one blip over the limit, but it was enough.

I woke up the next day to my mugshot all over the tabloids, and all the work spent cleaning up my image for the last two years had been wiped out overnight.

I could admit that my first few years of fame weren't my proudest. I was a wreck back then: throwing parties that left hotel rooms trashed, going from one model to another – women and cars. I'd really tested the limits of Derek's powers. But I'd cleaned up my act, and I couldn't remember the last time my face had been plastered all over the internet.

Until now.

'We're topping the charts,' I tried again. 'We went platinum last month, and we're in the middle of an international tour. Isn't that enough?'

'No,' said Derek simply, pushing back his dark hair. 'It's good, but it's not enough. When people search These Exiles, the first article that surfaces is still the arrest. We need to kill that story, and quick. We can't go into the next leg of your tour with this hanging over us. Besides, you're not the only one having to make sacrifices. Ben is hosting a series of charity events; Matt, wherever the hell he is, is going to be on that new celebrity reality show –'

'God help him,' I couldn't help but mumble.

'– and Wes will be shipping out with the UN tomorrow for one of their celebrity missions. You got off lightly,' Derek said pointedly. 'You get to date a celebrity of your choosing. Consider yourself lucky you're not being bundled off to rehab.'

'This is not what we signed up for, Patrick,' Ben muttered from the side of the room. He was sitting on the floor, legs kicked out, eyes not leaving his phone. The dark tattoo that spiralled down his neck was just visible, and the bags under his eyes suggested it had been another heavy night. 'None of this is.'

He was right.

Four lads from a small town with no regular buses and a sports centre that spent more time closed than open – we hadn't expected any of this.

Starting the band had just been for a laugh – something to do. We all loved music, we all were bored out of our minds, and college was just an excuse to see our friends. But then things changed overnight and, before we knew it, we had a record deal, and our first album was coming out just as we should have been starting uni.

That was four years ago now. I hadn't taken a full week off in . . . I couldn't remember how long. My neck ached, my DMs were apparently full of scams – not that I'd been allowed to read them for years now – and I was having to wear more and more ridiculous hats to stop being recognized.

I dropped my gaze, reaching into a box for a length of cable that no one had bothered to wrap properly, and started pulling it into loops.

'Think of the next album deal. You think the record label is going to let you negotiate better terms after a DUI?'

The unfairness of it was gnawing at me. I glanced up at Ben. His eyes were filled with guilt.

I couldn't hold it against him. I'd hardly been picture perfect, and he hadn't forced me to take the blame.

The door opened. Matt wandered in, breaking the tension.

'New idea?' I asked. *That's it. Turn the conversation back to music.*

'Bad idea,' Matt said with a sigh, his dark eyes and gangly frame marking him out as the heartthrob of the group – much to his discomfort. 'Again. What does he want?' He flopped on to the beanbag next to me.

One thing I appreciated about Matt: he was at home everywhere he went.

'Derek's giving us our penance – our "make the world love us again" assignments,' Wes said with a grin. 'And Patrick gets to date a celebrity.'

'Look,' Derek wheedled, coming over to me and kneeling down like I was a toddler. 'I know last time was a bit of a –'

'Shitshow,' I snapped.

'The record label needs to be able to *sell* you,' Derek said. 'And after that drink-driving disaster, and, let's be fair, your less than stellar record –'

'It's been years,' I bit out, not looking at him. I mean, what did they expect would happen when they gave a teenager millions to do with as he liked? Safe investments?

'– and you're more marketable if your lead singer is in a romantic relationship with another celebrity. Have you ever heard of Brangelina? Kayne and Kim? J-Lo and Ben, both times?'

'I do not –' I said firmly, rolling my eyes at Derek's painfully outdated celeb gossip – 'want to be Brangelina.' A shudder went through me at the thought.

'If These Exiles can survive this, we can look at truly global advertising,' wheedled Derek, moving away from me and heading over to Matt, who glared stonily at him from his keyboard. 'Hot sauces, fancy undrinkable gins, fragrances, the works!'

Wes snorted. 'I don't want to be the face of a fragrance!'

'No one wants you to be the face of a fragrance,' Ben shot over from his corner.

I let them bicker as I picked up my coffee. When I lifted the lid, I could smell the grapefruit notes.

This is what I need.

'– don't want to fall into the same trap as Patrick –'

I couldn't tell who'd said it. It didn't really matter. They were right, whichever one of them it was.

'Celine was Satan's mistress,' Ben was saying darkly, 'and you know it.'

She was a mistake. But like the very best of mistakes, I hadn't known it at the time. A gorgeous blonde with a smile that lit up rooms and a talent that lit up the box office. I'd bumped into her at one of those pre-award parties ... or at least that was the story we'd spun for the blogs. Our first encounter might actually have been at our agency's office, but the story had become a little truer when we'd woken up in bed together the morning after a night out.

That was how it started: friends with benefits. Then, just when I'd realized perhaps there was more – at least on my side – she ran off with her co-star. I didn't know what hurt more. Her leaving me, or the cliché of it all.

I couldn't do that again.

Derek was smiling uneasily. 'Look, Patrick, it's your name we've got to rehabilitate.'

I swore under my breath.

'You're the frontman. The lead singer. You're the most visible member of the group,' he said in a rush. 'You're the one everyone remembers –'

It didn't help that I was our main songwriter. It was my words we sang up there every night on tour, my words the crowds sang back to us – some fans had even tattooed my lyrics on to their bodies, which made me slightly uncomfortable.

I thought they were good, obviously ... but even I hadn't imprinted any of them permanently on my skin.

Besides, no good lyrics had come to me in weeks. I wasn't panicking about it – just quietly anxious. Because there was always another album needed. Another chart-topper the label was waiting for.

'Fine,' said Derek with his hands up. 'What about a compromise?'

I looked up. Derek had that pleading look on his face. *Hell.* 'What kind of compromise?'

Whatever it was, it couldn't be worse than another Celine situation.

'Hokapp,' Derek said triumphantly.

There was only one appropriate response to that. I swore.

'What, the celeb-only dating app?' Ben said, looking up from his phone for the first time, curiosity tinging his voice.

Trust Ben to only be interested when a dating app was mentioned. This was much more his playing field than mine.

'Look, you'll join Hokapp, you'll find someone with a great profile, huge social media following – but it will be organic, you can pick the person you like the most. Hell, it doesn't have to last long – just till the Songwriter Awards, that's nice and public, and it's only next month. All you have to do is sign up.' Derek made it sound so easy. 'Come on, Patrick. I don't think they're asking for much – they *had* been talking about hosting auditions for this new woman of yours. I know you wouldn't like that.'

My stomach rolled. I really wouldn't. 'So, I just sign up to a dating app? That's it?'

'That's it!' Derek said with a desperate smile. 'Just think about it.'

I looked around the recording studio. The nice, easy day I'd planned to have sorting our equipment had vanished into thin air.

TIME PASSES STRANGELY IN a recording studio. With no windows, no sense of the sun moving, it's easy to forget there even is an outside world – especially with Matt and Wes experimenting with some new melodies. Like this, I could forget all about Hurricane Derek and his demands.

'And here, the bridge – Ben, will you cut it out?'

'Sorry,' Ben muttered, looking not even slightly apologetic. 'It's my sister. She's complaining about this new guy she's started seeing and wants me to hook her up with –'

'Absolutely not,' Matt said with a grin. 'Not going to date your sis–'

'Do you think I'd let you?' Ben was always so easy to get a rise out of. 'She's too good for you, and I already spend way too much time with you idiots.'

'What happened? I thought she was excited about this one,' I asked distractedly. Emma had joined us for our last show in New York and flown back with us. She'd spent the whole time messaging back and forth with some guy.

'Yeah, but she says he's started flaking on her ever since they came off the app –' Ben broke off abruptly and I looked up – to see him grinning at me.

'What?' Nothing good ever came from a smile like that.

'*Butterflies*. That's it – that's how you get out of this relationship crap with the label.' Ben carried on looking at me, phone forgotten. 'Emma met this guy on Butterflies. It's a dating app one of her old friends launched recently. She begged Emma to join, said she wasn't getting enough engagement or something. I'd join it too, but Emma said she'd throw up if she ever saw my profile on a dating app.' He laughed. 'It's a new app, anyway – you probably won't even get a match.'

Wes glanced at me curiously. 'It's actually not a bad idea.'

I paused, a cable half-twisted in my fingers. He was right.

'Well, I guess I didn't promise Derek I'd use Hokapp, did I? If he asks, I could always say I'd joined *an* app.'

Ben slung his arm around my shoulder. 'Don't worry, Paddy boy, no one's even heard of it. It's the perfect app for you.'

'If Emma's thinking about ending it with that guy, think you could put in a good word for me?'

Ben turned to glare at Wes, who had a smirk teasing at his lips. 'The hell I will –'

The argument – well, bickering really – echoed about me. I wasn't paying attention. Ben's words were ricocheting around my head. I pulled out my phone and tapped in a quick search. It took a couple of scrolls on the app store to even find what I was looking for. Perfect.

There – Butterflies. A nondescript icon that looked out of place next to the slickly professional logos surrounding it. *Thank you, Ben.* Before I knew it, I had the app downloaded and was faced with an empty profile.

Right, then: no mention of the band, just generic statements that could apply to anyone.

I like . . . music. I like cats. I like coffee. All true.

Ben glanced over my shoulder. 'Don't forget to choose old or bad quality photos of you. Last thing you need is some fan stalking you on there.'

Where was that shot that Wes took of me in Saint-Tropez last year? The white glare of the sun had left exposure spots all over the image – conveniently placed over half my face. You could barely tell it was me. And I'm sure I had a pic somewhere of the time I'd let my beard grow out of control, before Derek had insisted I go back to being clean-shaven for the tour. And what about that one of the four of us at the top of the Empire State Building, backs to the camera . . . there we go. Upload photos . . . crop carefully . . .

There. *Profile complete.*

I scrolled through it one last time. Boring, sparse and not the least bit interesting. No one in their right mind would bother matching with me.

This was fine. I could do this. All I had to do was put up with a few conversations that would always fizzle into nothing. After a couple months, I'd feed the label some bullshit about not finding any connections, which would be true. After a couple months they'd forget about it all, and I wouldn't have to endure the embarrassment of another failed fake relationship.

Most importantly, Derek would be happy and keep bringing me coffee.

DAY HAD SLIPPED INTO night while I was in the studio, which had saved me hiding my face as I walked round the corner to my flat. It wasn't quite a home yet, but it was better than nothing.

Pizza, then bed. Tomorrow I could wake up with absolutely nothing to do for weeks, a blessed relief after –

Ping!

I checked my phone.

Butterflies: You and Jessy just matched!

THREE

Do you think in every world we're dancing like this, laughing like this, do you think in every universe I found you like this?
– from 'Serendipity', by These Exiles

Monday

I WAS GOING TO kill Laura.

Of all the ways to be spending my days, I never thought I'd find myself here, swiping endlessly and responding to painfully dull conversation openers. I'd finally got fed up yesterday and turned off the notifications. Guilt had gnawed at me all day, though, and now I was sat watching the timer run out on my latest match. I couldn't believe I was going to have to start the conversation. Again.

Fuck it.

> **Jessy**
> How's your day going?

I hit send. Well, it was pretty innocuous. But it was a message – Laura had never said how long they had to be.

Ping.

> **Paddy**
> Good, thanks. You?

Not even a minute had gone by. Keen much? I couldn't even remember which of the countless profiles I'd swiped on this was. I switched tabs and went to scroll through his –

'Jessica!'

The shout was so loud I almost dropped my phone on to my desk. I looked up as my manager glared at me over my desktop.

'It's Jessy, Karun.' Seriously, how hard was it to remember I preferred Jessy?

'Is the report ready?'

I smiled sweetly. 'Yes, it's in your inbox.' Which he'd know if he spent time actually at his desk and not monitoring us like a prison warden.

Karun sniffed. 'Good. And that pivot table is needed by Wednesday. If you need help with it –'

'I'll be fine, thanks,' I said, looking back at my screen as though I had very important emails to address. Truth was my display had turned itself off – I'd left it inactive too long.

'No phones at the desk,' he said curtly before striding away.

I gave the mouse a wiggle and watched the screen come to life.

The day dragged.

I'd been so excited to get this grad job. Proper employment, with a proper salary. I could afford not to depend upon Laura any more; I'd moved out of the flat and got my own room.

Yes, it was still a houseshare, but at least it was in a nicer part of the city – which had felt like freedom . . .

Now it just felt like a collar, squeezing tightly round my neck.

It was only hours later, when I'd dropped, exhausted, on to my bed, that I realized I'd never replied to Paddy.

Shit. And I'd promised Laura. I groaned before flipping myself over to grab my phone.

> **Paddy**
> Good, thanks. You?

I rolled my eyes. Honestly – was this the kind of scintillating conversation I had to look forward to?

Well, the world wasn't going to end if I didn't answer today. That could be Future Jessy's problem.

Tuesday

> **Jessy**
> Sorry, busy day yesterday

> **Paddy**
> No worries

Wednesday

> **Jessy**
> So, how'd you like your coffee?

It was weird. I'd tapped on one of the pre-written questions the app gave me – dull but serviceable – after his non-reply, but nothing.

I looked down at the message again. *Read*. But no reply.

Seriously weird. He'd taken half a second to reply to my first message and now, nothing?

I was not going to double message. The point was just to engage with the matches, not actually care about them.

I closed the app.

Thursday

> **Paddy**
> The best coffee is that made by someone else

> **Jessy**
> Strong disagree. No one makes coffee like me, except Maria

> **Paddy**
> Maria?

Jessy
The owner of my favourite café and all round goddess. Life isn't worth living without Maria 😍

Paddy
Well damn. Maybe I should be in Maria's DMs. Is she single?

Jessy
Wow, can't believe I've been outdone by an Italian grandmother

Paddy
Wait

Paddy
What?

Jessy
She's hot though, if you're into that

Paddy
I feel set up

> **Paddy**
> I guess I'll just have to have some of your famous coffee then

I looked down at the message. We'd been texting back and forth all morning and I found my lips turning up into a smile with every one.

This had always been my favourite part of dating. The attention . . .

'Eyes on the computer, Jessica,' barked Karun from across the open-plan office, throwing me a glare. 'Here at GSR Financials we value results.'

'It's Jessy,' I muttered as I glanced back at the numbers, putting my earbuds in. The opening tune to 'Honey and Spice' came on and I relaxed. Patrick Tetlow, lyricist extraordinaire – now that was a man who had a way with words.

I spent the next few hours unpicking data from a spreadsheet. I knew I should be grateful – there were thousands of people desperate for a job like this.

Stability. Reliability. A pension that meant I would only have to work until I was seventy . . .

I *should* be grateful.

The sacrifices Laura had made, all those hours I'd spent studying, the money we'd poured into my degree to get me here – and it was just a little bit . . . shit.

My phone pinged again and after checking that Karun was chewing out someone else, I glanced down.

> **Paddy**
> Sorry if that was a bit much. I swear I wasn't looking for an invite

> **Jessy**
> No, no, I just got yelled at for not focusing on work

> **Paddy**
> That arsehole boss still on your case?

> **Jessy**
> Yup. Hard to believe I only have, what, sixty years of this left?

Cathy opposite me gave me a disapproving frown as she cleared her throat. Busy cow.

'Just thinking of how best to colour-code this spreadsheet,' I lied with a bright smile.

Cathy snorted. 'Sure.'

> **Paddy**
> Is this the time to tell you that I've got really into creative tie-dyeing?

'No phones at the –'

'Just turning it off, Karun,' I said hurriedly, throwing it into my desk drawer as he loomed over me. 'What do you think, Cathy, maroon or scarlet for negative numbers?'

Cathy's sniff echoed across the desk as Karun made a pompous speech about taking my job seriously before wandering off to print something no one would look at. Only when I was certain he'd gone – pushing down the prickles of worry that I would definitely be put on warning if I was spotted – did I pull out my phone and look at Paddy's last message again.

> **Paddy**
> Is this the time to tell you that I've got really into creative tie-dyeing?

I couldn't for the life of me figure this guy out. He texted at all times of the day. He was funny, seemed normal, and hadn't asked for any nudes – yet. He started hobbies like he had all the time in the world – but he didn't really seem like he was down on his luck. I was tempted to ask what kind of job he had, but I wasn't sure I wanted to open that can of worms. Our conversations so far had been pretty superficial, and that suited me fine.

> **Jessy**
> How did we go from you angling to come over to tie-dyeing?

> **Paddy**
> ...

Still typing?

> **Paddy**
> Look, I feel like I should be honest with you. You're gorgeous and you seem cool, but I'm not really looking for a relationship right now

Huh.

And the proverbial balloon burst. Guess he wasn't all that different to every other guy on here. As I looked at his message, a stray thought popped into my head.

Laura hadn't intended Butterflies for hook-ups, but honestly, if he could scratch that itch . . .

He'd seemed nice enough. And he didn't want anything serious.

I messaged back quickly, before I could change my mind.

> **Jessy**
> So you're just looking for a hook-up? I could get down with that

I deserved it, I told myself. A meaningless one-night stand with a guy that I wasn't repulsed by. No big deal.

Friday

My phone vibrated against my chest. I'd fallen asleep last night while scrolling the timeline.

Through sleep still gathered in my eyes, I blinked blearily at my phone. The little Butterflies icon sat there, informing me of a chat notification. My heart skipped as I swiped through the app and opened my list of chats.

And groaned . . . I had neglected eight chats. I'd accepted every match the app had offered me – Laura's guilt trip was working perfectly – but I'd been so distracted by Paddy that I'd already lost two matches for not responding quickly enough.

Laura was not going to be happy.

Pushing myself up in bed and wincing slightly at the brilliant summer sun already pouring through my lacklustre curtains, I opened each of the other chats to see what we were working with.

I winced, the prickle of distaste bitter in my mouth. Dear God, no wonder half of this city was single. Talking to these men was worse than watching paint dry.

After shooting off the most basic reply to each of them – and in Tom's case a quick unmatch, because even if I was down to fuck, I certainly wouldn't with someone who couldn't at least write in full sentences – my shoulders loosened as I opened my most recent chat.

And . . . he hadn't replied. My last message glared back at me brightly on the screen.

> **Jessy**
> So you're just looking for a hook-up? I could get down with that

That was fine. Maybe he'd been distracted before he could respond.

Or maybe this was just a good old-fashioned case of ghosting. Embarrassment threatened to heat my face at the thought.

Groaning as I pulled myself out of bed, I waited for my housemate to be done in the bathroom, then stood in the barely warm shower.

Once I was out, I got another inane message from a guy whose profile picture was him topless, wearing sunglasses, playing golf. I rolled my eyes. Of course it was.

But I had been neglecting my other matches, and I felt guilty – Laura had worked so hard on this app, and she needed my support. So I got over the cringe and chatted with the wannabe golfer as I popped my earrings in and wondered if I had time for breakfast before heading out.

*

Saturday

The Butterflies ping filled the small room, and I looked to see if it was – no. Still not Paddy.

'And who, precisely,' my sister asked sweetly, 'is messaging you?'

I almost dropped my phone on my pizza – a terrible waste of both food and phone. 'No one.' No one interesting, anyway.

'It's not no one!' Laura paused the TV and stared through her glasses, half incredulous, half delighted. 'Who is it?'

'Just press *play*. I've been looking forward to watching the new episode all day.'

That was true. The latest episode of *Temptation Hotel* had dropped, and Laura and I had a long-standing tradition of watching it together – Anna too, but her appearances had been growing rarer and rarer lately, now work was so busy. It was the kind of reality TV that left you a little dumber than when you first started it, but there was something so addictive about watching other people's love lives implode.

But Laura was like a hound. 'I'm not hitting play until you tell me who –'

Ping. Ping. Ping.

My twin had the biggest grin on her face. 'You're messaging a guy on Butterflies, aren't you?'

'No.'

It was a stupid lie.

'You know I picked out that notification tone, don't you?' she said lightly.

Duh, how could you forget that little detail, Jessy?

Grabbing another slice of the pizza that was our monthly

pay-day treat, Laura took a bite before asking, 'So, what's his name?'

'There is no *him* – it's not – there's no one.' MI5 would not be calling for my skills any time soon. The funny thing was, there really was no one. 'You asked me to message people; I'm messaging people,' I said firmly, grabbing the remote and hitting play myself. 'You ask for a favour and then you interrogate me!'

'It's not an interrogation, it's just a question.' Laura rolled her eyes. 'You know what, fine. Keep your secrets. Besides, I could just download the data from my servers.' She waggled her eyebrows, but I knew she was just joking. She would never invade my privacy like that.

Maybe it was a consequence of being a twin and never really having things to yourself. We'd shared everything as kids – toys, clothes, even friends – and it could be stifling sometimes. We'd learnt to give each other space as we grew up. Mostly.

'OK, now let's see if Maddie's finally going to tell Harry how she feels – I've been avoiding spoilers all day!' Laura grinned, pushing her glasses up her nose.

I snuggled in, grateful for the chance to think about someone else's trainwreck of a love life for the next hour.

Sunday

I stretched out my legs in Maria's Cafe, my favourite blend in my blue coffee cup and These Exiles blaring over the speakers. I'd introduced Maria to the band last year and she'd taken to playing their songs whenever I came in, a gesture so sweet and motherly it'd brought tears to my ears the first time I'd realized.

I sipped the peppery fermented coffee and smiled. I wasn't lying when I'd said Maria made the best coffee. The woman was heaven-sent.

I spent the next few hours working on a presentation for Karun. It wasn't that I was behind on work – but I hadn't exactly been paying attention much during the week. I was only broken out of my focus when I looked down at my coffee cup and found it empty.

Rising to join the queue behind some guy in an awful tie-dye T-shirt, I glanced at my phone as I waited for him to finish ordering.

More messages on Butterflies. None of them from Paddy.

This was ridiculous. Rejection wasn't a big deal. OK, so I'd clearly got the vibe wrong – but still, ignoring me was just rude. I wasn't ever going to date this guy, but I had a duty to all womankind to improve this man before I dropped him back in the sea.

I steeled myself and tapped out a short message into the chat as the guy in front stepped to the left, waiting for his order to be made.

Maria's wrinkled face broke out into a smile when she saw me, her glasses on a gold chain glittering in the afternoon sun. 'Jessy! Same again?'

'Thanks, Maria,' I said gratefully as I hit send. Satisfied, I put my phone away.

> **Jessy**
> Ghosting is a really shitty move

Ping.

Weird. That sounded exactly like the Butterflies chime. Dread pooled in my stomach – what if one of my awful matches was in here? Oh, please not the golf guy . . .

For the first time, I looked around the cafe properly. My eyes found themselves drawn to my left, where that guy was standing –

There was something familiar about him, but I couldn't get a good look without seeming like a weirdo. He had a cap pulled down low, hiding most of his face, attention downcast as he flicked through something on his phone.

I really hoped this wasn't Dan . . . or Jason . . . or . . . shit, if it was golfing bro I was going to have to throw myself out the window.

'Order for Paddy – grapefruit cold brew?' Maria called.

My jaw dropped.

It couldn't be.

I felt my heartbeat pick up. There had to be more than one Paddy in a city this big. It had to be a fairly common name, right . . . right?

My thoughts spiralled as I watched him look up to grab his coffee. As the shop lights revealed more of his face, my world spun again.

Patrick Tetlow.

The lead singer of These Exiles and last year's world's sexiest man was ordering coffee in my favourite place.

Patrick Tetlow was standing less than a metre away from me and – fuck – he was hot. Even hotter in real life. My stomach churned. Seriously, social media pics did not do him justice. Laura and Anna were going to freak out when I told them. How long had we complained about never spotting any celebs?

I tried to get my facial expressions back under control and behave like an actual human woman.

Be normal, you weirdo. No one else in the coffee shop seemed to be affected by the presence of a bona fide celebrity, and I wasn't going to be the one to embarrass myself.

I tried to act nonchalant as *the* Patrick Tetlow turned back around, heading towards the exit as he tapped on his phone.

Ping.

Almost without thinking, I pulled out my phone and unlocked it.

> **Paddy**
> Sorry, things are just a bit complicated right now

Yeah, right – I could not give less of a fuck about whatever excuses Paddy wanted to give when the man of my dreams was about to walk past me.

I willed my eyes to look literally anywhere else, but as the singer made his way out of Maria's, I couldn't help but glance back. After all, when would I ever have the chance to see him again?

Damn. Even his back was beautiful.

Before I could look away again, our eyes met.

Confirmed. Best moment of my life.

A flush of heat ran through me as he held eye contact, and I swore I saw some of that heat reflecting back at me. His eyes darted around my face before dipping down my body, taking me in fully. I would have been flattered if the look of interest hadn't morphed into something a lot less pleasant all of a sudden.

'Jessy?'

Jessy? How the hell did he – and it hit me like a sledgehammer.

I'd heard the *ping* . . . just as I'd messaged Paddy. And he'd messaged – and my phone –

Paddy . . . as in Patrick . . . as in Patrick Tetlow.

A-lister, bad boy, the guy singing over the cafe speakers right now.

Fuck me.

'Oh my God,' I found myself saying aloud. My voice sounded funny to my own ears.

'Shit,' Patrick Tetlow said, his eyes widening. 'Jessy.'

'You're Patrick Tetlow,' I blurted out, like a complete idiot. 'Patrick Tetlow. You're –'

Oh shit. I'd been messaging *the* Patrick Tetlow.

I'd asked *the* Patrick Tetlow for a quick fuck.

And now *the* Patrick Tetlow was grabbing my hand – my hand! – and pulling me into one of Maria's booths.

This was not happening. This did not happen. Not to me.

'Jessy, look,' Patrick was saying hurriedly, leaning close to me to keep his voice low.

His breath fluttered on my neck and that familiar heat coursed through me again. This was insane. This was Patrick Tetlow, of These Exiles. My favourite band.

And now we were curled up close in a booth in my favourite cafe as he muttered hastily under his breath.

'– appreciate it if you didn't post about this,' he was saying quietly, his earnest eyes far too dazzling. I mean, a girl could fall in there and do herself some serious damage. 'Last thing I want – I'm sure you understand –'

'What? Yeah. Yeah, fine,' I managed to say, a little stunned. 'Yeah, I won't post about this.'

Post about this? No, just dream about it, fantasize about it, be unable to stop seeing the vision of it painted on my retinas whenever I closed my eyes . . .

I mean, I was definitely going to tell Laura. And Anna. But that wasn't the same thing.

Patrick's shoulders slumped with obvious relief. 'Great. Because I do not need this right now.'

Wow, rude. 'No problem. I get it.' I mean, I didn't, but it was fine. There was no way people would even believe me. The pictures on his profile hadn't looked anything like him. What the hell was he even doing on Butterflies?

God, Laura was going to freak.

'OK, great. Well, I've got to head off –' Patrick moved to stand, looking around at the other cafegoers before tipping his head back down at me – 'but, thanks and . . . and sorry about this,' he finished awkwardly, like he wasn't quite sure what we he was apologizing for.

Was it for forcing a vow of silence upon me, or the ghosting I'd called him out on?

Guess I'd never know.

'Seriously, it's no problem. And, yeah, I've got to go too,' I lied. The last thing I wanted to do was stay here and overthink everything that had just happened.

We made our way to the cafe doors, weird silence hovering between us. This was insane. Had I fallen asleep in my booth? Oh God, was I drooling?

This had to be a dream.

'I've got it.' Patrick was holding the door open. I blinked, before smiling.

'Thank –' I went to thank him but was assailed by shouts the instant we stepped outside.

'Patrick – Patrick, look here!'
'Over here, Patrick, smile –'
'Who's the woman, Patrick?'
'Dating again, Patrick? Are you over Celine?'
No. No, this was not happening –
'Patrick Tetlow, new girlfriend? Smile for the front page!'
And my vision was blinded by the camera flash.

FOUR

*I'll take the fire, I'll take the quake, I'll take
the storm but for heaven's sake – don't leave me,
don't leave me in this disaster, run faster,
no master, don't leave me in this disaster . . .*
– from 'Disaster', by These Exiles

'I DON'T SEE THE problem,' this Derek guy was saying, smiling at my sister, who was smiling back.

Traitor.

'You don't see the problem?' I repeated, my voice echoing strangely around the hotel room that the These Exiles publicist had booked for our meeting.

Meeting. More like ambush.

'I guess it is a reasonable offer,' Laura said, smiling uncertainly at Derek. 'But my sister and I need to talk about it. Jessy, I know you don't want to – but it doesn't seem like they are asking for too much –'

'Not too much? You're not the one being asked to fake a relationship with a global hottie!' I pointed out heatedly.

This couldn't be happening.

I mean, celebrities don't date normal people. They're too busy dating other celebrities.

'Patrick needs his image softening,' Derek was saying, leaning back in his armchair and shrugging, as though he matchmade for celebrities all the time. Hell, maybe he did. 'You've probably heard the rumours about all his partying – that hotel room will never be the same again. And we never did find out where he got the llama from.' He muttered the last bit to himself.

I couldn't help it. Despite myself, I leaned forward on the sofa that Laura and I were sharing. 'Wait, that was true?' Who hadn't heard about Patrick's wild antics in the early days of his fame?

'My point is –' Derek moved on hastily – 'he needs a more relatable image, and there's nothing more relatable than finding love.'

I rolled my eyes and grinned at my sister, expecting Laura to snort with me.

Laura wasn't laughing. She was biting her lip as she took off her glasses to rub them on her top.

'You seriously think I should do this.' I looked at my twin in disbelief.

'You *have* always had a crush on him,' she said, like that was a totally fair thing to point out in this moment.

'Laura!'

'And there's a contract and everything. You'd be protected,' she continued, as Derek nodded in agreement. 'We can put it out that you met on Butterflies. Just think about it: the downloads will skyrocket. My investors will be happy; Patrick's record label will be happy; the fans will go nuts thinking there's a chance they could date a celebrity on my app . . . But ultimately, Jessy, it's your choice.'

My stomach twisted.

She wasn't going to push. I knew that. It was obvious she wanted me to do it – but this wasn't something Laura would ever force on me.

I knew in my gut that she wouldn't have to.

I focused my attention back on this Derek guy. 'This is all legit, right?'

Next to me, Laura let out a small gasp that I firmly ignored.

'If by "legit" you mean "carefully considered and entirely designed for your mutual benefit", then sure,' said Derek confidently.

My gaze dropped to the contract in his hands. Then I looked up at him. 'Can you PDF this to me?'

I'd expected him to ask why, but he simply nodded and pulled out a tablet.

'Email address?'

I recited it to him. It came through within seconds, but I didn't even bother opening it. Forward . . . forward to . . .

Anna rang me two minutes later. Two excruciating minutes of Laura and Derek concocting some sort of plan that I had completely zoned out from.

Was this clinical shock?

'What the hell is this?' Anna asked me without any other introduction. 'You're pimping yourself out to celebrities now?'

'Not just any celebrity – Patrick Tetlow!' Laura called out with a grin. 'Is that Anna? Tell her she's got to give my black heels back, I need them for –'

'Is this really the time?' I hissed. I gave her my best glare, then turned and tried to concentrate on the flow of words pouring from my friend.

'– not your personal lawyer. Believe it or not, I actually get paid most of the time –'

'Anna,' I interrupted, trying to ignore the tension creeping up my spine. 'Anna, please.'

Silence. Then a heavy sigh. 'The things I do for you.'

'And I'm so grateful, thank you, Anna, thank you so –'

'It's fine. You can pay me back with a lifetime's supply of Maria's coffee. Now, give me five minutes of silence.'

I listened to her mutter as she rattled through the paperwork.

'. . . party of the first . . . co-signed . . . have set their hands to these presents as a deed on the day month and year hereinbefore mentioned . . .'

'God, I'm so glad it's you not me understanding this.'

Anna's chuckle was low. 'That's why I became a lawyer. And speaking of the law – I would sign this.'

I groaned.

Anna chuckled at my theatrics before she continued. 'Listen, babe, you could do a lot worse. The whole thing boils down to: date Patrick in public, and get paid a shit-ton of money.'

I dropped my head into my hands.

'You know you've got nothing better to do.' That was the trouble with Anna – she was so . . . so blunt. 'Hell, girl, isn't this the dream? Hot famous guy asks that you date him, and you get paid for it?'

Except Patrick wasn't really asking me, was he? His publicist was.

'He'd take you to all the best bars – you know, that place that only opened –'

Trust Anna to be thinking about all the perks.

'– and I just *know* that he's good in bed, the way he moves his hips on stage –'

'I am not going to sleep with Patrick Tetlow!' I hissed, louder than I intended.

Derek raised an eyebrow. *Fuck.* 'No one is asking you to sleep with –'

'She is!' I gestured at the phone as Laura stared at me, utterly lost.

'Hey, don't knock it till you've tried it,' came Anna's cheerful voice down the phone. 'It's not like you're inundated with offers right now.'

'Thanks, Anna,' I said, rubbing the spot between my eyes. 'Super helpful.'

'Am I wrong?'

'What's she saying?' Laura leaned closer, trying to hear. 'Anna, are you telling her to –'

'My professional legal opinion is *yes*, sign it,' my friend said with a chuckle. 'I've got to go in a sec, Jessy. Don't you have to be at work?'

Work? What the hell did that matter when my life had been turned upside down?

'Actually, I think it would be a good idea for you to take time off work while you're wrapped up in this,' Anna said. 'Call it a sabbatical.'

I blinked. 'Why – what?'

I could almost hear Anna's eyeroll. 'You seriously need to read this contract for yourself. Weekly dates, public events, all hours of the day? You're not going to have time for work.'

This was insane.

'We'll talk more about it later,' Anna said, breaking

through my thoughts. 'I need to get back to work. It'll be fine, don't worry about it too much, OK?'

'OK, bye,' I said numbly, ending the call. Then I looked up and saw Laura and Derek's eager faces.

'Look, I need to know one way or the other,' Derek said brightly. 'I think you'll find the monetary reward quite –'

'I'm not going to be paid to date him,' I said firmly. 'I'm not – that's just icky.' Despite what Anna had said, I was not pimping myself out here.

'Fine.' Derek shrugged. 'We'll invest it in Butterflies.'

Try as I might, I couldn't avoid my sister's face.

Or my own memories. The horror of being surrounded by paparazzi had pushed my encounter with Patrick to the back of my mind. But it was all flooding back now. Being that close to him had been . . .

I mean, everyone had a celebrity crush, right? You just never expected to actually meet them. Let alone date them.

'Fine, I'll do it.' Oh, I was so fucked.

FIVE

You thought I had a plan but can you not see that
I'm lost, the frost of your eyes so unnerving,
I'm learning that I'm alone here . . .
– from 'Frost', by These Exiles

'JUST REMEMBER TO SMILE,' Derek muttered under his breath as he led me into the hotel lobby. 'Try not to scare them off.'

'I'm not going to –'

'And have you sent the new song ideas to the label? You know they're waiting on you – marketing too – and the US team have asked –'

'I'll send them the lyrics when they're ready,' I snapped, trying not to think of the writer's block I definitely wasn't suffering from.

I was screwed. I needed good lyrics. Matter of fact, any lyrics would do right now.

'You're supposed to be smiling, remember, not whatever constipated look this is.'

My temper, never that far away, flared. 'Stop fucking telling me –'

'Look, Jessy is all for it, and you don't have much choice here,' Derek said sharply.

I swore under my breath. Of course she was all for it. Who would pass up the chance to get their five minutes of fame? Who didn't want to attend film premieres, or get invited to industry parties – and afterparties?

'– and we're not even having to pay her an extortionate fee,' Derek continued as we entered the lift and he jabbed nine.

Wait. Fee?

'Derek.' I glared at him as he smoothed back his hair. 'Please don't tell me that you're paying this woman to date me.'

'I don't have to; she's not taking a fee,' he said firmly as the lift dinged and we stepped out into an identical corridor.

I followed Derek to the last door and watched as he swiped the key card to enter.

My stomach jolted. 'OK, but you offered her –'

'Here we are!' Derek stepped into a room and beamed at its inhabitants. 'Apologies for being late – there was the little matter of a crowd of paps outside the hotel. And how are you today, Ms Donovan?'

There was nothing I could do. I followed him inside.

I'd been expecting one of the bedrooms, but this was a sort of meeting room. A large table was placed in the centre, and two people were already sitting at it. But I was only interested in one.

Jessy Donovan: the woman I'd left on read, then run into at her recommended café, and who I was now splashed everywhere online with.

And she was . . . shit. Just as gorgeous as I had remembered.

Dark hair, clearly unbrushed and curling in all directions. A sundress skimming over curves that woke up parts of my body that had been dormant for ... I didn't want to think about how long. Eyes that I knew were piercing but flickered everywhere in the room but at me. Fingers covered in silver rings that she tapped on the edge of her chair.

'We are very well, thanks,' said the woman sitting next to Jessy, a curious look in her dark, almost black eyes, gold eyeliner popping as she swept her box braids over her shoulder.

Derek looked at me and pointed at one of the empty chairs meaningfully.

I could storm out. Rage. Mutter curses, refuse to co-operate, and ... never see Jessy again.

I sat down.

'Now that we're all happy with the contract –' Derek began, but he was immediately interrupted.

'Patrick doesn't exactly seem like he wants to date me,' Jessy said archly, picking up the coffee Derek had brought her and sipping at it. 'In fact,' she went on, fixing her gaze on me properly for the first time, 'you look like you'd rather be anywhere else right now.'

Finally, she'd acknowledged me.

Her voice was light – almost a lilt. It was the sort of thing you noticed when you were a singer – the cadence of someone's voice. Some people's made me want to rip my ears off, the grating in their tone just painful – but Jessy's voice was almost melodic.

Didn't hurt that she was gorgeous. Her photos hadn't lied – I'd kind of assumed she'd pushed them through a filter or five to give her that carefully freckled look with the wide eyes and rosebud mouth.

Apparently not.

'Look, I know this hasn't been the easiest few days for

either of you,' interrupted Derek hastily, leaning forward across the table. 'But this is a brilliant opportunity for you both. Patrick dating a normie is –'

'Excuse you?'

I almost smiled at the outrage on Jessy's face. It drew her cupid's bow into perfect relief, and the way she leaned forward made her chest swell just –

Eyes up, Tetlow.

'Sorry, it's only – well,' Derek said, regret colouring his tone. 'We really need this to work.'

Jessy threw a hand in my direction. 'He's Patrick Tetlow. He dates bombshells, real hotties, models, influencers – and in between that he writes some of the best lyrics in the world.'

Do not preen. Do not smile. Do not –

'And he's reckless and smashes up hotel rooms and doesn't care about the consequences. He's so different to me it's not even funny,' Jessy continued, pricking the balloon of my ego with just a few words. 'How the hell am I supposed to date him?'

'Fake date him,' her friend – or lawyer? – said, her curt, professional manner belied by a twinkle in her eye and the half smirk that ghosted across her lips.

'None of this is real, Ms Donovan – you think half the celebrity pairings on the red carpet are real?'

Jessy blinked. 'They're – they're not?'

'Babe, don't be naïve,' muttered her friend, tapping away at her laptop with a grin.

'We don't need front page headlines,' Derek continued reassuringly.

Jessy seemed placated, the worried furrow between her eyebrows smoothing out. 'Oh. Good.'

'Just pages two, four and maybe six in several nationals each week –'

I almost grinned as her outrage spilled out again. 'I am not going to be – be creating *scenes* all over the place just so you can get your headlines!'

Derek stepped in. 'No, absolutely not, no creating scenes.'

Thank God.

'*Be* the scene!' he said brightly.

For fuck's sake . . .

'You look unhappy.' Her words were directed at me.

My gaze flicked back to Jessy, and I found myself caught in her eyes again. She was observing me closely, with none of the caution that I'd expected.

'Why wouldn't I be?' I muttered back, anger creating an edge in my tone. 'I'm a product, and Derek is about to sell me to the highest bidder.'

'Let the record show I haven't actually offered any money for you,' Jessy pointed out, raising an eyebrow.

No, but what have you been offered?

'It's simple, really,' Derek insisted. 'Two dates a week – I'll be sending you to events, you won't have to worry about organizing anything. Public suggestions of affection –'

'I'm sorry,' Jessy interrupted. '*Public suggestions of affection?* Is that not PDA?'

'We would never actually ask you to kiss Patrick. Consent issues and all that,' Derek said soothingly.

Do not think about kissing her. Do not look at her lips. Do not think about –

'The music industry needs to see the two of you together,' he went on. 'It can't all be candlelit dinners in expensive restaurants.'

'Candlelit dinners, you say?'

I glared at Jessy. *Of course she's into it – and why wouldn't she be?* Wined and dined by a celebrity, the dream of half the women in the world.

'What?' she said defensively, shrugging again. 'I like wine. I like dinners. Sue me.'

'– then there's the album launch for Cassandra's Chorus, following week the after-party for Fashion Week, you've got the interview on primetime TV, then you'll be attending –'

Christ, he really had organized it all. A fabricated love story with a choreographed relationship. Why was I surprised? I'd ridden this rodeo before.

'– until the Songwriter Awards next month,' Derek said brightly. 'To prove to the fans that it's real, even if it ends straight after. Hell, it can't continue when you start the Southeast Asia tour in two months anyway.'

'And I'll get wine.' Jessy grinned, sweeping a hand through her hair and messing it up.

I hated that it looked better that way.

My brain was melting, all coherent arguments fading away with every passing second – and Jessy hitching up her spaghetti straps as one fell from her shoulder didn't help.

I needed to think straight – I needed a way out of this nightmare. The sensation of being trapped was returning: something I thought I'd escaped years ago.

'Sure, it's not the most romantic document in the world.' Derek's voice broke through my thoughts. 'But this isn't a real relationship. You won't actually be dating – no feelings, no emotions, no hearts to break. Isn't that what you wanted?'

Isn't that what you wanted?

I swallowed hard, ignoring the bile in my mouth and trying not to look at the woman beside me.

I wanted to be left alone. I wanted to make music, not to have to act as though I was in love, or whatever, with someone who was probably only into this for the bragging rights.

And the wine.

'What are you thinking, Patrick?' Jessy murmured.

My whole body twitched.

I swallowed hard, forcing myself to look up at her. Blue eyes, freckles, rosebud mouth. Body to die for. She was probably looking for a way to break into trashy reality TV . . . and I would be spending the next five weeks with her on my arm.

'He'll sign,' Derek said quietly, pushing a pen into my hand.

My temper flared immediately, but it quietened just as quickly.

He was right. Butterflies had been my chance to avoid the label's machinations. They weren't going to give me another.

I stared over the contract at the woman I was signing away my soul to.

Jessy sighed dramatically, rolled her eyes and pulled the pen out of my hands. 'I'll go first. It's just five weeks,' she said firmly, clearly avoiding the triumphant glint in her friend's eye. 'I can put up with you for five weeks.'

Well. It wasn't the best start.

SIX

*Let me wine you, dine you, align you to the very
best of me, the worst of who I could have been but
I chose to be here for you . . .*
– from 'The Worst Best First Date',
by These Exiles

WELL, THIS WASN'T THE best start.

Look, I'd never been someone to forbid someone else from being on their phone all the time. I'd had enough dressing-downs from Karun to know that my phone was rarely out of my hand.

But this? This was just plain rude.

I slowly turned my fork around and around in my fingertips as I stared at the man sitting opposite me, his eyes flickering as he scrolled on his phone.

Patrick Tetlow.

They say you should never meet your heroes, and now I knew why.

It was unfair how hot he was. All chiselled jawbone and effortlessly cool hair. That smile he gave on socials – it always looked so cheeky, so unbelievably easy.

But I was quickly finding that it was all a facade.

This Patrick, the real Patrick, was aloof. Cold. And, currently, ignoring me.

Maybe it was because the restaurant was busy, and I'd already noticed people at other tables taking what they clearly thought were secret photos. My chest burned at the way they looked at me. Appraisingly.

What is she doing with him?

I looked back at the man in question. I'd hardly known what to expect from our first 'date', but it wasn't this.

Patrick Tetlow. Party-crashing, hotel-smashing, model-pulling, assistant-hassling Patrick Tetlow. If this evening had been full of manic energy and ended in a visit from the police, then, yeah, I would have believed it.

Instead, we were forty minutes into a meal that felt like it would last forever, and we'd exchanged, what, no more than a dozen words?

'What are you doing?'

I almost dropped the fork. Patrick was glaring at me from the other side of the expensive table in a restaurant that was so exclusive you couldn't find it online. 'What?'

'You're counting on your fingers.'

So? 'Just counting.'

Patrick's glower could stop traffic. 'Counting what?'

Counting down the minutes until this is over. Was this the type of scintillating conversation I had to look forward to over the next five weeks? I'd had better chats with Cathy.

Instead of answering, I simply shrugged and placed my fork on my almost empty plate. Patrick had clearly lost interest, or perhaps he'd never had any.

I tried not to think about how self-conscious I felt in this dress I'd borrowed from Anna. It was sexier than anything I owned or was comfortable in, but she'd insisted I wear it. The thought of having another picture of me in just my regular clothes plastered everywhere had been enough to have me say yes.

I shuffled in my seat.

'Was your food good?' I winced at my pathetic attempt to get something from him. It had been so long since I'd had to pretend to be interested in what a man said, and it wasn't any easier now.

Dating wasn't something I had planned on, and after Ross – I shook my head, trying to physically dislodge any thoughts of my ex. This date was going terribly enough without taking a trip down *that* memory lane.

Patrick sighed, and I looked up, only to see him swipe something on his phone, snort and keep scrolling.

A prickle of annoyance flashed through me as I glanced about the place again. It was nice – like, really nice. Not showy nice, but genuinely 'we've thought about the decor, the menu changes every week' nice. A place a guy would bring a woman he really liked.

Shame *my* date was contractually obligated to be here.

'Have you seen the stuff online?' Patrick's voice was like liquid lava pouring through me.

I held in a shiver, determined not to let him affect me. 'He speaks!'

'What?' Patrick blinked, looking at me like I was nonsensical.

'Doesn't matter,' I said awkwardly, shifting in my seat and trying to pull Anna's dress down my thighs a few inches. *Seriously, does the girl date pussy-out?* 'Have I seen what stuff online?'

Patrick – you know, the world-famous celebrity whose lyrics were so eloquent and refined – looked utterly bewildered. 'You seriously haven't searched your own name?' He gestured with his phone.

I probably shouldn't have done it. But who could honestly stop themselves? Even as Patrick said in a rush, 'No, don't – once you look, you can't –'

It was too late. I'd already grabbed his phone. He'd searched my name – why couldn't I look?

The thumbnail was bad enough, but I full-body winced when the guy started talking, the captions quickly reminding me why even looking at social media was a bad idea.

'*– does she think she is, dating Patrick Tetlow? She's clearly not in his league; her dress sense is –*'

I was suddenly grateful for Anna and her ridiculously sexy dress. There had been enough paps outside the restaurant when we'd arrived – surely by the time we left my sartorial rating would have gone up.

> **Message from Cassie Fletcher**

Cassie, huh? I flicked the notification away, trying not to care that he was messaging another woman. None of this was real, after all.

Not that the world knew that.

'Seriously,' muttered Patrick, his face looking almost apologetic as I glanced up. 'It's better to ignore it.'

'It's me they're talking about,' I said, almost accusingly. 'Why can't I –'

'Once you see that shit, you can never *unsee*,' he said

darkly, picking up a fork and jabbing it at the mashed potato he'd left on his plate. 'Just give me back my phone.'

But I couldn't. It was all too easy to keep scrolling.

'We've seen the gorgeous women he's dated in the past, and this Jessica is no Celine –'

Celine. Patrick's most recent ex.

I purposely hadn't searched her online, but I didn't need to. I could still picture her, all waif-like model beauty and large eyes.

'That is *my* phone, Jessy.'

I ignored him. Scroll.

'Now I'm not one to tear a girl down, but I think we can all agree this is not the sort of woman any of us expected Patrick Tetlow to be dating. She's not even a D-list celebrity. Does anyone know where she came from?'

The video was interrupted.

> **Message from Cassie Fletcher**

I was torn between continuing my doomscrolling and finding out who Cassie was.

And what she wanted from Patrick so badly.

'The last time I searched my own name, I couldn't write lyrics for a week.' Patrick's voice came from a long way away. 'It's like people don't even realize we're human.'

This was why Anna and Laura had told me not to search my own name. Hell, it had only been five days – how could half the world have formed an opinion about me in less than a week?

'Can I have my phone back now?'

Oh. Right. 'Sorry,' I muttered, handing it over.

He smiled. It was brief, gone like the Tube you'd almost definitely been going to catch. 'It's fine, I get it. Sorry you saw that.'

Ping. Now it was my phone that was blowing up with messages.

At least I had the good manners to look at them under the table.

> **Laura**
> How's it going?!??!?!

Too much punctuation. She'd gone back to her vape again, I knew it.

> **Jessy**
> Fine

> **Laura**
> Use protection!!

> **Jessy**
> Fuck off

> **Laura**
> You're welcome – 70K extra downloads of Butterflies in the last 24 hours!

I blinked. My sister had promised that it would do wonders for her app . . . but I hadn't thought it would be that quick.

There was another message, too.

> **Anna**
> Please tell me the dress works

I grinned.

> **Jessy**
> I've never felt more naked

It didn't take long for her to reply.

> **Anna**
> Good

My snort of laughter went utterly ignored.

Patrick was too busy muttering under his breath. 'I can't believe it's gone viral this quickly.'

I tried to focus as a waiter stepped silently to our table and started removing what was left of my main – something in French that I could never hope to pronounce but had wolfed down.

'You can't believe it? Thanks.' I smiled at the waiter before turning back to my . . . date, I guess? 'But you've gone viral loads of times.'

There was – was that a flush across Patrick's cheeks?

Surely not.

'Not like this,' he mumbled, gaze still fixed on his phone. 'Not for anything . . . personal.'

Just a moment of sympathy, that was all I allowed him. Shit, I wouldn't want my private life splashed all over the internet, a Wikipedia page telling the world what school I went to and who I'd dated.

The sympathy departed quickly.

'So,' Patrick said bracingly. 'Are you enjoying it?'

My jaw dropped. 'You think I *like* this – that this is fun for me? I'm being hounded!'

Patrick blinked, confusion sweeping across his face. 'Hounded?'

'Yeah, there are journalists and paps and weirdos literally camping outside my house,' I said quietly, remembering with an uncomfortable twist in my chest just how difficult it had been to get out of there this morning. 'My housemates aren't happy, I can't go to work –'

'I meant the food.' Patrick pointed awkwardly at the table between us. 'Are you enjoying it? The food?'

Oh. Right. Embarrassment flooded through me. 'Yeah, the food was amazing.'

The company less so.

Not that I should care. This whole thing was only for Laura's sake – something I had reminded her of sternly this morning. There was nothing in the contract that said we had to have a good time, even if I'd had dreams about riding this man until dawn.

But that was just the hormones talking. A nice, perfectly normal stranger was what I needed to scratch that particular itch.

But I wouldn't be doing anything like that for the next five weeks. Thanks to Section 18.

Section 18: Other connections
Patrick Tetlow and Jessica Donovan, subsequently known as the co-signed, will agree to pause and not return to any other romantic or sexual relationships for the duration of the strategy.

My gaze roamed over the man sitting before me.

Other romantic or sexual relationships. Not something I had to worry about: Ross had done a brilliant job of making sure of that. But had Patrick been forced to shut down a relationship just to make this work?

Was that who this Cassie Fletcher was? A woman he'd been seeing until I'd come along and ruined it all?

God, it was moments like this that made me desperate to have Mum back. She wouldn't have had anything useful to say, her own dating life had always been a disaster. But still. We could have laughed together.

'Dessert menu, *mademoiselle*,' murmured the waiter.

I jumped. I hadn't noticed him return. 'Oh – thanks. Patrick?'

Patrick shrugged without looking up. 'Whatever you want.'

The waiter cast me a sympathetic look.

I smiled sweetly. Well, it wasn't like I was paying – and if I wasn't interesting enough to warrant Patrick engaging even his most basic conversation skills, I would simply have to make my own fun.

'One of everything, please,' I said lightly to the waiter, whose eyes glittered.

'But – but, *mademoiselle*, each of them costs at least –'

'You're right,' I interrupted, grinning as I remembered Section 56. 'Better make it two of everything.'

That caught Patrick's attention. 'What the hell?'

'Like I told you: I like wine, I like to dine,' I said as smoothly as I could manage without giggling. 'And here is dessert.'

Patrick was staring in mingled shock and horror at the stream of plates and bowls being placed down before us. Another pair of waiters was carefully moving another table next to ours . . . to fit the sheer number of desserts. 'I thought you were joking. Surely you were jok–'

'Two of everything,' my original waiter announced with the merest hint of a wink. 'As the *mademoiselle* ordered.'

Patrick's gaze sharpened for perhaps the first time since we'd sat down. 'Fuck off.'

'There was a sweetness lacking in the conversation, and I have made up for it,' I said, perhaps a little tartly. *Oh look, a lemon tart!*

I picked up my spoon and started to attack a crème brûlée. Dear God, this trash date was suddenly truly worth it. 'You aren't going to try any of this? Come on, it's not like we're paying. Section fifty-six.'

Ice cream, parfait, three kinds of tart, two types of custardy thing, a cake that looked decadent and a peachy thing that looked criminal –

Patrick didn't move an inch. 'Section fifty-six?'

My eyes rolled to the back of my head as sharp raspberry burst on my tongue. *Mmm, that is good cake.* 'Section fifty-six – These Exiles foots the bill.'

For some reason, Patrick had gone still. 'I beg your fucking pardon?'

'OK, fine, that's not the exact wording,' I acknowledged. 'I'm pretty sure it's the record label that pays for dates, not you. The point is, I don't pay for any of this.'

And this was delicious. Maybe we could have all our dates here?

Nope, I thought, as I remembered the industry events clause. Fine, but everything else?

When I glanced up, there was dull disappointment in his eyes. 'Well, that makes sense,' he said quietly. 'Good to know you're just out for what you can get.'

'Erm, hello? Are you going to try this cake?' I pushed it towards him, almost knocking it over, the bowl was so fragile. 'Whoops! But seriously. You don't get this sort of food on tour, right?'

It had been tempting: to ask him all the questions that had ever rushed through my mind when listening to These Exiles. They were a great band, one of the best. The lyrics were just incredible – telling my story without me having to crack my own heart open.

And I was on a date with the guy who wrote them.

If only he'd stop scowling. 'Tour food is shite.'

'Then eat! *Eat and be merry*. That's Shakespeare, isn't it?' I shrugged. 'Anything you don't eat I'll be taking back for my housemates, so now's your chance. Oooh, is that a sundae?'

It had to be – a tall glass bowl with one of those special long spoons beside it. Raspberry cake abandoned, I reached out for it.

Damn.

Apparently Patrick'd had the same idea. He'd reached out for the long spoon at the same time, his fingertips brushing mine as we both went for the handle.

Heat, heat and need. That was all I could taste now, the merest touch somehow enough to set all my nerve endings alight.

I looked up, my lips parting, and saw a reflection of that same want in Patrick's face. The memory of our first meeting at Maria's flashed through my mind as his gaze twitched down to my lips, and I couldn't help myself. I licked them, the taste of raspberry blooming in my mouth. A soft moan escaped me.

A nerve throbbed in Patrick's jaw. The space between us seemed to shrink, the air taut with energy.

One second, Patrick looked like he was about to leap over the table, and the next he was leaning back, crossing his arms over his chest. 'I'm not hungry. Besides, this date is almost over. Tick it off the contractually required list.'

So, we were going to lie about what had just happened? We were going to pretend there wasn't something here? It might have been ages since my last relationship, but I knew what it looked like when a man wanted me. And from the looks of it, Patrick wanted me . . . badly.

'Fine,' I said lightly, taking the long spoon and pulling the sundae towards me. 'Have it your way.'

It took all my self-control to make sure that I did not look at him while I ate the sundae.

Do not think about it.

I swallowed another mouthful of ice cream and toffee before glancing up in time to catch Patrick looking at my lips.

When our eyes met again, he said without flinching, 'Well, I think this date has gone on long enough to keep Derek happy. Shall I ask for the bill?'

SEVEN

And the next time I decide to listen to you, remind me,
this is why we stepped away, stepped back,
stepped off the cliff...
– from 'Clifftop Ode', by These Exiles

> **Jessy**
> We need to talk

I STARED ONCE AGAIN at the message as I paced back and forth between two lamp posts along the river, tugging my hat lower across my face as I waited for my fake girlfriend to turn up.

Need to talk?

Shit, this was the sort of stuff that people in *actual* relationships had to put up with. I wasn't – I didn't care about this woman. I was being forced to be in a relationship with her – what was the point of dealing with all the crap that came with it?

All that crap, a horrible little voice in the back of my mind reminded me, *that you desperately wanted with Celine?*

I forced the thought away.

Unlocking my phone, I glanced down at the lyric I'd tapped out without much thought.

I'd rather argue with you than receive anyone's smiles

It wasn't bad. It wasn't good – it needed a little extra. Hell, I was just grateful to have something come to me, after weeks of nothing.

What came next?

I had no idea. I locked my phone. It would keep.

I had almost forgotten how gorgeous it was along here. The river wasn't the most beautiful stretch of water in the world, but with the sun shining, and the gentle chatter as people had lunch together, the laughter and screams from a trio of women catching up on the corner, and the two guys arguing vociferously about where one of them should propose to his boyfriend . . .

Seriously. Did the whole world run on romance?

Stupid thing to think. Didn't I make money singing about just that sort of stuff?

> **Wes**
> So how's the fake girlfriend?

I groaned. Of course he had to ask that in our group chat.

> **Matt**
> Wait, he went through with it?

> **Ben**
> Is she hot?

The messages came through thick and fast.

> **Wes**
> What does it matter if she's hot?

> **Ben**
> It doesn't, I just want to know

> **Wes**
> Looks like the world's media has bought it

> **Matt**
> Do you like her?

My thumbs hovered over my screen, but I didn't type anything. *Do I like her?* What sort of question was that?

> **Patrick**
> She's cool

> **Wes**
> Uh oh

> **Ben**
> Is she catching feelings?

> **Ben**
> No scratch that – are you catching feelings??

> **Matt**
> Way more believable

I snorted.

> **Patrick**
> Thanks guys. The support is appreciated

> **Ben**
> Always happy to give some tips for the bedroom

> **Wes**
> Yuck

> **Matt**
> Muting this chat if Ben even thinks about it

> **Ben**
> I'm just saying, I've had no complaints

> **Wes**
> When were you going to give me your sister's number again?

> **Ben**
> Fuck off

I sighed, closing the chat. Yeah, hoping for a bit of a distraction courtesy of my bandmates probably wasn't the best idea. But I was missing them; we usually spent our downtime between shows all relaxing together. Instead, Derek had us all running around on the so-called penance tour.

I leaned out against the railing by the river and tried not to think about whatever it was that Jessy wanted to talk about.

'Excuse me?'

I opened my eyes – only for my heart to sink.

Two girls, probably only about fourteen, stood in front of me. One of them was tugging her friend's arm, clearly uncomfortable, yet she hadn't walked away.

Of course she hadn't. Both of them were wearing merch T-shirts from our last UK tour.

The hat I'd pulled low across my brow hadn't worked, then.

'I just – oh my God, it's actually you – hello,' the braver one said breathlessly.

I forced myself to smile. I'd been trained for this – we all had been. The moment These Exiles had taken off, it had been the first thing Derek had made us prepare for.

Fan engagement.

'Hello,' I said brightly, as though it was about to make my day that two girls had accosted me in public. 'Do you want a photo?'

They didn't reply. At least, they didn't use words – but their squeals of delight were already making heads turn.

Stomach sinking, I carefully moved myself between them, ensuring my hands were clasped before me.

Always be perfect.

Always be charming.

And never, ever let a fan walk away from you with a bad experience . . .

It took the girls a few goes to get the selfie they wanted, and by the time they scampered away, my heart was sinking. People were staring, a guy over there was taking what he thought was a surreptitious photo, and if I was unlucky those girls were going to tag both me and my location online within five minutes.

Where was she?

> **Patrick**
> I thought you said 1pm by the Thirsty Bear?

> **Jessy**
> I'm running late

No shit.

I swallowed, looking back across the river. It was easier to do that than face the people sitting about staring at me.

Just . . . staring. Why –

'Patrick?'

My stomach lurched, and not because someone had called my name.

Because of the person who had called it.

'Patrick, it *is* you!' A woman was beaming at me as though she had never seen anyone she cared for more. 'I saw someone tag you here!'

I winced.

'Why didn't you tell me you were in the area, darling?' She leaned forward for an air kiss.

I couldn't exactly back into the river, but I side-stepped her just in time. 'Cassie.'

My mother's face fell. 'Cassie? On a first-name basis still, are we?'

'Full names on the restraining order request,' I said quietly, my jaw tight. 'I'd hoped you wouldn't be allowed within fifty feet of me.'

It had been painful, asking for Derek's help with that one. Not just because it meant asking for help – something I hated doing.

No, because I'd had to tell him . . . not everything. Not quite.

Half the story was enough.

But the judge hadn't granted it. And now here she was.

My mother's smile was too wide, too cheerful, too false. Her perfume was strong – jasmine, as always. 'But that didn't stick, petal –'

'I think you'll find I can apply again,' I shot back, taking another step to the side.

After being so desperate for Jessy to turn up these last twenty minutes, now it was the last thing I wanted.

Cassie and Jessy, in one place?

Absolutely not.

Cassie's face had already turned to pleading, an expression I knew well. 'But, darling, I saw the news.'

I blinked. 'The news?'

'Your new girlfriend, this Jessica girl,' Cassie said, brushing a curl out of her eyes. 'Does she make you happy?'

I swallowed, blindsided yet again. 'Happy?'

When was the last time she had asked about that? When was the last time she'd cared about anything to do with my wellbeing?

Cassie was nodding. 'Yes, happy. Can we sit, somewhere, love? These shoes aren't really made for walking.'

I glanced down and almost laughed, despite myself. No, they weren't. Spindly heels and tiny straps, it was a wonder anyone could get about in them.

'Look, there's a bench free over there – come on!'

Her hand had taken my arm before I could stop her . . . and I couldn't. Not really.

Despite everything, she was my mum. There was something almost surreal about seeing her here, in real life, after seven months of no contact.

Well. Other than the voicemails I kept deleting and the messages I kept ignoring.

Cassie tottered over to the bench, dragging me along with her, and I let her. It was just – shit – so nice for her to actually care about something going on in my life. No matter how much older I got, a small part of me was still five years old, waiting on the sports day field after everyone else had gone, blinking away tears that she hadn't seen me win the beanbag race. I hated how much I wanted her approval.

'Jessica,' she said promptly, her smile broad. 'You like her?'

I swallowed. 'Yeah. Sure.' I knew better than to divulge the truth of my 'relationship' to my mother. She couldn't be trusted. I'd learnt that the hard way.

'She treating you well?' Cassie persisted.

It was bizarre to hear such concern in her voice. Cassie was not someone who had ever been that interested in my happiness: not when I was a kid, not when I'd started playing music more seriously, not when I'd slipped into stardom and gone off to tour the world.

No, that had not been her priority.

'She's . . .' I hesitated before continuing. 'Yeah, she's great. Jessy's great.'

'Oh, darling, I *am* pleased,' said Cassie brightly, rubbing my arm. She still hadn't let go. I thought I would have minded, but somehow, I didn't. Her hand on me felt simultaneously soothing and branding. 'You deserve to be happy.'

Such a short sentence shouldn't make genuine joy spring through me, but it did.

God, I was such a loser. One kind word from her and I'd reverted back to being a kid.

'Thanks,' I said quietly.

Perhaps this was genuine from her. God knows I'd done a lot of growing up recently – there wasn't any reason to think she wasn't capable of it too. Perhaps this was the fresh start we needed.

'I'm glad, honey, so glad. And since things are going so well for you, do you think you could lend your moth–'

I jerked my arm from her grip and stood up. 'I fucking knew it.'

'No – no, it's not – Patrick, darling, calm down –'

'I should have known,' I snarled. 'Why am I not surprised?'

But I was, and that was perhaps what hurt the most. Just for a moment, I had truly thought my mother cared about my happiness, no strings attached.

Damnit, when am I going to learn?

Cassie had risen now, wobbly on the shoes she'd probably bought on credit and couldn't pay off. 'I just thought –'

'Well, you thought wrong – now go away.'

My mother's face sharpened, the cruelty that had been bubbling away underneath finally breaking the surface. 'Don't you dare talk to me like that. I'm your mother, not one of your fucking groupies.'

I laughed darkly. There was the Cassie I knew. 'Tell me when you've improved your mothering, and I'll reassess my skills as a son.'

'Patrick –'

'My security is only a phone call away.' I pulled out my phone. As I glanced down at it, I saw an unopened message from Jessy.

Either she wasn't coming, or she was about to arrive – either way, I had to get out of here.

'Patrick!'

Ignoring Cassie calling after me was easy. I'd been doing it the last three years.

Today wasn't any different.

As I strode away, I unlocked my phone.

> **Jessy**
> Meet me in five mins?

> **Paddy**
> k

I couldn't be bothered to type more than a letter. Rage was pouring through me, hot lead coursing in my veins.

How could she think – and I'd almost let her –

'Woah there, tiger.'

I felt someone grab my arm and flinched. I wrenched it back and exploded. 'Don't fucking touch me!'

Jessy placed both her hands up in immediate surrender, her arms wide. 'Hey. Sorry.'

I was breathing heavily and knew I needed to rein it in, but I couldn't calm down quick enough. Stars were appearing in the corners of my eyes, heat in my chest –

'You OK?'

'I'm fine.' I took deep breaths, settling myself before I snapped at the innocent woman in front of me. Again.

Jessy hadn't done anything to deserve my foul mood. I tried to look at her reassuringly, my eyes tracing over her face, and then her –

Damn. The little sundress she was wearing was doing nothing to help me cool off. I took in the rest of her. No bra straps, no shoes – no shoes?

'I broke my sandal,' Jessy said with a half grin as she saw my gaze dart down. 'I can fix it, though – this isn't the first time.'

My chest was heaving, my throat parched, and my brain was having a hard time keeping up with my violent swings between emotions.

All I wanted to do was go back home and write through the pain, pour it out into music.

All those girls, crying out my name and inking my words, my lyrics, on their bodies. They thought they came from love. How wrong they were.

'I thought – can we get a drink?' Jessy bit her lip, her smile fading. 'We can even count it as one of our dates, if you want. Save you seeing me again later this week.'

Another woman who wanted nothing but to profit off me. It was probably unfair to cast Jessy in the same light as Cassie, but the hurt was still churning in my chest.

And yet she was smiling. Unaware of her effect on me.

And she was right. We could count it as a date, even if the record label hadn't organized it. One less chance to make a fool of myself in front of her.

'Sure,' I said, subdued, and held the door open.

The pub was busy, as everywhere always was, but Jessy pointed at two barstools in a corner. 'You grab those, I'll get drinks.'

She was gone before I could say more.

When she made her way back, she had a drink in each hand and a white piece of paper dangling from her mouth.

'This better?' Jessy took the paper out of her mouth and stuffed it in her cleavage as she sat down.

Fuck. Don't look.

'It's the receipt,' she said, clinking her glass of tepid white wine with mine. 'For Derek. Cheers!'

She took a sip of the wine, but I barely touched my own. The reminder of Derek, the bullshit contract and the fact that Jessy was only here for the clout all soured my mood further.

Was every woman in my life determined to hurt me?

'God, it's so nice not to be working in the middle of the day,' Jessy said brightly. 'I mean, you'd think working in finance would be all fancy lunches and day-drinking, but it turns out not.'

'You wanted to talk,' I said woodenly, my patience for small talk low.

Jessy nodded as she took another sip. 'Yeah, I just – after our first date, I thought –'

'It wasn't a date,' I pointed out. 'Not really.'

Was it rude? Perhaps. Was it unnecessary? For sure. But I needed the reminder. Any desire I felt, any connection that seemed real here, was anything but. This was a woman who was only out for what she could get.

Cassie. Celine. Jessy. They were all the same.

'Yeah, I know that, obviously,' Jessy continued without pause. 'It's just – this fake dating.' She lowered her voice, and I resisted the urge to lean closer to hear her. The pub wasn't that loud, but her perfume was intoxicating. Or maybe that was just her. 'I think we need to work on it. Don't you?'

Work on it?

I blinked. What the hell was she talking about?

Confusion must have been painted on my face, because she flushed – and it travelled from her cheeks down to her shoulders. How had I not noticed that before?

'It's just, well, if we're going to convince people that this –' Jessy gestured between the two of us, the three silver rings on her right hand glinting – 'is real, we need to start acting like we actually like each other.'

Her gaze was steady, her point reasonable, and I wanted to stride away and punch Derek in the gut.

'Do you see what I mean?' Jessy prompted, sipping her wine and smiling at me a little nervously. 'I mean, you saw Derek's email.'

I blinked. Derek's email?

'Or not . . .' Her smile was a little too knowing. 'Look, here.'

Jessy pulled out her phone and tapped on it before she handed it over. The screen was open at a long, desperate email from my publicist.

> *Well, great. The two of you are a disaster – you didn't see the photographer outside that restaurant, did you? No, I guess not. The pair of you look miserable, you're not even holding hands. Do you understand what fake dating is? Heck, do you even understand what dating is? Because it doesn't seem like it from here.*
>
> *The label isn't happy. I'm not happy. You two are clearly unhappy – but that's your own fault.*
>
> *Get better at this. Hold hands. Smile as though you mean it. Get coffee together, wear Patrick's jacket – something, for God's sake.*
>
> *Here's a list of the ways this needs to go.*

I stopped reading at that point. 'He doesn't seem happy.'

'No, he's not.' Jessy's voice was wry as she held out her hand for her phone. 'So we've got to be . . . well, better at this.'

I leaned back, drink still untouched. 'So you're saying that I need to be a better boyfriend?'

There it was again. That flush. Only now it was reaching her chest and –

'I'm just saying, Derek seems pretty insistent we –'

'Because I don't remember being particularly wowed by your dating skills,' I lied, forcing my gaze back up to her face.

Jessy's smile vanished. 'Me? What did I do?'

'You weren't charm itself. Your conversational skills –'

'I am not going to be marked down on my conversational skills by a guy who didn't even notice that the waiter was offering him dessert!' Jessy hissed.

And it felt good, somehow, to get angry. All this rage within me, all the frustration with Cassie, it had to flow somewhere.

And Jessy was here, contractually obligated to be with me.

Well, if she wanted to bask in the rays of a celebrity, she would have to take the heat.

'You're only doing this for clout, and honestly, I'm already sick of it,' I spat out, knowing I should stop, unable to. 'You might be hot –'

'You think I'm hot?'

Shit.

'– but I am not here to pretend to be obsessed with a woman who couldn't find another guy to date her,' I finished doggedly, ignoring all the warning bells that were yelling *shut the fuck up*.

Jessy blinked.

It was hardly the best insult, and not based in truth – or any truth I was aware of, at least. But the ugly beast that had been gnawing at me since this sham had started was out for blood.

I sat waiting for Jessy to throw something back at me – a well-deserved insult, or even her drink.

Instead, her piercing blue eyes began blinking. Shit. Were those tears? Guilt stabbed me in the chest. She hadn't done anything to deserve that.

'Fuck you.'

I watched on, paralysed, as she gathered her things and rose from the barstool. 'Jessy –'

'You know, Patrick,' said Jessy, with a smile that carried no warmth, 'on Butterflies you always came across as someone out of his depth, but still a genuinely nice guy. I guess now I know the truth. You're just like the rest of them. An arsehole.'

Without another word, she wove her way through the crowd – disappearing out of sight with just a few steps.

'Great.' I picked up my drink and downed it in one.

EIGHT

What do you mean, we're over? Over is just four letters and I have more for you: love, need, stay . . .
– from 'Four Letter Word',
by These Exiles

'THERE YOU ARE!'

I'd never been happier to see Anna – or the two coffees in front of her – when I walked into Maria's. Sliding into our usual booth, I grabbed the nearest –

'Nope, this one's yours,' Anna said with a grin, pushing the other cup towards me. 'Unless you want a drink laced with blueberry syrup. And can I ask why we are meeting this early – I thought you'd taken time off work?'

'I have.' Karun hadn't been particularly pleased about that, but he was the least of my problems these days. 'I've got to meet Patrick at some TV studio and –'

'Ah, the life of the rich and famous,' Anna teased. 'Why you want to give it all up, I'll never understand.'

I rolled my eyes as Laura dropped down next to Anna. 'You try dealing with that man-child and see if you don't start to get it.'

'I should never have asked you to do this,' Laura fretted, tugging her hands through her hair as she forced her unruly curls into a bun. 'This is way too much –'

'I can handle it,' I found myself saying, almost despite myself. 'You don't have to worry about me.'

But my reassurances did nothing. Worry still clouded my sister's face.

That was Laura all over. Always worrying, always stressing, always determined to fix things before they even became problems.

I smiled softly. 'Seriously, sis, you don't need to worry about me. I'm not quitting. I thought – well, that I'd just see what my options were when I called Anna last night. Not that she really gave me much advice . . . since she had a *friend* over.' I waggled my eyebrows suggestively. I'd been disappointed when Anna had confirmed there was no way of getting out of the contract, but I'd been quickly distracted by the sound of a man's voice in her bedroom.

'I did not!'

'I heard him!' I snorted, delighted to see a dark flush on Anna's cheeks.

'That was just the TV –'

Laura groaned, her eyes closing momentarily behind her glasses. 'You are not sleeping with your housemate again, are you?'

Anna plastered a look of fake shock on her face . . . but the twinkle in her eye gave it away. '*Moi*, slip into bed with Casimir again? I would never!'

Both my sister and I groaned, but as we chattered on, my phone pinged. I sighed heavily and pulled it from my pocket. My lock screen blinked at me.

> **You have five missed calls**
> **Eleven unopened messages**
> **Four voicemails**

This was getting ridiculous. The first thing I did when I stormed out of our last fake date was delete Patrick's number. I'd been deliberately ignoring all his messages since, determined to keep our contact to a minimum outside of our contracted duties.

'For fuck's sake,' I whispered to myself. Why now, after being such a prick, was he blowing up my phone?

My phone pinged again.

'Ooh, is that lover boy?' Anna leaned forward as I went to open the messages and saw they were from – Ross.

My stomach dropped.

Ross.

It hadn't been Patrick who had been hassling me.

It was Ross.

Just seeing his name on my screen was enough to send my mind spinning. It had been . . . what. Six months? Seven?

'You won't hear from me.' His parting words echoed in my mind, making my lungs tight, every breath a struggle. 'And I don't want to hear from you. Don't contact me.'

> **Five messages from**
> **Ross Bradley**

> **Eleven missed calls from**
> **Ross Bradley**

> **Four voicemails from Ross Bradley**

'Jessy?'

My thumb hovered over the icon, half-desperate to know what he could possibly have said – needed to say – based on the number of calls? And the messages. What could he –

'Jessy!'

My phone disappeared. 'What the f–'

'I thought so.' Anna frowned, her gaze fixed on my unlocked phone. 'I knew it, I knew he'd come crawling back.'

'What, Patrick?' Laura said, confused, but one look at my phone from over Anna's shoulder and she too was cursing out my ex.

'That little –'

I tried to push aside the unsettling disappointment that it had been Ross, and not Patrick, who had desperately wanted to contact me. A feeling I wasn't going to examine too closely – especially after our disastrous last encounter.

'I'm going to block him,' said Anna firmly.

I lunged for my phone. 'Anna!'

'It's for your own good,' my best friend argued. And she was probably right. Still –

'Anna, give it back –'

'Oh don't get your knickers in a twist, you can always unblock him later if you really want,' Anna said, her tone betraying her true feelings about the idea. When she handed back my phone, all the messages were gone.

If I want. What did I want? Did I want Ross to contact me? Did I want to hear anything he had to say? I wasn't sure the answer was yes. But I wasn't sure it was a no either.

Anna flashed a smile before she and Laura rose from our little booth. 'Listen, we've got to go – do not be late for your big TV thing because you're moping here.'

'I'm not –'

'And don't think about that dick,' my sister said sharply, giving me that big mother hen glare.

'Which one? Patrick or Ross?' I asked sarcastically.

When I looked up at Laura, there was laughter in her eyes. 'I think it was pretty obvious I was talking about Ross,' she said. 'But sounds like you've got a certain hot celeb on the mind anyway.'

Kissing the top of my head, Laura whirled away, pulling Anna with her.

Well, fuck. She had me there. All those messages from Ross, and it was Patrick I was still thinking about.

I glanced at the time on my lock screen.

Shit. I was late.

'YOU'RE LATE,' SAID THE woman on the door with a frown. She was wearing a headset, had a pen stuffed into her bun, and had on a belt to rival Batman's, stuffed with masking tape, two walkie-talkies and a hammer, even if her clipboard had definitely seen better days.

'Yeah, I'm sorry, I –'

'Ms Donovan, over here, please. We're running behind schedule,' said another headset-and-clipboard guy with a shake of the head as he grabbed my arm and pulled me along a corridor.

'Sorry, I –'

'You're late,' said Patrick flatly as I was dragged into a make-up chair beside him.

He was dressed in a simple white tee and a pair of smart trousers, and it was unfair how good he looked, how utterly relaxed in this mad world of corridors and clipboards.

I dragged my eyes away quickly. 'I know,' I said quietly.

Awkward silence sat between us. Both of us refused to acknowledge the elephant in the room.

'Two minutes,' said the guy with the clipboard, his jaw tight as his gaze zigzagged down what had to be a schedule. 'Ready, Mr Tetlow?'

'As I'll ever be.' Patrick exhaled, rising to his feet.

Panic bloomed in my chest. What was I supposed to be doing here? Derek's notes had been brief: *Act like a supportive girlfriend.*

How the hell was I supposed to do that when Patrick could barely stand to be in a room with me?

My nerves must have been written all over my face, because Patrick took one look at me before turning round to the producer. 'Can I have one minute with Jessy, please? I promise I'll be right out.' He waited for the door to close before sitting back down next to me.

'Look, I'm really sorry,' he said, true regret in his voice. 'About how I spoke to you. At the Thirsty Bear. I didn't mean what I said.'

He seemed earnest, like he truly hadn't meant to hurt me. Honestly, I didn't know what to make of it.

'I – I appreciate that, thanks,' I replied simply. What else was there to say?

Some of the worry lines disappeared from Patrick's

forehead. 'I know this is your first time on set. It can be pretty overwhelming with all the lights, and noise, and everything else going on.' He leaned towards me, his cologne and something deeper – muskier – flooding my nose. Heat seeped deep into me, at every place our bodies met – his shoulders, arms and thighs all leaving invisible brands on me. I struggled to focus on his words.

'If it gets too much, just throw me a signal or a look. I'll get you out of there, Derek be damned.'

Where was the arsehole? What the hell was going on?

'Who are you and what have you done with my Patrick?' The possessive pronoun slipped out before I could catch it. I could feel myself flush.

Patrick chuckled – a deep, low thing – before continuing. 'I know what it's like feeling like you don't belong here. I've been in the limelight for years now and I still don't enjoy this shit. Probably never will.'

Huh. Well, that matched up with everything I had learnt about him so far – not that he'd given me much.

'I imagine you've already had to give up so much because of me. I . . . I don't want you to have to be any more uncomfortable than you already are.' His voice was soft, softer than I had heard it before.

This. This was the Patrick I'd imagined when I first met him. This was the guy I'd been secretly longing to appear since that first fake date.

And now I had him, I didn't know what to do with him.

A loud knock interrupted us. I swivelled my head to see clipboard guy peeking in. 'We really need to get you mic'd up, Mr Tetlow, and we've got a seat for you at the front of the audience, Ms Donovan.'

Patrick took in a long, slow breath. Then the smile I knew so well – the smile I now knew was fake – appeared as he held out his hand. 'Let's go make Derek happy and get this over with.'

I looked up at him and placed my hands in his softly. His grip tightened and energy crackled between us, just for a second, before he turned and led us out the door.

My hand stayed in his all the way to set.

NINE

*I'm watching from the sidelines of my own mind,
and surprise, surprise, it's a disaster . . .*
– from 'Observer', by These Exiles

I WAS TRYING. I really was trying to be better. But I had told Derek I didn't want to wear a suit.

I hate formalwear.

'It's the dress code, Patrick, what do you want me to say?' Derek's voice rang through on loudspeaker. 'Just wear it. You look great in suits, and we need to get some good shots of you tonight.'

I'd be more inclined to believe him if it wasn't his job to keep me sweet.

My eyes flicked over the outfit. It was . . . fashionable. Probably hot off some runway. As I picked the jacket up, I wondered what Jessy would think about it.

Damnit. I was doing that a lot recently. Wondering about Jessy – what she thought of me.

Stupid.

'You don't want to embarrass Jessy, do you?' Derek's voice said slyly. Like he knew something I didn't.

My jaw tightened. 'I don't know what you mean.'

'Word on the street is that the two of you were getting pretty cosy on that chat show.' I could hear the glee dripping from his voice.

Cosy. That was one word for it.

Yeah, I'd checked in on Jessy throughout the ad breaks, and someone in the audience must have snapped some photos of us, because pictures had been circling the internet since. The shots painted a certain narrative – one that Derek and the label were all too happy about.

What Jessy thought about it, I didn't know. I hadn't asked.

'No one says "word on the street" any more, Derek,' I replied smartly. I was not going to be discussing whatever pseudo-truce Jessy and I had fallen into with my publicist. It would just encourage him to trot us out in front of the world some more.

'Anyway –' Derek's voice was smug – 'I've seen the dress Jessy is going to be wearing and I'm telling you, wear the suit.'

I tried – and failed – not to imagine how she'd be dressed tonight. The sexy dress she had worn on our first date came to mind, followed by that polka dot sundress. And the sky-blue sundress with ribbony sleeve things. Shit, everything she wore did all sorts of things to my body.

'Just remember to behave tonight, OK?' Derek's voice came through the speaker. 'And try not to piss her off, yeah? We are finally getting some positive traction now the two of you don't look like you hate each other.'

I focused my gaze back on my phone. 'Yeah.'

'I mean it, Patrick. It shouldn't be difficult, dating a beautiful woman –'

'Fake dating –'

The snort told me everything I needed to know. 'Everything

is fake in this industry, kid. Just be polite, be nice, smile, kiss her on the cheek and tell her she's beautiful. It shouldn't be this hard to woo her – she already had a crush on you –'

'What?' My fingers tightened around the phone.

'Oh, there's my six o'clock – remember, show me the love, Patrick! I'll be watching online.' The call ended and my phone returned to my lock screen.

She already had a crush on you.

What the hell did that mean?

I'D ONLY HAD AN hour to shower, dress in Derek's suit and get across town to where this event was being held – some sort of rooftop on a fancy hotel.

When the car finally rolled to a stop outside the venue, I thanked my driver and took a deep breath before opening the door. I'd learnt to look down at the ground when I first stepped out of a car. Not just because I didn't want to trip and make an arse of myself – but because it prevented me from being blinded.

'Patrick! Patrick, over here!' The shouts of my name never grew familiar.

'And here is Patrick Tetlow, lead singer-songwriter for These Exiles, wearing a Crespianella suit –'

I walked past, paying them all no mind. Erika, Derek's assistant – and my babysitter for tonight – met me at the doors. 'Your date is just pulling up now, Patrick.'

I nodded distractedly. 'Right. Thank you.' I turned to see another luxury car where mine had been just a short moment ago.

As its occupant opened the door and stepped out, all rational thought exited my brain.

Jessy.

She was a vision. I could do nothing but behold her.

She was wearing a slip dress – all silk and spangled straps – in a dark forest green that complimented her so well it was like the colour had been made solely for her. Her hair had been pinned up in some sort of fancy style, all curls threatening to drip down her back, and as she turned to thank her driver –

She definitely wasn't wearing underwear.

I swallowed hard, my whole body stiffening at the shift of her dress.

Jessy turned and, from the sidelines, I saw the mild panic in her eyes as she was faced with all the cameras. I knew that feeling.

When she stepped over to me, it was all I could do not to pull her into my arms and make a real scene. God, her perfume – what *was* that? I had to stifle the sudden urge to bury my nose into her hair. When was the last time a woman had affected me like this? It was hard to think of anyone else, with Jessy so perfectly snug at my side.

'Hi.' Jessy's smile, small as it was, was already fading.

All I could do was stare.

'You ... you look ...' Fuck. I was supposed to be a lyricist. I literally wrote pretty things for a living.

'Shall we go in?' Jessy asked breezily, not waiting for me to collect myself as she grabbed my hand and pulled me forward.

'Just a second.' Erika appeared from beside me. 'We just need the two of you to take some pictures together and then we'll get you indoors.'

Of course they did. I don't know why I expected anything else.

The next few minutes were excruciating. Holding hands, smiling, laughing for the cameras, when all I really wanted to do was drag Jessy to some dark corner and trace my hands up her thighs.

This was going to be a long night.

'Smile! Smile, Patrick!'

Was I not smiling?

Finally, Erika gave us the go-ahead and I dropped my arm from around Jessy's shoulder. The lack of the physical connection was a wrench, an absence I couldn't stand. Without looking, I grabbed her hand. If she asked, I would say it was in case any paps were still watching.

But she didn't.

The hotel lobby was busy, but one look at us – look at me – and a member of staff led us to the rooftop. The sky gardens were beautiful, all flowers and strings of lights. Servers wandered around offering champagne, and some sort of light jazz was playing through speakers I couldn't see. There were people here I recognized – some I had worked with, others I'd schmoozed with, and the rest were from the upper echelons of celebrity.

Beside me, I felt Jessy press closer. I looked down and, seeing her deer-in-headlights expression, I led her over to a friendly face.

And not solely for her benefit.

'Vince – thank God there's real people here.' I grinned, shaking the hand of a man wearing large dark-rimmed glasses. 'Dogs still misbehaving?'

'I swore I wouldn't get another puppy.' Vince chuckled. 'So I've got two!'

I shook my head with a grin and turned back to Jessy.

'Jessy, this is Vince. He's done the cover artwork for most of our albums and some of our posters too.' I moved my hand to the centre of her back, keeping my touch light. 'Vince, this is . . . my girlfriend, Jessy.'

'It's lovely to meet you.' Her voice fluttered softly in the air, and I couldn't help but lean in.

Who *could* help it? *My girlfriend Jessy.* Was that the first time I'd introduced her that way?

'You too, Jessy. And let me just say, you look gorgeous tonight. Practically showing up pretty boy here, and that's not easy.'

Jealousy shot through me as Vince fired compliments her way. As the two branched into more conversation, that ugly little green-eyed monster continued to rear its head. It was so . . . easy for him. Did he notice the way her head tilted back as she laughed? Could he hear the soft lilt in her voice? Or was I the only one who paid that kind of attention?

It was almost an hour later when Vince finally made his excuses and went off to sweet-talk some exec. The tension pinching the back of my neck loosened with every step he took away from us.

I was being ridiculous. Vince was a friend. He would never look twice at a girl I was dating. But memories of Celine, and her betrayal, haunted me.

I would not go through that humiliation again.

As I watched him disappear into the crowd, Jessy stepped away, hailing a waiter.

She turned back to me, champagne flute in hand, and paused at my expression. 'What?'

'He was right, by the way.'

She tilted her head, flute still dangling delicately between her fingers. God, she was just so cute.

My throat was dry. 'You do look beautiful. I should have told you sooner.' *But I was too blown away to string a sentence together.*

Jessy's smile was back, but it was far too wise. 'You know, for a Grammy-nominated songwriter, you're not the smoothest of guys.'

She had me there.

'Look, Patrick. I know this is just another contractually obligated date. But this is one of the coolest things that has ever happened to me. So let's just try and enjoy the night, yeah?'

I nodded. It was the least she deserved. 'Jessy Donovan, I promise to give you the time of your life tonight.' I winked. My smile grew wider when the laugh I'd been angling for burst free from her.

'Charmer. So, what the hell are we doing here?' She hooked her arm through mine.

When I shrugged, the suit felt far too tight. 'Album launch.'

'Not for These Exiles, though? There's been no rumours of a new album – besides, I would have thought the rest of the band would be here,' Jessy said with a light laugh that made my whole body stiffen, just for a second. 'How are they, anyway?'

'Fine,' I lied. They were most definitely not. Our group chat was filled with nothing but bitching about their penance-making – though Ben was a little quieter than usual. 'They're fine,' I repeated.

I wasn't sure if I'd convinced Jessy. Her expression certainly didn't look like I had, but she moved on.

'So whose album launch is this?'

'Cassandra's Chorus. They're supposed to be here by now.' I glanced about, looking for signs the band had arrived. The two lads and their sister had supported us on the last tour, and I'd promised to come to their album launch.

'Oh, people you actually know?'

I focused on her face and tried not to notice the smattering of freckles across her nose. 'Not everything in this business is mutual backscratching –'

'Yeah, but they're not here!' Jessy looked half-amused, half-scandalized. 'How can you turn up to someone's party and the hosts aren't even here yet?'

I shrugged, definitely not looking at her lips. 'It's pretty normal actually. They'll be doing interviews somewhere. Press always overruns.'

I could still vaguely remember being confused about this sort of thing when These Exiles had first gone platinum. Journalists asking you a thousand and one questions. Being late to your own stuff. Other people turning up to an event just to be there, just to be seen – it hadn't made any sense.

Now it was pretty much the only reason that I went anywhere.

Jessy was still staring at me, nonplussed.

'It's just – it's a way to support each other,' I explained, incredibly poorly. 'You know, in the music industry –'

'Patrick Tetlow! And Patrick's new girlfriend, how delicious,' said a voice I didn't recognize.

How the hell had one of them got in?

It was easy to spot them; the journos always looked like they'd had to clamber over a fence to creep their way into an event like this, which, now I thought about it, was probably the case.

I acted instinctively, pulling Jessy into me and away from the pap. 'No comment,' I said, sternly.

'Oh Patrick, don't be –'

'No comment.' My tone sharpened. Seriously, would these guys ever get the fucking message? 'No . . . comment,' I repeated, slower this time, so the idiot *would* get the message.

The look of disappointment that swept across the journo's face was swiftly replaced with an expression of warm delight – as he turned his attention to Jessy. 'Jessica Donovan, isn't it?'

'She has no comment for you either,' I snapped, my grip on Jessy's warm shoulder tightening despite myself. 'Now get out, before I call security.'

Tension throbbed taut across my temple as I glared at the guy. After what felt like an age he stuffed his phone into his pocket and stalked off.

Only then did I realize three things.

Firstly, that I was breathing way too hard.

Secondly, that I had absolutely no desire to let go of Jessy.

And thirdly, that she was standing so close to me I could feel *her* breathing.

Fuck. The way her breasts were pushed up against my chest . . . blood rushed down my body. Feeling her breathe against me should not be so sexy.

'What – what just happened?'

The shake in her voice cooled me down immediately.

'The way he just . . . are they all like that?' Jessy looked up at me in horror. 'I – how do you stand it?'

I hoped my face was nonchalant. 'It's just what it is.'

'*What it is?*' I felt Jessy's shudder as well as saw it, her eyes almost blinking back tears. 'I'm sorry, I just –'

'Don't worry, you're fine. It's the shock. The intrusion, it affects all of us weirdly. I'm . . . I'm sorry you had to deal with that,' I muttered quietly.

More sorry than she could know. God, if I could protect her from all this – but hadn't I tried avoiding the press even before this whole fake dating thing started? Dating a 'normal' – Wes's term, not mine – was never going to stop the headlines.

'He . . . he just reminded me of Ross,' she whispered, so quietly I almost missed her words. I hadn't, though.

'Ross?'

She didn't even need to speak. I could tell by the look on her face.

'Oh. An ex. Right.'

Obviously she had dated before. Jessy was an absolute stunner; there was no way she hadn't. Still, the thought of another man's hand on hers, another man kissing –

OK, time to chill the fuck out, Patrick.

'He was just like that,' Jessy said, still quiet, nodding at the back of the man who was now attempting to get a photo with a pair of models. 'Intrusive. Demanding. Pushy.' She stepped even closer to me, and my breath hitched in my throat as she whispered, 'Thank you. For handling that.'

I was not going to take pride in it. That I'd protected this woman who had somehow stopped being a stranger, and was now . . . I don't know. Not a friend.

Friends didn't kiss like I wanted to kiss her.

'I get it,' I said, as lightly as I could. 'Part of the job is to keep the fans happy, you know. Selfies, and signing stuff – I never want These Exiles to get a reputation for not stopping for their fans. But paps are different.'

'I just . . . I wish they'd give it up. They swarm my house

every morning and I swear they're doing it in shifts, there's always someone there,' Jessy was saying, with that bracing look I was starting to recognize. 'I wish I had somewhere else to go, but I don't want them turning up at my sister's house. Or my best friend's.'

I hadn't realized the paps were still hounding her. The thought of her going back home alone tonight left me . . . unsettled.

'Book a hotel.' An easy solution.

She laughed, her hand splayed against my chest. When had that happened? 'Book a room in a hotel for weeks on end. Sure.'

'Just get Derek to sort it,' I said with another shrug. 'The record label will cover it. This is all their fault, after all.' That wasn't technically true, but what did it matter? They could afford it.

And if Derek kicked up a fuss, I'd just pay it. I could afford it too.

Jessy's lips parted in astonishment. 'Wh-What?'

'Consider it one of the perks of dating me.' I grinned, trying to lighten the mood.

Well, I wouldn't say being hounded by the world's media was a perk . . . but hell, if this was just a taste of what she'd be facing, I wanted her in a hotel. Safe.

'So, what do I do?' Jessy asked awkwardly. 'Just . . . ring Derek and ask for a hotel room?' Disbelief coloured her voice.

I tried to reassure her with a smile. 'Yeah, that's what I do if things get too much. I mean, I'm hounded by these people – day in, day out, I'm bombarded with it. Journos, paps, fans –'

The dark red flush that tinged Jessy's cheeks was impossible to ignore.

Oh, yeah. She was a fan.

I swallowed. 'Not fans like you, though. Obviously.'

A shy smile broke out on her face. 'Why not fans like me?'

Cheers erupted to my left as a gaggle of people started leaning closer together, chattering wildly. Cassandra's Chorus must have turned up – finally.

'It's just – you're different.'

Different because you don't stare at me like I'm some sort of sex god. Different because you haven't quoted my own lyrics back to me, or asked for a selfie, or started to dog my every footstep.

Different than I thought. Different because you're not here to get a story, but to experience one. And that's attractive in a way I hadn't expected.

All things I should have said. But didn't.

Jessy grinned. 'What, you're telling me that most of your fans don't appreciate your tie-dye disasters?'

'Artwork, I think you'll find it's called,' I shot back, even as she stepped out of my arms.

Which was probably a good idea. I'd started to feel really comfortable holding her.

'Oh, *artwork*? So it's supposed to look like a cat has –'

'Hey, art is subjective, remember!' I joked back at her, warmth spreading through me. It was all too easy to slip into familiar banter.

'Those T-shirts are monstrosities.' Jessy giggled, her whole body involved in the movement as she grinned at me. 'Seriously, how can a guy as hot as you wear such . . . I mean, you're an artist. Your lyrics. And then those T-shirts . . .'

'All I'm hearing is that you think I'm hot.' I lived for the flush that travelled down her chest at having been caught out.

For once, I didn't try to head off my appreciative stare, letting the success of this night loosen my inhibitions. The silence grew between us, but instead of the usual awkwardness, this was filled with something else.

Something good.

Fuck. This never happened. I hadn't expected to actually like this girl.

Her flush was deepening with every second I continued to gaze at her.

'What time is it?' She sounded winded.

I slipped my phone out of my pocket. 'Half-eleven.'

'Well,' Jessy said brightly, 'that should be enough time for Derek.'

She moved away – but only managed three steps before she had to stop. She looked down at where my hand was grabbing on to her wrist.

'Where are you going?'

Jessy turned, her smile hitting me in the chest all over again. 'Going? I'm leaving. We've fulfilled our contractual duties for the night, right?'

Leaving?

'The night doesn't have to end yet,' I said, before I could stop myself.

'Why?' she said lightly. 'It's all fake. It's not real, Patrick, none of this is. Any time we spend together is because of that contract, remember?' Her soft words rang harshly in my ears.

A chill whispered across my skin, and it had nothing to do with the evening air. 'Right.'

'We're just doing it to be seen, to help Laura – that's what this is for. For Laura.' Jessy held her head high, no shame in her statement. 'Well, we've been seen. We've done what –'

A phone rang. Mine. Damn.

'What?' I asked, irritation sharpening my tone as I picked up.

'Why hello, Patrick,' Derek responded cheerfully. 'Loving the official shots of you and Jessy. The two of you look nice and intimate standing close together like that. Well done.' The brightness in his tone was pissing me off even more.

I swore under my breath as I looked around. 'You seriously need to get a life, mate.'

'You and your bandmates are my life,' Derek said, sounding far too happy about it. 'Anyways, I won't take up much of your time. I was just calling to let you know I've had a taxi pick your mother up just outside of your location.'

My chest tightened. 'You what?'

'Yes, you can thank me later,' he said smoothly. 'Don't worry about her – worry about Jessy. Now all we need is a few more public suggestions of affection, and you'll be done for the night.'

My mouth went dry. 'You can't be –'

'Go on, get on with it.' The line went dead.

'Patrick?'

I shoved my phone in my pocket as I looked into the eyes of the woman I was starting to find a little too enticing.

Go on, get on with it.

'That was Derek.' I pointed – unnecessarily, probably – to my pocket. 'He was just warning me –' I cut myself off. I wasn't ready to get into my mummy issues with Jessy. Especially not when I was already feeling so raw from her rejection. 'He wanted to remind us of . . . erm . . . the public suggestions of affection.' Which was true.

Jessy swallowed. 'Oh. Right.'

'But you don't have to –' I began.

'I know. But it's OK,' she said with a small smile.

What kind of smile? My brain tried to analyse it even as she stepped into my arms. Delighted? Worried? Cornered? Perhaps –

The kiss on my cheek should have been nothing. It was hardly even a kiss, just her lips brushing the stubble I hadn't bothered to shave.

But, fucking hell, it was something. It was everything.

The warmth of her body pressed against mine, the shift of her breasts, her palm splayed on my chest, that scent, the way my hands immediately moved to capture her waist –

She'd been about to step back, but I halted her, keeping her close, nuzzling her cheek with my neck. God, I wanted this moment to last forever.

I felt – heard, sensed – the hitch in her breathing.

'Patrick –'

'I just wanted to say thank you,' I murmured, my pulse skipping a beat. 'For making this bearable. For being ... yeah. Great.'

Jessy tilted her head up, her gaze meeting mine, and for a moment – a moment that ached far more keenly than it should have – I thought she was going to lean forward and press those pink lips to mine ...

Jessy stepped out of my arms and gave me a teasing smile.

'There. Public suggestions of affection complete,' said the most beautiful woman I had ever seen, before she stepped away, leaving me emptier than I had ever felt.

TEN

Whoops, that was never meant to happen – can we pretend it never did?
– from 'The Mistake', by These Exiles

'JUST ONE MORE DRINK!' Anna begged as I glanced at my phone and saw it was near midnight. 'Come on, it's Friday night!'

It *was* Friday night, and it had been a damned long day. Once I'd got settled in the hotel Derek had arranged for me after the 'date of epic complications' – as Laura and Anna had dubbed it – I had taken to completely avoiding Patrick. Again.

A little difficult, when I was supposed to be dating him. Even more difficult when I could not stop thinking about a kiss that wasn't actually a kiss but maybe should have been a kiss. And practically impossible when your sister and best friend kept sending you trending videos about him.

Him, and you.

'One more drink and one more video!' Anna giggled, pulling out her phone and scrolling rapidly.

Laura groaned. She was sitting opposite the two of us as we lounged in the bar that had been our favourite since we'd first moved into our old flat. 'Please, God –'

'He's not listening to you right now, so you better listen to me.' Anna grinned as I tried my best to pretend I wasn't at all intrigued to see what video she was going to show me. 'Look at this!'

The moment I saw the opening frame, I knew.

Oh, fuck.

My heart fluttered, pulse racing as I watched a tiny, slightly blurry version of myself step forward in a green dress that admittedly made my boobs and butt look incredible, press a kiss upon Patrick Tetlow's cheek, get pulled against his chest as he appeared to whisper sweet nothings into my ear, then stride away from him.

And that was it. That was it!

'First kiss!' Anna crowed, waving her porn star martini at me. 'How was it?'

'It was a kiss on the cheek, you idiot,' I countered, trying to ignore the margarita the waiter had just placed before me. 'I didn't order –'

'From the ladies over there,' the waiter said with a grin. 'They said, and I quote, "For the girl who's bedding Patrick Tetlow."'

My face could have heated a kettle as Anna collapsed into giggles and Laura craned her neck to look.

'Which girls? Do you think I should talk to them about Butterflies?' Laura's one-track mind was no better with alcohol coursing through her system.

'No,' Anna and I said in unison as we pushed my twin back into her seat.

I glanced at the margarita. 'Do you think this is safe to drink?'

You could never be too careful, right? Even if the girls did look normal enough.

'Absolutely not,' Anna said firmly. 'Excuse me – yes, excuse me.'

I watched, amused, as my bestie argued with the waiter about making a fresh drink.

Laura nudged my shoulder, pulling my attention back to her. 'So, seriously. Kissing Patrick Tetlow. What was it like?'

What was it like?

Like . . . like nothing I had ever felt before. Like my whole body was buzzing with electricity just from being so near to him. Like the way he whispered to me, and only me, was my own private These Exiles concert. And after that, he'd just stood there and done nothing – well, he'd pulled me closer for a moment, a heartbeat, but then it had been over. A secret part of me had wanted him to pull me in tighter, longer, turn the innocent kiss into something not so chaste.

But he had done none of that. He hadn't called out to me – like in one of those cheesy romcoms when the hot guy chases after the heroine on a deserted street in the rain.

It hadn't even been raining. And nowhere in this city was ever deserted. And he hadn't followed me.

But I'd wanted him to. And that scared me.

'It was fine.' Maybe if I kept saying that, it would become true. 'It wasn't even a real kiss.' I needed the reminder as much as they did.

'So, you're not . . . you know . . .'

'In lurrrve –' the two said in unison. They could be so annoying when they wanted to be.

'Come on!' I exclaimed as the waiter brought over the fresh margarita. 'Thanks.' I took a sip, to avoid the inquisition taking place.

'We're just saying, he's gorgeous,' Laura said, raising her voice as the bar's music increased in volume.

'And rich,' Anna said, winking like a pantomime dame.

'And you've always fancied him,' added Laura, like that was the be all and end all.

I groaned. 'Is this all you two can think about?'

Seriously, when was the last time we'd talked about something other than my bullshit relationship?

'It just looked like you were having a good time, that's all,' my twin answered, and I couldn't deny it.

I was starting to have a good time. With Patrick.

Was the room really hot, or were these drinks super strong? 'He's just – Patrick is – I like him.'

I did. There was no point arguing against it when I'd spent all morning looking at the photos from the previous night. I couldn't remember the last time a man had looked at me like that. Like there was nothing else in the world but me. Did Patrick know what his face was giving away? Or maybe he was just that good an actor? I had seen first-hand the mask he pulled over his face for the cameras.

Maybe this was all just part of his performance. Maybe none of it was real.

It didn't matter. It was already starting to feel real to me.

'Like him? Oh girl, just admit you want inside his pants!' Brushing her box braids away from her eyes, Anna reached into her handbag, grabbed the tequila she always brought on a night out, and tipped a far too generous measure into my margarita.

'Down it!' She grinned. 'For tonight, let's try to forget guys, forget work and forget dating apps that take up way too much of your time –' Anna threw a pointed look at Laura.

'Hey!'

'– and let's just hang. We're only young once!'

'Young and hot,' Laura corrected as she lifted her glass of wine.

'Young, hot and famous,' I said with a grin, lifting my own, now intensely alcoholic, margarita.

Anna raised her glass and tapped it against ours. 'Clink, clink, bitch!'

And . . . the rest of the night was a blur.

WHEN I WOKE UP, face down in my pillow with last night's make-up crusted around my eyes, the low moan I uttered earned nothing but silence from my hotel room.

'Arrghhh.' I tried to force myself to sit up, but my tongue felt like velvet and my shoulder ached.

When the fuck had I hurt my shoulder? What was I, fifty?

I tried to recall the rest of my night with the girls, but only snippets came to mind. Hopping from bar to bar . . . stumbling back to the hotel . . . picking up my phone to message –

Oh, shit.

Scrabbling to find my phone in my rumpled duvet and eventually locating it in my right sandal by the bedroom door, I scrolled down the messages I'd sent last night.

Oh, shit shit shit –

> **Paddy**
> So, we're on for eleven tomorrow, right?

> **Jessy**
> Anything for you, king!

> **Paddy**
> What?

> **Paddy**
> You OK?

OK. Not the worst case of drunk texting.

Wait.

Eleven?

I looked at the clock on the top left of my screen and groaned.

Yup, I was going to be late.

'YOU WERE SUPPOSED TO be here at eleven,' said Patrick as I skidded to a halt just before him – my hands on my ribs, lungs pulling in as much oxygen as they could, my cross-body bag somehow still attached to me. 'That was thirty minutes ago –'

'I know – I'm sorry –' I really needed to get into the gym. Panting like this was not OK. 'So,' I wheezed. 'What – what's the plan?'

He hadn't shared much about what our next outing would be. My hangover was fading fast thanks to the large coffee I'd inhaled before I left the hotel, but I wasn't sure I had the strength to do more than just smile in a corner today.

Did he need me to smile in a corner?

'We're attending a lunch with my record label,' Patrick said with a sigh. 'They throw a fancy midday shindig every year, ahead of awards season. For all their artists.'

I paused, waiting for my brain to kick in before asking, 'If the lunch starts at midday, why did you ask me to meet you here at eleven?'

'Because first I want us to do *that*.' He pointed to a sign behind us.

Thanks to the coffee now coursing through my veins, it took me a moment to focus on the words.

Abseiling. *Abseiling?*

'You cannot be serious!' There was not enough money in the world –

'What?' A slow smile spread across his face. 'You've never wanted to launch yourself off a building?'

Was that supposed to be a rhetorical question?

'I like the ground,' I said firmly. 'Besides, we have this lunch –'

'Look, instead of just going from one contractual obligation to another, I figured we should actually do something fun for once,' Patrick said, a wry smile lifting his lips.

'Fun?' I repeated, trying to take it in.

'Yes, Jessy. Fun. Have you ever heard of the concept?'

Fun. Falling from a building?

I was starting to get whiplash from all the sides of Patrick I was being introduced to. Spontaneous, teasing Patrick was a new personality . . . but one that was winning me over.

'So . . . we're not going to have lunch with your record label?' I asked, glancing up at the tall building we were standing beside. I couldn't tell if my head was pounding from last night's antics or from the imminent death that awaited me.

'Nah,' said Patrick, his smile smaller, but still there. 'I mean, we'll still have lunch with them, but we'll be fashionably late.'

It was the easy way he took my hand. It was the way my skin warmed to his – the way his fingers felt right, solid, in my palm.

As though his hand should have always been there.

I found myself nodding, almost without thought. Anna was always telling me I needed to make the most of this experience. Perhaps it was time to start listening.

As we stepped into the lobby, a guy wearing sunglasses – indoors? – waved us towards a lift.

'So, do you take all your girlfriends here?' I teased, trying not to be so conscious of my hand in his. 'Abseiling?'

'No.' Patrick pressed the button to call the lift. My heart twisted before he continued. 'I haven't been dating anyone in a while, Jessy,' he said, his voice almost . . . was he laughing? 'Don't believe everything you read online.'

I mean – sure. Right. Not that I had been able to avoid him online.

The lift doors opened, and we stepped inside. Patrick pressed 'Roof'.

'Are you sure about this?' I glanced up at him, conscious we were . . . alone.

Which was ridiculous. We'd been alone before – but not since the almost-kiss. And not on a non-sanctioned date.

This was private. This was . . . intimate.

It was sending all sorts of mixed messages to my brain – which was unhelpfully supplying me with many, many ideas of what we could be doing in this lift right now. I imagined him pushing me up against the mirrored wall and dragging my hands up his chest until I had to wind my legs around his waist to hold myself up. The image came in such startling clarity that I was almost breathless with want.

'Jessy?'

'Yep!' I jumped, disorientated. 'What?'

'We're here.'

The doors opened to reveal . . .

Nothing.

I mean, not nothing. It was a rooftop, just like any other rooftop in the city. There were air-conditioning ducts and fire escapes, and a pretty impressive view. This place wouldn't have been a bad location for the fireworks at New Year. But there wasn't anything about it that particularly screamed *come jump off me*.

Then I focused my gaze on the two women standing right by the edge of the roof holding equipment that could only be for one thing.

My stomach rolled and I took a step back towards the lift. 'I'm not sure I can do this, actually.' In fact, I was entirely sure I couldn't do this. I had never been afraid of heights before but, suddenly, being this high up was making me shake. Maybe I just hadn't had the chance to properly feel the fear. 'Yeah, no. I change my mind. Throw me straight into the lunch, not off a building!'

Patrick's grin was fucking stunning. My whole body lit up as the strength of his full smile hit me.

'Come on, you've never tried abseiling?' he said cheerfully, as though he'd suggested a game of minigolf instead of certain death. 'It's pretty exhilarating –'

'Nope, nope, absolutely not.' Where had this fear come from? Laura wasn't afraid of heights – had Mum been? I'd promised myself I'd never forget a single detail, but just a couple of years later and the intricacies of her character were slipping through my fingers.

'Jessy?'

I managed to drag my terrified gaze away from the clips the women were holding – which apparently somehow kept you safe a million miles from the ground – and looked at Patrick.

He looked . . . disappointed.

The excitement had faded from his eyes, but the smile still lingered.

The smile I was very quickly realizing I was obsessed with. *Fuck.*

'You – you've done this before?' I managed to ask.

Patrick shrugged. 'Yeah, a bunch of times. We . . . well. We had to do it for a music video, but it turned out I get a real kick out of it.'

It was coming back to me now – the music video for 'Adventure'. It had looked fun – and totally bonkers. For someone stood firmly on the ground, obviously.

'I know it's a bit sad, trying it for a music video,' Patrick was saying, as though I got my thrills in a far more exciting manner, and not from trying to avoid Karun finding out that I was using the work printer for Laura's business. 'But it really is fun. I'll be right there with you,' he reassured me. 'We'll be doing it together. I could even hold your hand the whole way.'

His last-ditch attempt to get me on board was adorable, though probably impractical.

I swallowed, mouth dry. *How many floors did the lift go up?*

'But you don't have to. Obviously.' He stepped directly in front of me, breaking my connection with the outside world, hiding it from view. Immediately my breathing settled – *not*, I told myself firmly, *because he's closer to me.*

Because I couldn't see my ultimate doom.

'I would never make you do anything you don't want to do, Jessy,' he said intently, gazing down at me like he had that night at the Cassandra's Chorus album party. And just like then, I found myself getting lost in his eyes. My centre of gravity shifted towards him, pulling me further into his orbit.

Wait – concentrate!

'I just thought it could be something fun for us to do,' Patrick continued, his voice low. 'Without the pressure of Derek, cameras, the public – but if I was wrong, then I'm sorry. It's not a big deal, we can still head to lunch.' He shrugged, like it was nothing. Like it wasn't the sweetest thing he'd done for me.

And it did matter. To Patrick. I could see in his eyes that the disappointment I'd seen earlier hadn't actually gone away; he'd just hidden it from me.

Ugh. I was going to regret this.

'Fine,' I said quietly.

That wide smile was back. It was intensely intoxicating – and ninety per cent of the reason I'd eventually capitulated. 'Fine?'

'Fine, let's throw me off a building,' I said with a smile I hoped he was convinced by.

His laughter warmed me, even as we stepped out on to the blustery rooftop. 'I've got you.'

He spoke in reaction to my tight taking of his hand. A breeze tugged at my hair. How could Patrick just . . . just walk calmly, like we weren't going towards our deaths?

'Hey, there. Found us OK?' one of the abseiling women said as we approached. 'Careful of that line!' she yelled over the edge of the building. 'Great timing, there's only a few minutes' wait.'

'Great.' Patrick nodded.

The lady took another look at us – Patrick, really – before she exclaimed, 'Oh my God, it's Patrick Tetlow, right?'

Patrick stepped closer to me and curled his arm around my waist. 'Yeah.' Heat sparked everywhere his arm touched me. The white top I had hastily put on this morning had been pushed up by his forearm, leaving his hand on the strip of bare skin around my waist.

Which I had definitely not noticed. Obviously.

'Wow, my daughter is such a huge fan!' the woman gushed as I watched Patrick's face transform into . . .

Well. Work Patrick. I couldn't think of a better name for it. It was the look he got when he was interacting with the public, his fans – These Exiles fans. Professionalism descended and he was somehow distant, despite being physically close.

'Can I get a photo?' the woman was saying, her voice a little breathless now. 'For my daughter, of course. Could your – could you take it?' Her question was directed at me, and I instinctively looked up at Patrick – searching his face for approval.

I couldn't imagine how exhausting it had to be. Trying to just enjoy your day without having strangers always wanting something from you.

'Let's take a selfie,' Patrick said lightly, stepping just a few inches from me and smiling tightly.

'No one is going to believe this . . .'

The photo was taken in moments and Patrick returned to my side just as quickly. I tried not to delight at how protected, how close, I felt with him as he pulled me into his side again.

He was with me. He was mine.

The thought shimmered through my mind before I could stop it, but it felt so . . . right.

Patrick brushed his knuckles along my arm, and I grinned like an idiot. I was getting awfully used to this physical contact between us. And I wasn't sure it was a smart idea. There were no cameras here. No reporters, journalists or paps to peddle our love story in the next day's papers.

And I liked it.

'Amazing, thanks for that! Right, have you ever done this before?' the instructor asked, her silvery hair brilliant in the sunlight.

I shook my head, not trusting my tongue. If I opened my mouth now, one of two things would come out of it. A request for help, or projectile vomit.

Damn you, Anna, and your cheap handbag tequila.

'– and just like that, you'll be down on the ground.'

I blinked. Fuck. What had she said?

Patrick squeezed my hand, and I fought the desire to launch myself into his arms and beg him to take me.

Take me into the lift and downstairs to safety, to be specific.

'Why don't we go over it again?' Patrick said, clearly sensing my panic.

I threw him a grateful look.

He caught my gaze and gave me that uncertain little smile I was fast becoming addicted to, then jerked his head to the silvery-haired woman who was explaining how not to die.

This was ridiculous. I was about to go to my death on a spindly little rope, and I was far more interested in examining the colour of Patrick's eyes. Not quite green, not quite hazel. Was there even a word for that shade?

Right. Concentrate.

The next few minutes were – well, not exactly a blur. Deciding I would prefer to live than plummet to my untimely death, I really did pay attention to the instructor, whose name I now knew was Katarzyna, watching carefully to see how she used the ropes and various other pieces of equipment.

'I must be mad,' I muttered to myself, carefully snapping the hard-hat fastening around my chin.

Patrick, who somehow looked just as hot wearing the ridiculous bright orange headgear, grinned. My stomach fluttered. 'I didn't know you were afraid of heights.'

'Heights? Heights? No.' I peered over the edge of the rooftop at the ants driving about in toys cars below. 'Falling to the ground in an uncontrolled and terminal manner? Yes.'

His snort of laughter should not have made me feel better. 'I've got you.'

And those three little words should not have made me smile. Oh, hell. Here we go.

'– and then just swing yourself over the edge,' Katarzyna said, far too cheerfully. 'There you go!'

It was Patrick who had moved, smoothly and without a care in the world, up and over the side of the building.

My heart was hammering. 'Patrick?'

'I'm OK – honestly, I'm fine.' *Fine, fine,* was that all we could say today? 'Come on over, it's amazing.'

Fuck fuck fuck –

'Aarrgghhhhh!' I yelled to no one in particular as I swung myself over the edge.

The ropes held – and beside me was a grinning Patrick, a man who had never looked this free in the whole time I'd known him.

Or, you know. Stalked him online.

'Isn't this great?' he yelled, dropping a little further down.

'Patrick!'

Panic should not rise in my chest at the sight of a guy I did not care about dropping a few feet down a skyscraper.

'Just relax into it,' Patrick yelled up at me. 'I won't let you fall.'

Which wasn't true. The man had absolutely no control over my descent whatsoever.

Still. It made me feel better, in a way I was quickly learning only Patrick could.

Which was something I was absolutely not going to examine here and now, dangling off the side of a building.

Slowly, I began to walk down. *This is nuts! Laura and Anna are never going to believe it!*

But as I reached Patrick, then matched his pace as we continued to descend, I had to admit that this was kind of . . . fun.

Exhilarating.

Patrick chuckled, and his laughter warmed me. 'You're enjoying this!'

'I am not,' I shot back, holding a little tighter to my rope as we made it down another floor.

'I knew you'd like it,' he said happily. 'And I wanted you to actually enjoy yourself. I mean – you deserve to have fun. This wasn't your fault, after all – you didn't ask for any of this crap.'

I was hardly going to argue with him. Not fifty or so feet off the ground.

Besides, he was . . . different, like this. Freer. More open. This was a side of Patrick he clearly kept close to the chest, that few people were privileged enough to see.

I couldn't help but be grateful. Flattered, even.

And then he said something I was not expecting. 'Race you to the bottom.'

'Race to – Patrick!'

He was gone, swiftly yet controlled. Faster than I could ever even think to go.

'Patrick!'

Despite my better judgement, I did the stupid thing. I looked down.

The ground swam in dizzying circles and, in the centre, all I could see was Patrick.

Patrick. His eyes, shining up at me as he stood on the safe, solid ground.

'Jessy.' His voice sounded far away. 'You can do this, Jessy.'

The deep, shuddering breath I slowly inhaled wasn't enough – but nothing would be, not until I was back in his arms.

'I can do this,' I muttered quietly, gripping the rope tightly. 'I can do this.'

Slowly, slowly, and then faster, I stepped down, until I was almost leaping down the side of the building, my lungs burning and my mind spinning and my stomach soaring and –

And then I was on the ground, but I wasn't, because I was in Patrick's arms and he was holding me.

Holding me safe. Holding me close. Holding me in a way that Derek would have heartily approved of.

One arm gripped tightly around my waist, the other slid downwards. I looked up, heart pounding, a thank you on my lips ... and instead found myself kissing him.

A real kiss, this time.

And fuck me, what a kiss. Heat and relief and sweetness and passion, his tongue twisting pleasure in my mouth that I hadn't felt in – had I ever felt like this? Adrenaline pumping and spirits soaring and Patrick's hands holding me tight, as though he never wanted to let me go.

I lost myself to the kiss, eyes closed, head tilted, giving more of myself than I had ever thought possible, my whole body reacting to the heat, the vibrancy of this man –

I was kissing Patrick.

I had kissed Patrick.

This was not part of the plan.

I pulled away, cheeks burning, to see him with a stunned look in his eyes.

'That . . . that was –'

'A mistake,' I said hastily, breathless still.

Shit, what was I thinking? I could not go around passionately kissing this man! This was all fake! A sham!

We were playing pretend, and I'd let my fantasies run away with me.

Or maybe Anna's words had lodged themselves deeper in my mind than I'd realized. Either way, in less than a month we would be saying our goodbyes and never seeing each other again.

Patrick was blinking as though I'd knocked him on the head. Which, considering how swiftly I'd fallen those last few feet, maybe I had. 'Mistake?'

'Yeah, yeah, stressful situations can lead to intense and unexpected romance – have you never watched *Speed*?' I'm pretty sure I was misquoting Sandra Bullock, but I was even more sure the reference would be completely lost on him. 'It could happen to anyone.'

'Anyone,' Patrick repeated, staring at me as though I had grown another head.

Think, woman, think!

I glanced up at the building we'd just thrown ourselves off and groaned inwardly. There was only one way I was going to properly distract him from my brief loss of sanity.

Smiling as brightly as I could manage, I said, 'Should we get in round two before today's real dangerous activity – lunch with your record label?'

ELEVEN

Can you be alone in a crowd? I know the answer but it's not the truth, lights swirling as I smile, my teeth bared, ready for a fight . . .
– from 'Crowd', by These Exiles

THIS WAS A MISTAKE.

Well, not a mistake. But after a whole twenty-four hours of not seeing Jessy after a mildly successful lunch spent mostly trying not to make her smile, I'd cracked and gone against Derek's suggestion.

'Twice a week is more than enough – you don't have to see her again for three days, remember. Besides, it will start to look fake if she goes everywhere with you.' He'd had a point.

But three days was too long.

'Your next date is the Soundscape Awards after-party,' Derek had explained to me that morning. 'And this time, maybe don't arrive late? You know, try not to make me look incompetent?'

I should have felt bad, but I didn't. Still, I usually tried to avoid making Derek's job harder. 'Sorry, man, we . . . we didn't –'

'Right, tonight your life is your own. I managed to get you

out of Lily Ross's perfume launch, and don't think I won't be cashing in on that favour.'

Oh, I was sure he would.

'Just try and stay out of any trouble, understand?'

I did.

For the first time in – I don't know how long – I had a night all to myself. And I knew exactly how I wanted to spend it. I just had to hope that Jessy was free.

> **Paddy**
> What are you up to tonight?

> **Jessy**
> Nothing – well, hanging with Laura and Anna. Why?

> **Paddy**
> Fancy a night out?

'OK, IS THAT –'

'Yes,' I said, enjoying watching Jessy stare open-mouthed as some A-list actor passed us on the way to the dancefloor on the other side of the room. 'General rule at these kinds of things – if you think it's a celebrity you recognize, the answer is yes.'

'And that's – Jesus, I had no idea there would be so many famous people here tonight,' Jessy said, her eyes wide. 'Isn't this amazing?'

Amazing? No. This was pretty normal for me. But I was enjoying watching her take it all in. This type of event had long stopped being interesting for me, but seeing it through Jessy's eyes ... it somehow brought back some of that lost glamour.

I thought about introducing her to one of the singers who had opened for These Exiles on the European leg of our tour, but I was swiftly interrupted.

'We're going to dance,' Jessy's twin, Laura, said firmly, her face weirdly different without her glasses. 'Anna?'

'You know I will.' Anna grinned, jamming a gold clip into her hair. She'd taken her braids out, her hair styled in a fluffy 'fro. 'Thank you so much for getting us in here, Patrick, this is amazing.'

Well, Jessy had asked, and I was hardly going to say no. Her sister and friend were ... were pretty cool. And they seemed to be having a great time.

But I kind of hated that I didn't have Jessy to myself.

I watched as Anna whispered something into Laura's ear, who giggled before presumably repeating it in Jessy's ear ... who went scarlet.

Interesting. The same thing had been happening all night – quiet mutters that often left the trio breaking out in giggles.

'Go and dance, you dicks,' Jessy yelled over the loud music, grinning fondly as her friends departed for the moment.

Thank God.

'Right,' I said, suddenly unsure of myself now the two of us were alone, but not quite sure what to do about it. 'Another drink?'

'I'll have another mhhahhghh.' Jessy grinned, the gold glittery streaks across her cheek utterly distracting.

'What?' I leaned closer – to hear her better. Not because I'd been dying for an excuse to be near her all night.

'Marghhhmmth!'

The heavy beat of the club I'd suggested made it almost impossible to hear, but there weren't that many drinks that started with *marg*.

Had to be a margarita.

I gave her a thumbs up and rose from the corner booth I'd managed to snag – thank you, Derek, for calling ahead, I guess – to head to the bar, steps a little unbalanced thanks to the two large gin and tonics I'd already had.

The Forty Six wasn't a place that you could just turn up to. A haunt for celebrities only – usually your publicist had to make the call, and even then you still might not get in. That was how exclusive it was.

In a way, it was a relief to come here. No fans, no selfies, no stealthy photos taken over someone's shoulder – just people.

Rach was behind the bar, as always. She grinned at me, tilting her head to where Jessy still sat, waiting for me. 'She's hot.'

'What?' I blinked as I leaned heavily against the bar.

'Your date.' Rach gestured with a lemon before she crushed it into Jessy's drink. 'She's hot. You never bring girls here.'

I glanced over my shoulder, as though I needed to confirm for myself.

When, really, I'd thought she was hot the moment I'd swiped on her profile.

And when she'd pressed a kiss against my cheek.

And especially when she'd thrown herself into my arms and kissed me senseless.

And now – now she was being chatted up by some guy.

Of course, the downside of bringing your hot date – who you weren't really dating – to a bar like this was . . . some other famous, model-like man would make their move.

Perfect. The plans I'd had for us this evening were going down the drain.

'Margarita, and a gin and tonic,' Rach said, her grin far too knowing. 'On the house.'

Well, that was something. The price of drinks here normally made my eyes water.

Resisting the urge to rush back to Jessy's side and flex my arms in front of her new admirer, I carefully wove my way through the crowd. My eyes zeroed in on Jessy, watching out for any signs of discomfort from her. But she looked like she was enjoying herself.

Great.

'Hey,' I said as I finally reached our booth. 'Here's your drink.' I placed it on the table, before sliding in next to her and draping an arm around her shoulders. If I made sure to press the length of my side against hers, well no one could blame me.

Jessy grinned as she looked up at me, seemingly unconcerned by the presence of the stranger. 'Thanks!'

'Sorry, pal, I didn't get one for you,' I said, bolstered by the genuine happiness of having Jessy sitting here with me. I knew I was being a possessive arse, but I couldn't help it. My hackles were up.

The guy only grinned. Up close, I could admit he was handsome, but I couldn't really see Jessy going for the clean, preppy look. 'No worries, I'll get my own. Thanks, Jessy – you have a good night.'

His gaze flicked over me, and not in the aggressive, put-out manner that I'd expected. No, his expression had quite a different flavour.

'Oh,' I said quietly as he slipped out of our corner booth and over to another group, who welcomed him back with cheers.

Jessy's giggle was something I didn't just hear but felt, my hand gently caressing her shoulder like it had a mind of its own. 'Yeah.'

'I didn't realize –' I was an idiot.

Jessy picked up her drink and took out the freshly squeezed lemon before speaking. 'He wanted to know the brand of my body glitter.'

Do not think about body glitter. Do not think about all the delicious places it could be –

'Right,' I said. *Fuck.* I was an idiot.

Jessy's snort of laughter was somehow warming. 'You OK there, champ?'

'Not my finest moment,' I said, trying to see the funny side of it.

I didn't have to try very hard. Nestled up here with Jessy felt . . . good. The slow buzz of alcohol wasn't the only thing making my body tingle. She hadn't pulled away, hadn't told me I was being inappropriate – she was happily sipping her drink, her shoulder nestled into my chest, her head leaning against my neck . . .

Celine had never allowed anything like this, not in public – even when we'd slept together, it had to be a secret. I'd thought it was because she hadn't wanted the world to intrude on our love.

Big mistake.

'God, I could do with some air.'

I blinked and glanced down – suddenly conscious that Jessy's lips were far too close for comfort. Or not close enough. Memories of the kiss we'd shared flickered across my eyes.

A kiss I'd struggled to stop thinking of.

Jessy looked at me ruefully. 'Do you mind if we head outside for a bit?'

Outside?

That was a tough one. Outside was quieter, so we could actually talk. It was more private, fewer eyes, so we might be able to . . .

On the other hand, I was really enjoying the snuggled-up comfort we were enjoying right here.

Jessy's smile faded a little. 'Besides, we . . . we've had a lot to drink, and we could do with some sobering up. Stumbling out of here probably won't do anything for that reputation of yours.'

My frown furrowed. *What was she talking ab–*

Oh, shit. The DUI.

Jessy must think –

I glanced down at my gin and tonic. I mean, I liked a drink. Who didn't like a drink? Yeah, it was my third, and I could already feel the buzz tingling around the base of my skull – occupational hazard of not eating dinner. I'd been so looking forward to seeing Jessy that I'd kind of . . . forgotten.

I tried to think back to whether I'd had a drink on each of our dates and was pretty certain I had. Not before the abseiling, obviously, but the lunch afterwards had been pretty boozy.

She probably thought I had a problem.

Which should have been easy to sort out – but how the hell was I supposed to reassure her I wasn't an alcoholic without giving it up that it had been Ben behind the wheel that night?

If I couldn't tell her the actual truth, then I could at least take her outside for some of that fresh air.

I pushed the gin and tonic away from me. 'Let's head out.'

I knew I'd made the right decision when a smile broke out on her face.

Fuck. She's gorgeous. Like, unbelievably so.

It wasn't the first time I'd thought it, but it hit me hard, all the same. Maybe the fresh air would be good for me too.

It was so much quieter, once we stepped outside. In fact, there was no one else out here.

'You don't mind, do you, Patrick?' Jessy stepped over to the balcony, breathed in deeply, then looked up at me expectantly over her shoulder.

I dropped down on to one of the benches they had out here and shook my head. 'Nah, you go for it.'

Jessy looked out across the city, all glittering lights and sirens, and sat beside me. I had kind of hoped she'd be the one to say something, but no. She just . . . sat there. Next to me. Her hip pressed up against mine, her bare thighs just inches from my hand.

Inches from my hand.

Don't do it, Patrick. Don't be that guy. She said kissing you was a mistake.

A mistake that I wanted to repeat again, badly.

Do it. Touch her. The adrenaline shit was an excuse. She wants you. You've seen the heat behind her eyes, whenever you pull her in close.

'You've changed. You know?' Her soft voice drew me out of my rampant thoughts.

I turned to her and froze. Jessy was looking at me like . . . like she'd never looked at me before.

The gold body glitter shimmered in the low evening light and her eyes sparkled, but there was a directness and intelligence there that was painfully disarming.

As though she was picking me apart.

'Changed? How?' Hopefully for the better.

Jessy nodded, pushing her hair back behind her ears. 'Yeah, different. I mean, when you took me to that fancy restaurant for that first date –'

I winced at the memory.

'– you were so . . . so closed off. So absent, I mean. Not really there.'

I swallowed.

It had been deliberate. The distance. I had still been furious with Derek and the label for the whole fake relationship idea, and I'd wanted nothing more than to push Jessy away. Perhaps if she'd found my behaviour off-putting enough, she would have pulled the plug on the whole thing.

As I sat with her now, I was glad she hadn't.

'But when we went abseiling –'

I grinned. 'Ahh, the abseiling you hated every second of.' I let out a chuckle so she knew I was only teasing.

'I – I did not hate it!' Jessy protested, though there was a twinkle in her eyes that told a different story.

My smile widened. 'You absolutely hated it – but you did it. Twice!'

'You were a great encouragement.'

That should not have made me feel as warm and fuzzy as it did.

'So, what's the deal?'

I blinked. Jessy was looking at me expectantly, twisted on the bench now so she could look at me straight on.

I let my eyes trace her face. Her eyes, her cute button nose – and I couldn't help but glance at those rosy lips of hers. 'Deal?' I questioned, voice softer than I could imagine.

'Yeah. With you.'

With just us out here, alone on the Forty Six's balcony, the balmy evening had a magical feel to it. Like we were cocooned in our own little world.

Jessy's smile was that knowing one again. 'Patrick Tetlow, reformed player and bad boy of music, the dark and mysterious singer of These Exiles –'

I laughed at that. 'Fuck off.'

'Well, you know what I mean!' Jessy nudged me with her shoulder, and I tried not to notice how good it felt, to be in contact with her again, even for a brief moment. 'What gives, Patrick?'

My laughter faded as I looked up at her open and unguarded querying expression.

What gives.

So much. Not enough.

Any other situation, any other person, I would have shut down this line of conversation and merely laughed it off.

But the alcohol was still gently buzzing in my skull, and there was something even more intoxicating about this woman.

Jessy. Jessy Donovan.

I knew almost nothing about her, I realized with a twist in my gut. She worked in finance. She had a twin whose dating app she was trying to promote. She hated heights.

How could I be dating this woman – *fake dating*, I reminded myself sternly – and know so little about her?

Probably because she knew fuck all about me.

I knew then that if this was going to stay tolerable – hell, stay enjoyable, something I had not allowed myself to even think until now – Jessy needed to know something about me.

Not everything.

But something.

'I . . . I'm . . .'

Jessy waited for me with bright, curious eyes – a curiosity that only heightened my nerves.

'The distance is to protect myself.'

'What?' Jessy blinked, as though she hadn't expected my answer.

I explained. 'I . . . I'm not interested in all this fame. Maybe once upon a time, when I was younger. Before I really knew how much of myself I'd have to give up. But not any more.' It was the truest thing I'd said to her, probably, since we'd begun this sham, and I'd expected it to sting to be so open. But it felt right. 'Don't get me wrong, I love making music with the boys. They're the only thing that keeps me going, honestly. And I never want to get in the way of their success, so I've learnt to just hold back – it's so much easier that way. Does that make sense?'

I wasn't sure it made sense to me. God only knew what Jessy made of it.

'Yeah.' Jessy nodded, her smile still tugging at the corners of her mouth.

Was she laughing at me? Or did she get it?

Part of me didn't care. Here was someone, finally, who I actually wanted to talk to about this stuff. Who wanted to know more about the real me.

'The music,' I started slowly. 'That was why we – Wes, Ben, Matt, I mean – it's what we loved. Love.'

Jessy just . . . sat there. Looking at me. Listening.

When was the last time someone had completely listened to me?

'When I'm writing lyrics, when I can see how the chords will come together – it's like . . . like the most satisfying, incredible thing.' I grinned awkwardly. 'It's kind of like sex.'

Jessy raised an eyebrow. 'Oh yeah?'

'Like – like two people absolutely knowing what the other person wants. What they need. When a song comes together in the studio, I can feel it moving through me, like . . .' I scrabbled about for a word. 'Like the world inside me is finally out there in the world. For others to see.'

At some point, Jessy had taken my hand in hers. When had she done that?

'I know it sounds dramatic –'

'No, it doesn't.' A smile flickered across her face. 'It's probably the most real thing you've ever said. To me, I mean.'

I felt vulnerable, sitting here on a bench in the dark, pouring out my heart.

But it also felt right.

'It was supposed to be about the music, not – not the number of followers we had on socials, or whether or not *Musica Italia* would put us on the cover,' I said, my own smile returning as I spoke. 'It was never meant to be about our childhood friends selling stories to the papers –' or, if it came to it, my mother – 'or ex-girlfriends trying to use our dating history to land a reality-TV job.'

Jessy winced. 'Yeah, I remember reading about that.'

Of course she did. Everyone had.

But I couldn't blame her for it. Hell, sometimes even I couldn't avoid seeing my own face online, and I'd gone to all the effort of blocking my name from searches.

I glanced down at my hand. Jessy's hand. In the dark, I could barely tell. 'It all happened so quickly. Fame, I mean. It took me a while to realize no one really wanted to talk to me. They didn't care what I was about to say, just that I'd said it, and to *them* – like they were in some sort of fucking inner circle.'

'Sounds lonely.'

I blinked. Jessy was staring at me with sympathy – not pity for the poor famous guy who just had it so tough, but for a person who had spent the last four years holding themselves at a distance from the rest of the world.

I never thought anyone would get it. Get me.

'It is,' I said simply.

Silence fell between us, but it wasn't the awkward or uncomfortable silences we'd so often shared before. It was . . . different. Warm. Comforting. Like a hot tub I'd slowly lowered myself into. You didn't need to move to feel the benefit of the warmth, it just . . . was.

'So that's why you're so guarded,' Jessy said, a teasing lilt in her voice.

The track changed inside and whoops went up to herald the new song. The noise echoed out here on the balcony.

And I just stared at the woman now tangling and detangling her fingers with mine. 'You believe me?'

'Yeah.' Jessy shrugged, as though she hadn't just said something incredible. 'Who doesn't want to be believed?'

It was hard to take it in.

This was a woman who knew about These Exiles – who

on the planet didn't? – but she didn't seem to care. Sure, Jessy was a fan of the band, but it was like she wasn't affected by me at all. In a good way.

She hadn't asked to do any social media collabs, or take selfies together, or any of the stuff Celine had wanted. In fact, I hadn't seen her tag me in anything online. Had she even posted anything since this whole fake dating thing had started?

A quiet discomfort shifted through me. Everyone was out for something – that was something I'd had to learn, thanks to Cassie.

What did Jessy want?

I pushed the thought away. She'd shown me, more than once, that she wasn't here for my fame. In fact, if it wasn't for Butterflies and Jessy loving her sister dearly, I wasn't sure she would ever have agreed to it.

'It's . . . it's so weird talking to you about this,' I said, breathing a laugh into the silence. I hadn't let my walls down around anyone, other than the boys, in . . . I couldn't even remember how long. 'Talking to you is just so easy.'

Above us, the moon had come out from behind a cloud, and I gazed at Jessy now bathed in moonlight. Her skin was like a beacon, calling to me on the deepest, basest level. The music from inside faded into the background as the space between us narrowed.

Before I realized it, I had leaned forward to capture her warm lips. The kiss was softer, gentler, than the last. And she did not pull away.

Fuck, she tasted wonderful, and when my hand somehow found the nape of her neck to keep her close, she didn't fight me.

My whole body stiffened and then sagged as she broke the

kiss. She pressed her lips together as though she was about to say something, but then thought better of it.

A second later Jessy rose from the bench and stuck out a hand. 'Come on. Let's go back inside, I need to get the girls back to my hotel.'

Her gaze didn't quite meet mine.

Was she seriously going to ignore us kissing . . . again?

TWELVE

*You were never meant to be the centre of my world,
the moon in my sky, my affection waxing and
waning as my tides roar . . .*
– from 'Tidal', by These Exiles

'YOU KNOW, YOU HAVEN'T mentioned that we've officially fulfilled our weekly quota of dates,' I pointed out, heart fluttering traitorously as I sipped my iced coffee.

Patrick raised an eyebrow and absolutely melted my insides, the fucker. 'Haven't I?'

I shook my head as we wandered slowly down the path in the park. People kept glancing over at us, but for once I was confident it wasn't because I was walking with the lead singer of These Exiles. No, his hideous tie-dye T-shirt was doing that for us.

'Well, in that case, let me be the second to mention that we have officially fulfilled our – what did you call it?'

I hiccupped as a huge lump of ice almost went down the wrong way. 'Weekly quota.'

'*Fulfilled our weekly quota,*' finished Patrick, sipping his grapefruit cold brew coffee. 'To be honest, I hadn't noticed.'

Neither had I.

I mean, at least, until that moment.

I hadn't thought about it as I'd carefully chosen what to wear today, staring at myself in the huge, mirrored wardrobe of my hotel room and wondering if Anna would be proud of how low-cut this top was. I hadn't thought about it as I'd waited by the park gate watching people head home after work, heart hammering, knowing I was being a complete idiot.

Not at all.

'I suppose this is keeping Derek happy,' I suggested, trying not to pay attention to how close we were as we walked along in the late Thursday afternoon sunlight.

'Huh. Let's find out.' Patrick pulled out his phone and snorted.

I wasn't exactly looking, not really, but I couldn't help but catch what had been on his screen.

If you take this leap of faith as I abseil down your heart

That – that couldn't be about me. Could it?

'Yup – three emails, a message and a missed call. What about you?'

I pulled out my own phone.

> **Laura**
> 150K downloads this month so far! And 75% of them are women! Jessy is a star

> **Anna**
> Has she fucked him yet?

> **Laura**
> Anna!

> **Anna**
> I'm just saying, he's hot. And Jessy needs to get laid

Handing my coffee to Patrick without saying a word, I tapped out a quick message.

> **Jessy**
> You do know I'm in this group chat, right?

It only took five seconds before the reply came through.

> **Anna**
> I said what I said

I snorted.

'Well?'

Oh, yeah. Patrick was standing still, holding my coffee like some sort of waiter – or a doting boyfriend – gazing at me curiously.

'Messages from Laura and Anna,' I replied simply.

'App going well?'

'Yeah, really well.' Because that was what this was all about, wasn't it? Getting Butterflies up in the app charts, making women think they could meet a celeb by signing up, pleasing the investors, making my sister's dreams come true.

Not actually falling for a handsome singer who had way more layers than I'd first thought.

'So. I was thinking . . .' Patrick started.

I grabbed my coffee and began walking again, trying not to glance over at him too many times. 'Yeah?'

When I chanced a look at him again, though, Patrick seemed . . . curious. 'Tell me about your sister. You're twins, right?'

'Yeah. Non-identical, obviously,' I said with a shrug as we passed a volleyball match someone had set up on the grass. I halted, my wandering feet warring with my tongue, which won. 'She's great – I'm lucky, so many people don't like their siblings.'

'I wouldn't know.'

'Only child?' That made sense. Patrick hadn't mentioned any brother or sisters on any of our outings, and I was relieved to know he wasn't just hiding them from me. I was starting to get used to this new-found trust between us.

He nodded. 'Yeah. Probably a good thing.'

Now that was interesting. 'Come on.' I tried to say it lightly. 'You can't just leave me with that.'

When Patrick's gaze met mine, I had to remind myself to breathe.

There was something so . . . so enticing about him. Something that drew me to him, even in the most mundane of moments. When I wasn't with him, I was struggling to stop thinking about him, listening more and more to These Exiles, trying to remind myself that the guy I was listening to was not my actual boyfriend.

I seriously needed to get a grip. This whole charade was going to be over soon, and I would be going back to my regular, celebrity-fake-boyfriend-free life.

And oh, how I dreaded it.

Patrick shrugged and started walking again. 'There's no story, not really. What about your parents? Are they still together?'

Ah, deflection. I was the master – the mistress? – of that myself.

But something told me not to follow down the same old paths I'd always trodden. This wasn't Ross, or any one of my other failed relationships.

This was Patrick. And he had trusted me with parts of himself. It was only fair I did the same.

'Your parents,' he repeated. 'Still together?'

Right. Conversation. Words.

'My dad left when we were little. Like, really little,' I said, finishing up my iced coffee and dumping the empty cup in the bin we passed. 'I can barely remember him. He sent child maintenance, but other than that, nothing.'

'Ouch. Sorry, Jessy.'

'Don't be, honestly – it's not a sob story,' I said swiftly, trying to reassure him. 'It's all I've ever known, so I don't feel like I've missed out.'

And yet his gaze seemed to pierce through me far more effectively than I had hoped. 'Liar.'

My breath caught. *How had he –*

'Takes one to know one.' Patrick shrugged, dropping his own coffee cup into the next bin. 'My mum didn't even know who my dad was.'

'I'm sorry,' I said, feeling the awkwardness creep over my skin.

'Don't be,' said Patrick with half a smile as we wandered closer to a copse of trees. 'You can't miss what you never had.'

This time my smile was natural. 'You get it.'

'Oh yeah, *all* the daddy issues,' Patrick said with a laugh that drew one from me in response, all the tension in my shoulders melting away. 'Why didn't he stay, why didn't he want to find me –'

'Was it something I did,' I chimed in as we stopped by the trees, the wide canopy a welcome relief from the evening heat.

'What the hell did my mum do, how many guys are we talking,' said Patrick, making a face. 'Ohhh yeah, I've asked all the same questions.'

I couldn't help but smile up at him. 'You really have.'

Weird. I knew so many people whose parents had split, separated, divorced, sometimes remarried – but after not actually seeing my dad for fifteen years, I had no idea what he even looked like any more. There weren't that many people who couldn't pick their father out of a line-up.

And now there was Patrick.

'So, you must be really close to your mum,' he said brightly.

Oh shit. I always hated having to do this.

'Yeah, I was,' I said calmly, making sure there was absolutely no change in my voice. 'She died two years ago.'

And just as I knew it would, all the joy and warmth disappeared from the conversation.

Patrick's face had fallen. 'Oh, I'm so sorry –'

'Don't be,' I cut in, as I had done hundreds of times before. 'You didn't kill her. Cancer did.'

OK, it wasn't a great attempt at levity, but it tended to work. Now he would apologize again and splutter something awkward as hell, like, 'That must have been really hard' – yup – or 'That's crap' – double yup – or even my personal least favourite: 'She's in a better place.'

Patrick reached out and took my hand before he started to walk again, pulling me with him. After a second, he said quietly, 'Tell me about her.'

I could have melted right there on the pavement. *Tell me about her?*

No one ever asked me about my mum any more.

'She . . .' The smile that crept across my lips was broad. 'She was the best. I mean, don't get me wrong, she was irritating as hell sometimes. But she got me – both of us. She listened. Really listened, you know?'

Patrick nodded, his smile inexplicably wistful.

'She was a terrible singer – whenever she had a shower, we'd have to put the radio on to drown her out,' I remembered, a warmth curling in the pit of my stomach. 'But her pasta was to die for. She made it herself, flour everywhere – Laura would follow her with a damp cloth trying desperately to keep the kitchen clean. She . . . she always drank too much red wine on a Friday night and promised lifelong sobriety on Saturday morning. She loved shouting at documentaries, and she had this coat . . .'

My voice faded away as the lump that hadn't appeared in my throat for months suddenly made itself known.

We kept walking, one foot before the other. Somehow it was easier to just let Patrick pull me along.

Then his voice cut into the silence. 'What was her name?'

'Jessalyn.' Just saying her name was painful, a slice into my gut. Two years. You think you're over it, but you never are. 'That's how we got our names. Jessica and Laura-Lyn.'

'Pretty.'

Get a hold of yourself, Jessy – he was talking about your name, *not you.*

'And you never argued?'

I chuckled as we turned a corner and the wide expanse of the Serpentine lake appeared in the distance. 'Oh hell, we argued all the time, mostly about –'

Ross, I went to say, but hesitated.

But Patrick had noticed my pause. Of course he had. 'About?'

My gaze flickered over to him. This wasn't real.

Oh, my hand was in his and I liked him far too much, and if he kissed me again I wouldn't be complaining . . . but hadn't Patrick made it perfectly clear that this was all a PR thing?

Hadn't we both made it clear nothing could happen here?

His record label loved the idea of him dating a fan, the public loved the idea that they had a chance at bagging someone as famous as Patrick, and Laura's beloved app, which she had given her all to, got the recognition – and downloads – it deserved.

That was all this was.

I swallowed hard. 'About guys. We argued about guys,' I gave, prickles of discomfort warring with the warmth in my hand, which was still encased in his. 'She didn't like my ex.'

'Huh.'

I sighed heavily. 'I dated a guy – he seemed great – I thought he might be . . . I mean, not *the one*. Something like it, though.'

'You don't believe in the one?' Curiosity rather than judgement coloured his voice.

'Just one person for you in the whole world? A world populated by over seven billion people?' I shook my head. 'Nah, the odds are ridiculous. Say you have a statistical chance of meeting ten thousand people in your life, plus or minus fifteen per cent dependent on lifestyle, travel options, etc. – you'd have to live more than six hundred thousand lifetimes to meet even half the –'

'Shit, Jessy.' Patrick interrupted me with a laugh 'How the hell did you –'

'Maths degree. I told you, I work in finance,' I reminded him, startled at how delighted I was to have impressed him.

'So this guy wasn't the one,' he concluded.

Correct. 'I really thought it might go the distance, you know? And it's such a cliché, meeting someone when you're eighteen and thinking you'll be with them your whole life –'

'I have definitely contributed to that cliché,' Patrick broke in with a grin. 'Song lyrics are the worst for that.'

I tapped him on the arm, revelling in the chance to touch him again, even just casually. 'You're right, I blame you! Anyway. I got back to our flat seven or eight months ago and found . . . a note.'

Patrick winced. 'Oh shit.'

'Yeah. Trouble was, he was still writing it,' I said, breathing out slowly and trying to smile. It really was quite funny, now I thought about it. 'Suitcase packed, right by the door like a cheesy movie . . . but he was still writing the note.'

'Dick.'

'You and my mother had the same opinion.' I remembered my mum's choice of words for Ross when I'd told her about one of our earlier break-ups. 'Dick' didn't quite cover it. 'Oh, he had this whole explanation, but the gist was he'd met someone else. Had met several someone elses, actually,' I said, managing not to wince for the first time in . . . was this the first time that I'd talked about Ross without wanting to cry? Or hit something?

'Fucker.'

'I mean . . . yeah.' Patrick's obvious dislike for Ross, a guy he'd never met, warmed me. 'Hindsight is a wonderful thing, though. I mean, I look back at the way he had a problem with me always hanging out with Laura and Anna, the way he always wanted to know where I was going . . . He was toxic.' It seemed so obvious now, but Past Jessy, Young Jessy, hadn't seen the waving red flags for what they were.

'Anyway. I moved in with Laura just for a bit,' I continued, 'and then got myself a houseshare nearer work. Now I'm weirdly . . . fine.'

Super weirdly fine. When the hell had I got over Ross?

'I know the feeling.'

I glanced up. 'You do?' It was the first real glimpse into his past relationships I'd had.

Patrick shrugged. 'Yeah. Celine – Celine Dellacorte –'

'Yeah, I know.' Of course I knew. Everyone in the world knew.

'She cheated on me and, for a while after, I thought – I thought that trust was something idiotic. For the weak.' Patrick's smile was light, almost self-deprecating. 'And then there was you.'

Something fluttered deep in my chest, and I tried not to smile like an idiot. 'I know what you mean.'

We walked on in peaceful quiet. Walking in silence had never felt so right.

'You know, I'd completely forgotten about her,' Patrick said after a moment. 'Weird, isn't it? I mean, you fall in love with someone, she breaks your heart and you think it'll never be whole again . . . and then you haven't thought about her in weeks.'

In weeks. Was that because of me?

'So,' Patrick said, moving on. 'I'm guessing you're not dating anyone else right now. I mean, if you had been dating someone, I'd kind of assume they wouldn't be a huge fan of –'

His phone rang, cutting him off.

I smiled, almost relieved to be interrupted. We were getting into dangerously personal territory. 'Derek, right?'

Patrick swore under his breath. 'It's like he's got us bugged.'

'Honestly, I wouldn't put it past him,' I joked.

Making a face, Patrick picked up the call. 'Hello, my favourite person.'

I couldn't hear the convo – not properly. All I had was Patrick's side of it, but I was pretty certain I could guess the rest.

'Yeah we – already online? Oh right . . . yeah. Yeah. Yeah, I guess we could – uh-huh. Whatever you say.' Patrick's smile was wry as he ended the call. 'So, that was Derek.'

I laughed. 'Obviously. What did he want?' He hadn't needed to stage an intervention or force us to get along for a while now. We'd been perfectly obedient, matter of fact.

Patrick's smile softened as he stepped forward confidently, cupping my cheek with his hand and gazing deep into my eyes. 'I'll be honest, I've wanted to do this since we got coffee.'

My lips parted but no words came out. What the hell had his publicist said to him?

'And I'm tired of us pretending we don't want to do this,' Patrick said quietly, brushing my cheek with his thumb.

I gaped. 'Wh-What?'

He couldn't mean what I thought he meant.

Right?

Patrick just cocked his head to the side. 'You know, for your sister's app. For my reputation. Everyone's got to believe this. We've got to trick them. Trick the world into thinking this is real.'

'Y-Yeah, I guess,' I stammered, his thumb still swiping my cheek. I tried not to lean into the warmth of his hand, but utterly failed.

Patrick chuckled under his breath. 'I'm going to tell you what Derek told me, but to be clear, this is not why I want to kiss you, OK?' I could barely hear his words over the sound of my pulse roaring in my ears. 'Some pap is following us right now, and Derek wants us to give them a show. But that doesn't matter to me. I want to kiss you because you're gorgeous and because not having you in my arms is literally killing me. And I think it's killing you too.'

I swallowed. The desperation in his voice awakened something deep within me.

Something no one had ever awakened before. Not like this.

Furiously hating that I could feel the flush travelling down to my chest, I sighed out a breathless 'Yeah.'

'Yeah?' Patrick's murmur was low, suggestive, and it made my knees tremble.

Did he even realize he was doing this? Did he know the fire he was igniting in me?

'Just fucking do it already,' I said, voice just as low and soft.

Once I'd given him permission, he didn't hang around. Patrick leaned forward and closed the miniscule gap between us, his lips crushing mine with a fervour that set me alight.

I gasped into the kiss, welcoming him deeper as his tongue trailed along my parted lips. My hands reached out and grabbed his T-shirt, whether to pull him closer or to steady my own feet, I didn't know.

Patrick's nose nuzzled my face as he tilted his head, deepening the kiss, and I knew then: I was fucked.

He was delicious, and he made me feel like the most beautiful and alluring woman in the world.

Being kissed by him was the most electrifying, earth-shattering thing I had ever experienced.

And I never wanted to stop.

Somehow the kiss got away from me, away from us, out of control: he was biting and sucking on my lip while my fingers scraped and pulled at the hair at his nape. When his hand left my face to grasp my waist, his thumb swept under my top and left a teasing burning path, and all I wanted was for those fingers to trail lower.

God, I hadn't felt desire like this in so long –

This was electrifying. This was turning me on.

This was not going to end well.

THIRTEEN

Were you there? When the cut first went deep, when the agony swept in, running salt into scars – were you there?
– from 'The First Cut', by These Exiles

IT WAS A RELIEF to land, after the frantic dash to the airport and the overnight flight – though, to be honest, it was seeing Wes's face that truly made me smile.

'You dick,' I said as I hugged him in the hotel lobby. 'What have you brought me out here for?'

'Blame Derek,' Wes said lightly, clapping me on the back and grabbing my rucksack from my shoulder. 'Good flight?'

'Yeah, fine.' We were used to it now, the constant travel, though I had to admit I'd liked being in one place for more than two minutes. 'What am I here for, again? Derek said something about an opportunity –'

'A *photo* opportunity,' interrupted my bandmate as he rolled his eyes and jerked his head to the lift. 'Come on, you're crashing in my suite. He seriously didn't tell you it was a magazine spread?'

I groaned. 'Of course he didn't.'

Derek had to know that I wouldn't have obediently trotted on to the plane if I'd realized. He'd said something about Wes needing me at the UN project, and so I'd done what I was told – chastened, as usual, by the reminder that it had been my face plastered all over the papers after Ben had crashed the car that night – and now, here I was, hundreds of miles from Jessy, about to be trotted out like a show dog.

Same old, same old.

'By the way, I've been following your whirlwind romance,' Wes teased as he tapped his key card to the door and it clicked open. 'You and Jessy? Is it serious?'

'It's complicated,' I said as conversationally as I could, stepping into the room after my friend.

It was ... well, not exactly luxurious, but I supposed I couldn't expect much else when we're supposed to be at a UN event. The room had two double beds, an ensuite, a large TV and a kettle.

'If "complicated" means "fake", then you're a bloody good actor and you've missed your calling, bud,' Wes called over to me, dropping my rucksack on to the only made bed and lifting an eyebrow as he dropped on to his own – seriously messy – one. 'The way you look at her, seriously –'

I groaned. 'Please don't tell me you've been stalking me online.'

His grin was all I needed to know. 'Pretty difficult not to – you're trending everywhere.'

Great. I mean, that was the point, wasn't it? Bury the DUI story. Create hype for Butterflies. That was why Jessy and I were doing this. Even if we were starting to be something more.

'You like her, don't you?'

When I looked up from pulling my phone charger out of my rucksack, it was to see Wes looking at me with that quiet, serious face that I'd known for years. The sort of face I couldn't lie to, even if I wanted to.

'We're . . . having fun. She's fun.'

And Wes . . . cackled. 'Fun? What are you, fucking fourteen?'

'Shut up,' I muttered, throwing one of the pillows at him.

He caught it, still laughing.

'Seriously, shut up!' I said, trying not to grin as I plugged my phone in.

It immediately switched back on, and in flooded . . . oh shit.

'You must be in trouble,' Wes commented as my phone buzzed and lit up again and again, and again . . . with messages from Derek.

I swore under my breath and swiped open the phone. I was, apparently, *in trouble*.

> **Derek**
> Pick up the phone, Patrick.

> **Derek**
> You forgot to charge your phone, didn't you? I swear, you need babysitting.

> **Derek**
> Call me.

'I guess I better –'

But a video call was already incoming. Only, once I'd

accepted the call and settled on the bed, the face that appeared on screen was not the one I expected.

'Shit,' I said, hurriedly sitting up.

'Yes, I thought you'd say that.' Anna glared down the barrel of the camera. 'Hello, Patrick.'

'Anna! Anna, move over –'

Oh God, there were two of them. Laura appeared in frame next to Anna, her face far more concerned than angry.

This didn't bode well.

'What the hell?' I couldn't help but say, concern flickering in my chest. 'You – where's Derek?'

'Derek is currently being held hostage,' Anna said. 'We need to talk to –'

'I'm here, Patrick.' Derek's voice came from what had to be the other side of his office. 'Not actually being held hostage.'

That was little comfort. What on earth was he doing, letting Jessy's sister and best friend call me from his phone?

Panic flared through my body. 'Jessy – is she OK?'

'She is not,' Anna said smartly.

Laura looked shocked. 'Anna! Don't scare him –'

'She's not OK?' That was the only statement I could focus on. It wasn't panic rising within me now, it was something else. Something darker. 'What's wrong with her – do I need to get on a flight back?'

'Hey, you can't abandon me,' Wes started saying. 'We've got to –'

I waved a hand to get him to shut up. 'Laura, what's wrong with Jessy?'

'Nothing,' her sister said firmly, though the worry around her eyes suggested something else. She pushed her glasses up her nose with a thumb. 'Nothing, it's just –'

'It's just that she likes you,' Anna said with a feral grin. 'As in, *like* likes you.'

'OK – yes . . . I'd kind of got that already,' I stammered, unsure of how much Jessy had told her twin and best friend about our last conversations.

The kisses we'd shared.

How vulnerable I'd been.

'She likes you,' Laura said quietly. 'But she has terrible taste in men.'

'Hahaha, burn,' was Wes's super-helpful remark.

Well, that didn't do much for the ego.

'She's been hurt before, and we will not allow that to happen again,' Laura continued, staring down the camera lens as though she could reach through and throttle me. 'Do you understand, Patrick?'

'Because if you don't, we'll make you understand,' interjected Anna, somehow managing to look far more threatening through a phone screen than anyone had ever done in person.

I swallowed.

I'd never been given shit about hurting a girl before. And certainly not from her friends.

'I'm not going to – she knows what this is,' I said hastily, before trying again. 'When we signed the contract –'

'This has gone well beyond a contract, and you know it,' said Laura sharply. 'Jessy is the most important person in my life, Patrick. I half-raised her – well, got her out of more scrapes than I can count and got her through uni – and if you hurt her –'

'I'm not going to hurt her,' I interrupted.

For a moment, the two women held my gaze, as though considering whether or not to let me live. Then Laura nodded.

'Great. Well, that was it. Thanks for letting us borrow your phone, Derek.'

Relief flooded through me.

'Anything for an up-and-coming tech mogul like yourself.' Derek's voice came from off screen. 'So, should we have that chat about further investors now? There are a number of celebrities I manage who are looking for –'

The video call ended.

Wes snorted. 'So . . . Jessy *like* likes you, huh? And I'm guessing you *like* like her back?'

I threw my phone at him and laughed as it conked him on the head, a fantastic distraction from the flurry of thoughts that were roaring through my mind.

I KNEW I SHOULD be concentrating. And I was – but first, I just had to jot this down. Almost unable to help it, I slid my phone out of my pocket and tapped out a line.

> *As you let me into your world, I realized it was you*
> *Central sun, letting none into your orbit – until me*

God, that sundress made her look incredible.

'Patrick!'

'Wh-What?' When I looked up, my cheeks burning, there was a knowing smile on Jessy's lips that was far too comfortable.

'Eyes up here, bud.'

It was difficult to nod, difficult to agree, difficult not to take in her stunning form again. From the moment she had stepped into the restaurant today, four days after my bizarre call with Laura and Anna, all sun-kissed glow and smiles, it had been all I could do to pay attention to what she was saying.

'Hey!'

A noise – *damn. My ringtone.*

'Sorry,' I mumbled, shoving a hand in my pocket. 'I'll just check to see –'

A name flashed across the screen.

> **Incoming call: Unknown
> (Cassie Fletcher?)**

I declined the call.

'Important?'

'Not at all.' I put the phone back in my pocket, determined not to let my mother ruin my mood.

Besides, there was nothing she had to say that I wanted to hear. Now or ever again.

Before I could turn back, though, my phone buzzed again. I should have just put it on silent.

'If you need to get that –'

'I don't.'

> **Incoming call: Unknown
> (Cassie Fletcher?)**

One tap and then another put the thing on silent. When I looked back up at Jessy, curiosity was written on her face. But she didn't ask the question she clearly wanted to.

'I wish I'd known you back then,' she said instead.

That got my attention, though my brain was still busy with wondering why the hell Cassie was ringing me again. 'Then?'

Jessy nodded, pushing her plate forward slightly as her cheeks flushed. 'Back before you were famous. When you were just Patrick, not the lead lyricist of These Exiles.'

That was an interesting thought.

'You think we would have got on?'

'I think I would have been far too intimated to talk to you.' Man, I loved the way she blushed.

I leaned forward, the last of my spaghetti forgotten. 'Why?'

'Why do you think?' She rolled her eyes before looking at me intensely.

I swallowed.

This woman – she did something to me no one else ever had. My whole body came alive when I was kissing her – not like I was taking possession of something, but like I'd been gifted something so incredibly special instead.

Now, just sitting opposite her, I could still taste her on my tongue.

And I wanted more.

'I don't know. Why?'

Jessy's freckles only became starker as her blush deepened. 'You have a mirror.'

'So do you.' My voice dipped low. Didn't she know she was beautiful? Didn't she know what she did to me?

Well, the important thing was not to spill my guts and tell her just how often I'd daydreamed about her. About the sundresses she always wore, the way her hair gleamed in the summer sunlight. The way I'd tasted her lips but yearned for a taste of something sweeter – the kind of sweetness that came with a bed, warm skin and soft gasps into the air.

'Patrick?'

I blinked.

Jessy was grinning. 'Lost you there for a moment.'

'You could never lose me,' I said before I could stop myself.

'Good.'

Something stirred deep within me. Ever since we'd agreed to stop pretending, the chemistry between us had only heightened. The desire that had felt like a deep wave pulling me in now felt like a tsunami smashing through me. My every thought was consumed with Jessy.

'Thank you.' Jessy smiled politely at the waiter who had come to collect our plates.

'My pleasure, *mademoiselle*,' the waiter murmured back. 'And shall I bring over the dessert menu?'

Jessy's lips parted, but I got there first.

'No need,' I said graciously. 'We'll take two of everything.'

'Of . . . everything.' The waiter's eyes bulged as Jessy attempted, and failed, to stifle a giggle. I tried not to feel too proud of myself.

I nodded sagely. 'Yes, please.' I waited for him to leave before turning my eyes back to Jessy.

I tried to slow my breathing. *What is she doing to me?*

Had she put that body glitter stuff on her shoulders, or was that just the way her skin shimmered in the candlelight? Looking at her felt like gazing upon some great maestro's work. She was more than just beautiful, she was ethereal.

And right now, she was mine.

'So, what was I saying?' Jessy pressed her lips together, an adorable expression on her face as she tried to pick the conversation back up. 'Yeah. We probably would never have even met pre-fame. Maybe it's better that it went this way?' She cleared her throat. 'Obviously I didn't expect to meet in person, when we were on Butterflies – and then when I realized you weren't just some guy called Paddy, but one of the world's hottest men according to –'

My loud groan only sparked laughter.

'What! That's what you were voted!'

'Never remind Derek of that. I think I've finally got him to forget it,' I said, jokingly threatening, the twist of joy at her laughter making it hard not to laugh along with her.

As the desserts began to arrive, Jessy continued. 'I'm just saying – we never expected to meet this way. But I'm glad we did.'

Fuck, that felt good to hear. 'You are?'

Without hesitating, she responded, 'I am.'

I reached out across the table, avoiding the stacks of desserts I wasn't sure we would ever manage to finish.

But Jessy was already reaching for me.

The moment our fingers entangled, I knew. This wasn't just some deal Derek had concocted to save face – some mutually beneficial situationship.

This was something more. More than I'd ever had with Celine. More than I'd known before.

Everything I shared with Jessy was new, fresh – utterly unique.

Her sister and best friend hadn't needed to demand anything from me. I wasn't going to hurt Jessy. I couldn't imagine it. I wasn't going to do anything that could risk this feeling.

It made me want to pull out my phone and start tapping out more lyrics. The writer's block was well and truly gone, and all I'd needed was a gorgeous woman to cure it – which was perhaps a little pathetic.

Or perhaps it was inspiring. Perhaps all the poets had this, all musicians: that moment when you looked at someone and their smile held all the comfort of a home that you'd never known.

I was pulled out of my musings by the buzzing of my phone.

'I thought you put it on silent?' Jessy teased as I took it out of my pocket – again.

'I thought I had – but this piece of crap is dying on me.' I glared at my phone. Derek had tried to get me to replace it with some new, fancier model, but I was the type to hold on to something until the wheels had fallen off.

> Incoming call: Unknown
> (Cassie Fletcher?)

Fuck off.

I declined the call. I really needed to figure out how to block her number.

'Who's Cassie?'

My blood ran cold. Slowly, I lifted my head to meet Jessy's gaze.

Her cheeks were pink now, and she obviously felt a little awkward asking – but she'd seen the name on my phone.

Great.

'No one.'

'She has to be someone: she's been trying to get through to you for our entire date,' Jessy pointed out, entirely reasonably, as my mind raced. 'Friend?'

'No.' Not a lie.

Something strange flashed in Jessy's eyes before her expression shuttered off. 'Is she an ex? Or someone you were seeing before we –'

My phone screen flashed again in my hands.

> Incoming call: Unknown
> (Cassie Fletcher?)

I hit *decline call*.

'I'm not seeing –'

'Because she seems pretty persistent,' Jessy said, her voice growing colder. 'And I can't imagine that many people have your number.'

> Incoming call: Unknown
> (Cassie Fletcher?)

Decline call.

'She shouldn't have my number.' This was getting stupid. 'Look, let's talk about –'

'You do remember that you're not supposed to be dating anyone else, don't you?' Jessy's tone was pointed with accusation.

Fuck, how had this gone so wrong?

> Incoming call: Unknown
> (Cassie Fletcher?)

'Fuck off, Cassie,' I muttered under my breath, losing all patience.

There. Phone turned off. *Try and call me now.*

When I looked up, feeling more than a little triumphant that I had put an end to the constant interruptions, it was to see Jessy looking less than impressed.

She had her arms crossed. 'Is that how you're going to treat me, when all this is over? Telling me to *fuck off*?'

I fought the instinct to swear again. 'No.'

I had to be fair to her: she didn't know the context, and from the outside looking in I could see how Jessy had got the wrong idea. But still, I had hoped she knew me better than that.

'Because I can't think what this Cassie woman could have done –'

'Yeah, well, that's because you don't know shit,' I snapped, my temper like an exposed fuse whenever Cassie tried to get her claws back into my life. 'I don't want to talk about it. Please drop it.'

It was the wrong thing to say. Jessy's eyes widened – in shock, in hurt, I didn't know.

'I just asked –'

'No, you didn't – you *kept* asking, and I told you I don't want to talk about it. I don't want to talk about her,' I said stiffly, trying desperately to remind myself that it wasn't Jessy's fault the woman had been such a terrible mother. 'And I told you, she's not an ex, she's –'

'Right, and I'm supposed to believe you when you react like that,' Jessy said, her voice sharp. 'I just –'

'You just nothing.' My self-control slipped through my grasp. 'You're not my girlfriend. You don't get to dictate who I do or do not talk to – we are not actually in a relationship, remember?'

The words hung in the air around us, casting a pall over the whole table.

Was it my imagination, or was the restaurant somehow . . . quieter than before?

I glanced around, tension sharpening every one of my nerves, but no one seemed to have heard. Thank fuck – I did not want to know what Derek would have to say about me revealing to the world that the whole Patrick-Tetlow-dating-Jessy-Donovan thing was all fake.

But when my gaze turned back to Jessy, my stomach lurched.

She was pulling on her jacket.

'Jessy –'

'I'm tired,' she said curtly. 'I'm going back to the hotel.'

'Jessy – fuck, I'm sorry, it's just –'

'You just nothing,' Jessy said brightly, though her eyes were far too brilliant, glittering far too brightly. Was she – crying? 'You've made it perfectly clear what this is all about for you, and since we've gone over our quota, you don't have to worry about seeing me again for almost a week. Have a good one.'

FOURTEEN

Take me to the woodland where the fairies whisper,
whisper all the secrets I never told them . . .
– from 'Folktale', by These Exiles

'. . . AND AS PART OF our ecological initiative here at GSR Financials . . .'

I was trying to listen. I really was. But how long did a lecture about new printers actually have to take?

Sabbatical or not, I'd been called in for an important team meeting that, apparently, I absolutely had to be there for – at least, that's what Karun's curt voicemail had said. As far as I could tell, it was a never-ending lecture about the planet and how we should take care of it. Which was obviously a good thing. I liked the planet; I wanted it to continue. But I really was not in the mood. I hadn't been in the mood for anything recently.

I wonder why that is . . .

As carefully as I could, not wanting to draw Karun's beady eyes to me, I glanced at my phone. The lock screen said 10:41a.m.

Seriously? Only forty minutes?

'. . . and as you can see from this pie chart,' Karun said

smugly, as though he'd been the one to formulate the pivot table that had generated the data, 'we'll enjoy a full two point three per cent . . .'

You'd think after weeks off I'd be itching to get back to work, back to the routine of my own life, but it was all just so . . . so dull. My mind wandered, and this time there was little I could do to keep it on the topic of printers, even if I'd wanted to.

Not with the memories of my argument with Patrick still echoing between my ears.

'You're not my girlfriend. You don't get to dictate who I do or do not talk to – we're not actually in a relationship, remember?'

My stomach twisted: those words had hit me hard. I'd barely been able to hold my tears back as I fled the table. I was still reeling days later, the emotional bruise still twinging in my chest.

Patrick. The lack of him these last three days had been painful. His absence brought into stark relief just how much I'd got used to having him around. How much I'd let him into my life and I hadn't really noticed it – until he wasn't there.

'. . . efforts companywide are conglomerating at this synergising point to elevate our initiative by a factor of . . .'

Why hadn't he messaged me? Heck, why hadn't *Derek* called me? Surely this radio silence wasn't good for our image.

Ugh, I hated this – who was I, pining after a guy who couldn't even answer a reasonable question?

I'd promised myself I would never be that girl. Not again.

And yet here I was, missing him.

Maybe I should have messaged him.

Glancing about the table at the twenty or so colleagues who were all focused on Karun and his technicolour dream presentation, I carefully placed my pen on my notebook and slid my phone out of my pocket again. It only took a few taps to open.

Paddy was last online two days ago.

My stomach twisted.

He hadn't even been online to see if *I'd* been online.

Discomfort twisted in my chest as I tried not to think about it. Patrick didn't owe me anything. Sure, we had both wanted more than just fake dating, but maybe he'd only meant casually dating until our contract ran out. He hadn't made me any promises of exclusivity after that.

Even if I wanted us to be.

Exclusive.

I couldn't believe I'd caught feelings for a playboy musician who didn't even have the balls to message me.

A sudden rise in voices made me stuff my phone quickly in my pocket, and my heart skipped a beat as I picked up my pen – but the noise wasn't coming from in here. The room hushed as the crowd of voices outside our doors got louder.

What on earth is happening out there?

Whispers blossomed as people turned away from Karun's insomnia-inducing presentation.

'I wonder what –'

'Did you hear that?'

'What do you think it is?' Cathy whispered, eyes gleaming at the potential for office gossip.

I shrugged. Honestly, I didn't care. Nothing that happened at GSR Financials was ever that interesting.

But still, it was hard to ignore the noise that was coming through the door, even with Karun doing his best attempt at getting people to return their attention to the front of the room. 'Come on, team, focus! We still have forty-six slides to –'

The door opened and the floor fell away underneath me.

Patrick stepped into the room.

Patrick. In my office.

'Hey, sorry to interrupt.' He didn't look that sorry, I noted. As his gaze landed on me, he gave a small smile. 'I was just looking for Jessy.'

I wanted to curl up on the floor and die.

For a multitude of reasons.

This time the gasp was closer to me. Cathy grabbed my hand. 'Is – is that –'

'Patrick Tetlow,' breathed some guy from HR across the table from us.

What the hell did he think he was doing, coming to my job? How the hell had he even known I was here?

'Can you believe it?' squeaked Cathy.

'No,' I replied in an undertone, completely truthfully.

'Hey, Jessy,' Patrick said with that public performance smile I knew so well. 'Can we have a moment?'

The entire meeting room had gone silent and turned to stare at me.

Well, shit.

'Jessy, I wasn't sure whether to believe the gossip online,' said Karun brightly as he strode forward, hand outstretched. 'Karun Gupta, lovely to meet you – if there is anything I can help –'

'Right, you want a moment, come on then,' I interrupted Karun, desperate to escape the room, and rose to my feet. 'Meeting room three is probably –'

'Why not take the boardroom? I assume this is a business matter,' my boss suggested with a gleam in his eye.

Oh, crap. 'Erm –'

'Yes, of course. I would like to speak to Jessy about a small matter of business,' Patrick said lightly, as though there was nothing unusual about one of the world's biggest artists showing up to an office, unannounced and uninvited, and asking to speak to a low-level employee. 'Shouldn't take long.'

God, I was never going to hear the end of this when I came back. And what was all this about 'business'?

Is he here to call the contract off? Is that why he's found me at work, so I can't make a scene when he inevitably breaks up with me?

Is this even a break-up if we aren't dating?

I shuddered. 'We're going to want somewhere a little more private.' I looked at Karun, thinking about the boardroom's tall glass walls and the uninterrupted views they afforded. It would guarantee us being gawked at like animals in a zoo.

Karun nodded. 'How about the director's office? He's out with a client all morning.'

'That's very kind of you, thank you,' Patrick said with a warm smile.

It was hard to believe. The guy was guarded, he'd told me that – and I'd seen plenty of evidence to support his statement . . . and yet here he was, charming the literal pants off my boss.

And he was Karun's type, according to the photo of his husband on his desk.

'Patrick,' I said quickly. 'Come on.'

'Just a second, Jessica,' Karun interjected. He stepped between us. 'I didn't know you ran in these kinds of circles. You really should have told me.' He kept his voice low, and I could see Patrick raising his eyebrows in interest.

I focused my attention back on Karun. 'Right, sorry –'

'We've got a few celebrity clients that I'd like you to meet,' my boss continued quietly. 'I'll brief you on them soon.' Karun leaned away and turned back to Patrick. 'She's all yours.'

Flushing furiously, my cheeks so hot you could roast a marshmallow on them, I grabbed Patrick's arm and dragged him out of the room.

In stony silence, I led us around the corner and down a corridor, heading straight to the director's office – a place I'd only been once.

And it was nice. Large, with a wide window, a desk and three chairs – but, most importantly, thick walls. Made of bricks.

I shut the door hastily and whirled around.

Patrick's smile had faded somewhat, but it was still there. 'Hey, Jessy –'

'What the hell are you doing?' I hissed. 'Everyone in my office is talking about this,' I continued, pointing at the door. 'Right now! God knows how many photos and videos could be being uploaded this very –'

'Good.' Patrick's smile was only a flicker, but it had definitely been there. 'I want them to talk. I want them to know that you're important enough for me to come and see you.'

I swallowed hard, my righteous anger disappearing with his soft words.

Was this the grand apology that Laura had said I was owed? Was it really an apology if he hadn't said sorry?

I wasn't even sure I knew what I was owed. We weren't actually dating – I had to keep remembering that. Patrick didn't owe me any sort of exclusivity ... and he didn't owe me his life story.

I'd replayed our argument at dinner over and over again. I couldn't fault him for keeping the details of his past to himself. It was clear this Cassie was a sensitive topic for him. But I'd shared all kinds of things with him. I'd told him about Ross, about my mum. Clearly I had mistaken our physical attraction for a deeper connection.

Whoever this Cassie woman was, she was his business.

Not mine.

I took a deep breath. 'Look –'

'Cassie is my mum,' Patrick said quietly. 'She's my mum, Jessy.'

Oh. I had not expected that.

I hated to think how I must've looked. Shocked. Confused. Dumbstruck.

Perhaps that was why Patrick breathed a laugh, turning away from me to look out the window. 'Look, my childhood wasn't great. My mum wasn't great. Always a different guy, disappearing off for days at a time when she was convinced she could start a new life with him . . . sobbing and needing me to comfort her whenever it went to shit.'

I could tell by the look in his eye and the tension in his voice that it cost Patrick to reveal this part of himself, yet he went on speaking. 'Part of why These Exiles was so great was because . . . well, the music was an escape. I think I told you, once, that it was supposed to be about the music.'

When I spoke, my throat was inexplicably dry. 'Yeah.'

'That's because the music was always better than being at home. At the bedsit, or the room she'd managed to get, or some random bloke's house.' Patrick's smile was wistful. 'I'm not an idiot, I know she didn't have it easy. I thought, when These Exiles took off – I mean, so many of our problems had been because we'd never had a home, you know? Somewhere that was ours. Somewhere we couldn't get evicted from, or moved on from. I mean, she'd invite a guy back and he'd move in and then, somehow, we'd be the ones who had to leave.'

My lungs tightened. 'That . . . that sounds really hard.' After bonding over our absent fathers, I had just kind of assumed Patrick's relationship with his mother was something he'd never want to talk about. And yet here we were.

'It was. And I thought it would be easy,' Patrick said as he turned to me, his expression warm and yet somehow lost in the past. 'Easy, once I had money. I mean, money would solve, like, almost all those problems, right?'

'Right,' I found myself saying.

Patrick's smile faded. 'Wrong.'

He leaned against the director's chair, and I fought back the instinct to step closer to him, to comfort him.

I wasn't sure he would want my comfort. Not after the way I had pretty much accused him of lying.

I waited for him to continue instead, clasping my hands tightly together.

Patrick sighed deeply. 'I bought her a house – and when she asked for money for a car, for renovations, for decorating, I thought nothing of it. It was easy to hand it over. She was my mum. I wanted to look after her.'

'But something changed.' I could tell from the pain in his voice.

He nodded slowly. 'Yeah. It didn't happen all at one, but bit by bit. Soon she was never calling just to catch up with me, it was always to ask for money. She started taking out credit cards and forwarding the bills for me to pay. My accountant had to have a word with me, the money I was spending – the money she was spending – wasn't sustainable, even for me. But Cassie . . . Cassie doesn't like being told no.' Patrick took another deep breath. 'She refused to hear me when I tried to explain, so I just stopped trying. Cancelled the cards, stopped paying the bills, ignored the last notices. I refused to answer her calls, hoping she would get the message. But then she started turning up at the studio. At concerts. Everywhere I went, she was there, asking my team, my band, to see me. When that didn't work, she went to the newspapers –' His voice, strained but steady up until then, broke. And my heart broke with it.

No one deserved their own mother selling stories.

'I'm so sorry, Patrick.' A half sob formed in my throat, his pain was so potent. 'I didn't know. I've never seen those stories –' It was true. I'd never heard anything about Patrick's mother, or anything she'd sold to the tabloids about him.

'Gotta love an injunction. I mean, I know loads of awful people use it to hide shit, but it kept her lies out of the newspapers. Derek really saved my skin with that one.' Patrick's low laugh rang hollow. 'She stopped hounding me for a little while, but ever since you and I started up this whole –' he gestured to the space between us – 'fake relationship thing, she's been back to her usual antics. Maybe she thought being in love would soften me back up.'

I blinked, hardly able to take it in. His mother – his own mum, using him like this. Not interested in him, or his dreams . . . just what Patrick could give her?

Deep sorrow rose within me for him, making an ache in my chest reopen at the thoughts of my own mother. I wanted to reach out and take his hand.

'I even applied for a restraining order a while ago.' He spoke quietly, his jaw tight. 'What sort of a guy takes out a restraining order against his own mother?' Guilt racked his voice, like he wasn't sure whether he hated his mother or still loved her.

Now there was a question I would never ask.

I swallowed. 'It . . . it doesn't sound like she was acting much like a mum. But maybe she's changed, maybe seeing you all over the papers again has stirred up some –'

'No.' The syllable was absolute.

He was probably right. But my own grief from losing Mum made it hard, hearing someone talk about willingly cutting their parent off.

I continued delicately. 'I'm not saying reconcile with her tomorrow –'

'Please, Jessy. Don't. I've given Cassie so many chances, I can't risk giving her another one. It would destroy me.' Patrick's voice was little more than a whisper now, but his gaze was unwavering.

'I'm sorry. About all of it.' I really was. Embarrassment overwhelmed me as my accusations flooded back to me. 'I should never have pried; it wasn't any of my business –'

'It's OK. Honestly.' He leaned forward, brushing a hand down my arm, soothing me. 'I understand why you were upset. I should have explained.'

'And I shouldn't have pushed. Even if she wasn't your mum, even if it was an ex, or –' Why did he have to look at me like that? Smiling like that? 'What?'

'I mean, now that I think about it, jealous Jessy was kind of hot.' Patrick stepped forward.

My senses roared to life with every step he took closer,

but my brain managed to kick in and forced me to step back, maintaining the distance between us. 'I was not jealous.'

I wasn't. I'd just been . . . shocked, thinking he was seeing someone else, or talking to an ex.

Shock and jealousy were not the same thing.

My back hit the wall just as Patrick said, 'You were absolutely jealous.'

He was mere inches from me now, his hips almost pinning mine to the wall. My head was spinning – from his closeness or from the rapid change in emotions, I wasn't sure. I should not have been turned on. A second ago, we had been dumping our parent-related trauma on each other. And now?

Now, I was hot as fuck. And still in my boss's office.

'We – we can't do this here,' I whispered, looking up into his hazel eyes and wishing they weren't quite so beautiful.

Patrick's gaze flickered to my lips, then back to my eyes. 'Why not?' I imagined that the want in his eyes was clearly reflected in my own.

My breath hitched in my throat. 'Because –'

'Because I really want to kiss you right now, Jessy. Isn't that what couples do, when they sort out an argument?' Patrick said, pulling me off the wall and into his arms. 'Kiss and make up?'

I bit my lips almost without thought and Patrick let out a soft moan.

Slowly, slowly, inch by inch, Patrick lowered his mouth to mine – stopping a mere millimetre before they touched. 'Do you want me to stop?'

Hell no.

It seemed easier to show him rather than tell him, and he didn't seem disappointed when I pressed my lips against his.

Quite the reverse.

Before I knew it, Patrick had pinned my shoulder against the wall as he cupped my cheek with his other hand, tilting my face to deepen the kiss, his tongue invading my mouth in a rush of blissful pleasure that was surely criminal to experience in an office.

Fuck, it felt good to be wanted this badly. We kissed like we had hardly drawn breath since we'd been apart – his fingers in my hair, my hands tugging his shoulders closer, my knees weak as the kiss deepened.

Oh, this guy knew how to kiss. More, he knew how to kiss me. His teasing tongue knew all the right spots in my mouth, his lips pressing fluttering kisses that promised more down my neck before returning to my eager mouth.

'Jessy . . .'

Dear God, his growl was going to be the end of me. Perhaps it already had been; my eyes closed and I lost myself in him.

By the time we pulled apart, my body felt all soft and loose.

I tried to rein in the need still flickering through me as Patrick pressed his forehead against mine and murmured, 'If this is going to work, Jessy, you . . . you have to trust me.'

My heart fluttered. 'I can trust you,' I whispered, knowing that it was true.

His lips met mine again, hungrily, desperate for something that I was all too willing to give him. My own desperation matched his; my whole body craved his touch, and I could only thank the heat of the summer that I was wearing another sundress. Patrick's fingers caressed my shoulder, fluttering along my collarbone, stroking lower until he was cupping my breast, his thumb brushing my nipple through my bra sending heat straight to my core. I let my legs fall apart when –

The door to the office opened. 'Jessy, I need you to – oh.'

Patrick stepped back from me, hair tousled – whoops – and smiled at my boss. 'Mr Gupta, isn't it?'

'I just . . . I thought . . .' Karun thrust forward his office notebook. 'A signature? No, that's stupid – I'll wait outside. So sorry.'

We watched Karun retreat before bursting into laughter. When we'd got our giggles under control, I looked up to see Patrick gazing at me with a soft smile on his lips. 'Well, I'd better leave before –'

'I don't want you to go,' I said, before I could stop myself.

Patrick stepped closer, once again pinning me against the wall. 'So . . .' he whispered, pressing a scorching kiss against my lips before he stepped back and offered me his hand. 'Why don't we run away together? Unless you need to go back to that presentation, I mean.'

My face broke out into wide smile. 'How about we go for another round of abseiling?'

Patrick's chuckle made it a small miracle that I could walk forward. 'You just want to throw yourself into my arms at the bottom.'

Welp. Guilty.

FIFTEEN

*Because when we discover the truth, it'll be sweeter than
my favourite blend of coffee in your cup . . .*
– from 'Grapefruit Sweet, Grapefruit Sour',
by These Exiles

'AND WHO EXACTLY IS going to be there?'

Did I sound nervous? I definitely didn't want to sound nervous, but Jessy squeezed my hand as we walked along the pavement as though she knew I was.

'Not that many people,' Jessy said brightly as she wove the two of us through a gaggle of tourists attempting to take a photo of the entrance to Chinatown. 'Just friends. Family, really.'

Friends. Family.

I swallowed. I only had a few of the former, and none of the latter. Not really.

Since Celine . . . well, it had always been easier not to trust new people.

The reminder that I hadn't messaged Wes, Ben or Matt in days made the knots in my stomach twist even tighter. I really should check in on them – but any moment that I was on my phone was spent messaging Jessy.

And any moment that I *wasn't* messaging Jessy was because I was with her.

The familiar sensation of her hand tightening around mine made me smile, and as I looked to my left, it was to see Jessy smiling too. 'Seriously, Patrick. It'll be fine. You don't have to be nervous.'

I nodded, trying my best to relax my body.

It felt so natural now, walking about hand in hand, that I'd almost forgotten we were doing it. I tried not to think about how right it felt. Tried not to memorize the curl of her thumb, the warmth of her skin.

Add it to the long list of things I was trying not to think about. Like how her breath hitched whenever I leaned in to kiss her. Or how badly I wanted to make it past that, even if she was the hottest kiss of my life.

I tried to remind myself that sleeping with a woman I was contractually obliged to date had not gone well for me, historically . . . but there was a voice in the back of my mind that told me Jessy was different. That things with her would be different.

'Here – I think it's down here.' Jessy's voice interrupted my swirling thoughts. She peered down a lane that was barely a street. 'I think?'

'Who picked this place?' I raised an eyebrow.

'Oh, Anna always chooses where she wants to go for her birthday,' said Jessy, laughter bubbling up. 'So, it's you, me, Laura, Anna and Anna's two housemates. Don't worry, she's declared her birthday a phone-free zone, so there won't be any photos. Just a small dinner.'

My shoulders relaxed. 'OK.' That felt less nerve-racking.

'Not that it won't be rowdy,' Jessy added, grinning at me. 'This is Anna, after all.'

I felt honoured, in a weird sort of way. I couldn't remember the last time someone had invited me to their birthday dinner. The only close friends I'd kept post-fame – and the only people I really trusted – were my bandmates, and we weren't the type to be going out for fancy dinners. We got takeaway and watched trashy TV.

So here I was, going out with Jessy for something that wasn't a contracted date, and it felt . . . good.

'I can't remember the last time I was down here,' Jessy was saying. 'Here it is! Oh God . . .'

I peered through the window. The dim sum place looked good – or rather, the sign was broken and there was a pane of glass cardboarded up, which meant that the food had to be incredible. It was a general rule I subscribed to – the worse a restaurant looked on the outside, the better the food would be on the inside.

Sitting there in the window was a table of people laughing. Laura, looking nicely done up and without her glasses again, two guys, neither of whom I recognized, so they must have been the housemates, and Anna, who was wearing a flashing light-up headband that screamed BIRTHDAY GIRL in neon pink over her voluminous 'fro. She was quite the sight.

Jessy snorted as she pushed open the door. 'Classic Anna . . .'

The restaurant, if you could call it a restaurant – it almost felt like someone's living room – was small and dark, but it smelled amazing, all dumplings and buns and noodles.

The instant I stepped into the place, a cheer went up, and the hackles on the back of my neck rose. I did not want to be spotted, I did not want to be papped and interviewed, and –

'Jessy!'

'Jessy, you're here!'

'Thank fuck – Jessy, can you get her to take that awful headband off?'

Oh. That was humbling.

Jessy was laughing. 'It really is ridiculous, Anna –'

'I want everyone to know it's my birthday.' The birthday girl in question sniffed. Now she'd twisted around to greet us, I could see Anna was wearing a bright pink top with rhinestones that spelled out BIRTHDAY GIRL too.

'That's what I told her,' one of the guys was saying loudly. 'I told her – without the headband, who would know?' Sarcasm laced his voice.

I snorted and he looked up at me with a grin. His smile quickly morphed into one of recognition and I knew what was coming next.

'Hey, you're –'

'Yeah,' I said automatically.

I usually saved a lot of time that way.

The other guy sitting next to him looked between us as his friend continued. 'I'm –'

'No one cares who you are,' Anna quipped, her face flushed and her bright blue mascara making her dark brown eyes sparkle. 'Come on, you two, sit down, we were waiting for you to order.'

It wasn't exactly panic roaring through me, but it sure as hell felt close.

This . . . this wasn't my world. Ridiculous as it sounded, this wasn't my sort of Saturday night. I spent Saturday nights playing to sold out locations when on tour, and eating terrible oven pizza in my flat when not. I didn't – I never – I couldn't –

Jessy squeezed my hand. 'Come on.'

There was a seat, maybe a seat and a half, of space on a bench on one side of the table. Jessy pulled the two of us into it, leaving us pressed tightly together in a way that woke up parts of my body that should definitely not have been – not in public at least.

Anna was on my other side. She leaned forward, asking in a stage whisper that probably carried all the way through Chinatown, 'So have you two fucked yet?'

Jessy's face could have fried an egg. 'Anna, what the hell!'

Seeing her discomfort made my own bearable.

Wait – why had Anna asked that? Just how much of this fake relationship was Jessy sharing with her mates?

My gaze flickered over to Jessy. She was still pressed up against me in the most delicious way, and I opened my mouth before I could censor myself. 'Have you –'

'Ah, food!' Laura yelled and pointed to the waiter approaching our table.

'I thought you said that you were waiting for us?' Jessy said darkly, reaching forward and moving her glass so that the waiter could squeeze in another plate.

Anna shrugged. 'Toby and Cas must have ordered before we got here.'

'We are starving,' one of them grumbled. 'And we got here early. Besides, you always take ages to order.'

As conversation erupted around us, Jessy grabbed the waiter and requested a few dishes that were obviously favourites. Thankfully no one seemed to need much input from me. Laura was teasing Anna about something relating to a particular brand of strawberry lube, a story I wasn't sure I wanted to know more about, and Toby and Cas – whose full name I'd learnt was Casimir – were laughing along.

'I did never find that tube again,' Cas said with a sly grin aimed at Anna.

I watched as her cheeks went a darker red. Yeah, there was definitely something going on there.

'It was not my fault,' the birthday girl protested, headband still flashing.

'You already knew you were allergic to strawberries,' Jessy pointed out, using her chopsticks to grab a few dumplings. She placed two on my plate, and two on hers. 'Remember that time what's-his-face, Yang –'

The entire tabled groaned or giggled.

'I do not want to talk about Yang,' Anna said firmly.

'You said he could eat strawberries off your –'

'I said I don't want to talk about it!'

'The point is,' Jessy said with a grin, nudging me with her shoulder as she laughed, 'the A and E nurse was super understanding, and my girl Anna here promised me that she would never touch strawberries again!'

'But I did,' Anna said with wry smile. 'And I probably will again. Honestly, there's something about an allergic reaction tingle –'

The table collapsed into giggles and calls for her to shut up.

I smiled.

This was beyond odd. Being part of a group like this.

I couldn't remember the last time I had hung out with people outside of the industry. As we gorged on dumplings, and chatter – interspersed with laughter – rang out around me, a strange sort of realization hit me.

I'm a celebrity.

I was a celebrity. Everything about this dinner felt strange because I was so used to being the centre of attention. Forced to be funny and charming, making sure my good side was camera-forward, smiling at every inane comment . . .

None of that was me, and yet it had been my life for so long that I'd almost forgotten how much I hated it.

Or how nice this was.

'– and that is exactly why I will never hire you to be my lawyer,' Toby said with a snort. He picked up his glass before turning to me. 'So what do you do, Patrick?'

The table fell silent. Jessy paused with chopsticks full of spring roll halfway to her mouth. Anna snorted into her drink, gasping as she put it down, and wiped her mouth. Laura's lips had parted in silent shock.

Wait, is he being serious?

Toby looked around the table, as though mystified as to why everyone had halted their conversations. 'What? Can't a guy ask a question?'

I blinked. He was serious.

Of course he was. There were people who didn't listen to These Exiles. Who didn't know who I was, even if they recognized my face off a screen. I knew that. I just hadn't encountered one in . . . in a while.

'He's in the music business.'

I turned my head to look at Jessy just as she popped her spring roll into her mouth.

Well. She wasn't wrong.

Toby brightened. 'Oh yeah? Lawyer stuff like Anna, or finance stuff like Jessy?'

Laura and Anna started giggling, and I did my best not to look over at them.

'Something like that,' I said weakly.

The whole table was laughing now – well, except Toby, but he smiled good-naturedly and shook his head. I got the impression he was used to his friends' silliness.

'Patrick here is a writer, but he's hardly the most interesting person at this table,' Anna interjected, giving me a look that said much more. 'What I want to know is, where are my –'

'Presents!' Laura cut in with a knowing look. 'You are so materialistic!'

'I'm not materialistic! Some of us just have real jobs that earn real money so we can buy ourselves nice things!' the birthday girl retorted.

'And some of us have real jobs to buy presents just for you,' Cas said with a grin, pulling a small, wrapped gift out of his rucksack.

Anna fluttered her eyelashes at him. 'Aww, you should have.'

Laughter pooled around the table, and it seemed that I'd been forgotten again.

And I loved it.

This was ... nice. Being with Jessy was always a good time – when we stopped fighting – but I hadn't known what to expect from her friends. I should have known they would be an extension of her.

'That,' Jessy murmured beside me, low enough that no one else at our table could hear, 'can't happen too often.'

I glanced at Anna, who was unwrapping Laura's present now, and frowned. 'What?'

'Not being recognized.'

'Oh.' *Obviously*. 'Yeah, not that often. I don't know if that's good or bad.'

'Good, right?'

'Derek would suggest not,' I joked.

'There can't be too much that's bad about being recognizable, though?' Jessy asked, curiosity written across her face. 'Other than . . .' Her voice trailed off and her gaze melted away from mine. I frowned, curiosity of my own growing. When she looked back at me, Jessy almost seemed embarrassed. 'Obviously there are downsides. I mean – I shouldn't have mentioned – I . . . sorry, I know it must be –'

My complete confusion must have showed on my face, because Jessy lowered her voice even more and said in barely a whisper, 'The DUI.'

Oh. Right. That.

'It wasn't me.' The words slipped out without me thinking.

I mean, it couldn't hurt. Who was she going to tell?

Jessy was the one frowning now, and the instinct to tell her the truth, to open this part of my life to her, pushed me forward.

'I mean, it wasn't – the DUI. I wasn't the one driving,' I said quietly, leaning back against the wall and turning slightly, as though that could give us extra privacy.

It didn't seem to matter. Anna was laughing with the others about the presents they'd given her, attention elsewhere.

Jessy bit her lip. 'You weren't?'

I couldn't help myself. 'It was Ben.'

Fuck. I probably shouldn't have told her that.

But it was *Jessy*. She was just so easy to talk to. So easy to reveal things to.

I knew, deep down, I could trust her.

She was still worrying her lip. 'So, you – you what, switched places?'

I nodded.

'Why would you do that?' Her shock was palpable. 'Why would you agree?' she said in an undertone. 'Ross once asked me to – and I wouldn't do it. I wouldn't switch.'

For some reason, I felt a little . . . defensive. The mention of her ex threw me off-kilter. 'He's my friend. I would do anything for my boys.' They were the only family I had. 'I just . . . It would have wrecked him, being torn up on the internet and in the papers like that. And he already has points on his licence,' I explained. 'To be clear, he didn't ask. It wasn't like that. I just kind of stepped in and decided for him.'

The laughter and chatter of the birthday group continued around us as Jessy examined me, a mix of emotions swirling in her eyes.

Curiosity, and something else I didn't recognize.

'You just did it for him?' she said as Laura passed a plate of dumplings around the table. Neither of us took any – too engrossed in our own world. 'Accepted the DUI? Isn't that a criminal record?' Concern was evident in her voice, a concern I definitely shouldn't have been so glad to hear.

'A warning and public penance, as I had an otherwise clean record. Nothing I wouldn't do again, for a friend.'

After a second, her lips lifted into a smile. 'You're a good man, Patrick.'

My stomach swooped and for a moment I was speechless.

'I . . . I would do a lot. For the people I care about, I'd do anything.'

Jessy looked at me, her freckles sun-kissed and her lips so inviting, and there was warmth in her eyes that felt all for me and no one else.

The moment stretched.

We were so close, surrounded by people but somehow completely alone. Lost in our own bubble. It felt private. Intimate. Ours.

'Right, Patrick, your vote.'

And the bubble burst.

I blinked. Anna was grinning at me, and when I glanced back at Jessy, she had already turned to chat with Laura.

'Patrick?' Anna called my name again. 'Your vote is needed – is it or is it not weird that Toby still doesn't know how to do his own laundry?'

'I know how to –'

'Then why are all my undies pink now, you dimwit?' Anna turned back around to lightly smack her housemate's arm.

Apparently Anna didn't need my vote too badly, because she continued berating her housemate for some time. Which was perfect for me.

Not just because I didn't have a particularly good insight to share – I hadn't done my own washing in some time – but because Jessy had placed a hand on my thigh, and all coherent thought was driven away.

Save one.

'So have you two fucked yet?'

SIXTEEN

*The adventure isn't you, the adventure isn't us, the
adventure is me . . .*
– from 'Adventure', by These Exiles

'I MEAN . . . IT'S THE right name. It was definitely the Phoenix Hotel,' I told my sister, a little uncertainly. 'But this can't be where Patrick wanted to meet me . . . can it?

We were in a part of the city I'd never actually been in before. Now I was here, I knew why. Everyone walking about looked as though they got daily blow-dries to match their pearls – and not the cheap kind I'd bought a few years ago, but the real deal. The place was jammed with fancy cars without proper number plates, and boutiques without prices, and a patisserie that sold cakes that cost more than my rent.

And here was the Phoenix Hotel.

'There can't be that many Phoenix Hotels,' Laura said with a shrug as she gazed up at the building, her coffee from our breakfast run still in her hands. 'And he said he was meeting you here?'

I nodded. The hotel looked like something out of a Jane Austen novel – all pillars and marble. There was even a doorman dressed in some sort of livery. I pulled out my phone and reread Patrick's message. I was definitely in the right place.

> **Paddy**
> I've got a work thing at the Phoenix Hotel until eleven. Meet me there before we go to lunch?

I swallowed. This was . . . not the sort of place I would tend to hang out – but we weren't staying, were we? It was just somewhere to meet.

'So . . . a hotel room?' My sister asked with a twinkle in her eye. 'You don't think he –'

'No,' I said automatically.

Laura raised an eyebrow above her frames. 'You didn't know what I was going to –'

'I knew exactly what you were going to say,' I said with a wry smile. 'And the answer is still no. He said he had a work thing here.'

'OK, but still, you should really get on that man. He makes Ross look like an absolute loser, not that he needed much help there.'

I looked at her, unimpressed.

'I'm just saying: blocking Ross's calls is one of the best thing you've ever done.' Laura paused. 'Or the best thing Anna's done, anyway. He hasn't been bothering you lately, right?'

Nope. 'Ross is ancient history, I haven't even –'

'Did Derek mention that he's been trying to get into your hotel?'

I stopped in my tracks. 'What?' This was the first I'd heard of it, and cold gripped my heart.

'Yeah, he rang me to ask if Ross Bradley should be an approved person,' my sister said, something like guilt sweeping across her face. 'I'm sorry I didn't tell you sooner, but I wanted to make sure you weren't tempted to go back there. I wanted to protect you from –'

'You don't have to keep protecting me,' I said, vaguely annoyed she'd kept something so big from me. What if I had run into him in the lobby? Or outside the hotel?

Why the thought of my ex trying to worm his way back into my life made me so uncomfortable, I didn't know. I'd just got truly free of him, and it had taken work. And now, big surprise, he wanted back into my life.

No thank you.

'I know. I really am sorry – but anyway, forget him. You've got Patrick now. And doesn't Karun have you meeting with some famous clients for work?'

He did. We'd agreed I would take time during my sabbatical to meet and network with some of GSR's high-net-worth clients, and I hadn't argued. He hadn't given me much of a choice – and it wasn't like I'd had much else to do recently. In the lead-up to the Songwriter Awards, my chances to see Patrick were growing fewer and fewer.

'My little sister, on to bigger and better things!' Laura wiggled her eyebrows. 'Did you really meet –'

'You know I'm just meeting these people for work,' I shot back, trying not to notice a woman stare at us as we walked down the street. Her face felt familiar, but I couldn't quite place it. *Please, don't be a journalist, or, worse, a superfan . . .*

'You have to admit, you're moving in higher circles now.'

My sister grinned. 'Anyone would think that being wined and dined by the very –'

'You're Jessica Donovan, aren't you?'

My twin and I turned to see the woman I'd noticed earlier approach us. She wore the most delicate heels and looked likely to fall at any moment, her gaze fixed on me.

Oh God.

Patrick had warned me this might happen – that, eventually, people would begin to recognize me and might approach me in the street.

I'd laughed.

'Erm, hi,' I said awkwardly.

Laura stepped closer to me, her arm brushing up against mine. 'Who are you?'

Ever the protective sister.

'I'm a fan. Just a fan,' the woman said with a broad grin. 'Patrick, what a rockstar, eh?'

She didn't seem intoxicated or anything, just ... just fixated. A prickle of discomfort warred with my wish to be polite. I mean, I got it. Hadn't I acted the fool when I'd first met Patrick at Maria's?

God, that felt like a lifetime ago.

But this woman seemed a little older than the usual age of Patrick's fans. These Exiles were a popular band, but their core fanbase was under thirty. This woman was closer to being middle-aged.

'How is it going between you two? It must be so exciting, being with a celebrity. Do you love him?'

My laugh was awkward and damned uncomfortable. 'Erm ...'

What the hell was I supposed to say to that?

'Can I get a selfie?' The woman pulled a phone from her pocket and smiled brightly. 'Or your friend could take it for us?'

What was it Patrick had said – it was important fans always walked away with a positive experience.

My shoulders relaxed. Someone happy to hand their phone over to a stranger probably wasn't going to do something weird. 'Yeah, sure. Why not. Laura, do you mind?'

My twin gave me a look that said quite clearly that this was not what she'd signed up for, but she took the phone from the woman anyway and nodded. 'All right, smile, you two.'

The woman threw an arm around me and held me close, far closer than was comfortable, but she was grinning at the camera, so I smiled as hard as I could and tried not to breathe in her sharp jasmine perfume.

'Thank you so much, Jessy,' she said with a grin. 'I hope he's treating you well, petal. Showering you with jewels, that sort of thing.'

'Yeah,' I said, my stomach twisting. 'Well, it was nice to meet you.'

Thank goodness she got the hint, walking away with another quick thanks over her shoulder before turning the corner, her gaze fixed on her phone.

'Weird,' Laura muttered. 'But I guess you are now with Patrick Tetlow, international celebrity. Bound to happen eventually.'

'Yeah.' No wonder Patrick wore those ridiculous hats and pulled them low over his face. If that was just one person, and it made me feel that uncomfortable . . .

'Right, I gotta go. Those analysis spreadsheets won't review themselves,' Laura said, pulling me into a hug before glancing up at the Phoenix Hotel for a last time. 'Don't do anything I wouldn't do, yeah?'

This time my smile was natural. 'No promises.'

'Yes?' The doorman's gaze flickered over me in barely veiled disapproval as I stepped forward.

It was all I could do not to roll my eyes. I mean, what the hell did he think I was doing, other than walking towards the door? 'I'm meeting someone. A friend.'

A friend.

The doorman raised an eyebrow. 'Indeed.'

OK, fine, this was a fancier place than I had thought, and I definitely wasn't dressed for it. The sudden downpour of summer rain as I'd left my hotel meant I'd thrown on an old raincoat that had definitely seen better days, but underneath I was wearing a pretty passable sundress.

'Right. In y'go.'

It wasn't the warmest of welcomes, and it was perfectly matched by the unimpressed expression on the receptionist's face as I stepped towards the front desk.

'Are you lost?' he asked with a look of pity.

I did my best not to scowl. OK, I looked a little out of place – but some of the richest people in the world wore tatty old clothes, didn't they? Wasn't that the point of old money, that it looked like they didn't have any money at all?

'I'm here to meet Patrick Tetlow,' I said, pulling my raincoat around me a little tighter. 'I'm Jessy Donovan.'

The moment I dropped Patrick's name – or revealed mine – everything changed.

The receptionist rose to his feet and inclined his head as though he were bowing – actually bowing. What the –

'Of course, I quite understand,' he said, deference dripping from every syllable. 'I hadn't realized – but, of course. Upstairs, second room to the left. The Winter Suite.'

The staircase was one of those that swooped around, all marble handrails and red velvet carpet. The landing was opulent, there was no other word for it. Chandeliers and fancy paintings galore.

The Winter Suite.

Unsure of whether I was supposed to be waiting for Patrick outside the room or not, I opened the door slowly . . . and immediately wished the floor would swallow me up.

'– and that was the inspiration for – ah. Jessy.' Patrick's smile was warm as he glanced over at me from where he was sitting on the sofa.

But he wasn't alone.

Beside Patrick, sitting in an ornate armchair that looked as though Marie Antoinette might have used it to play whist, or whatever it was she did, was a woman. She looked roughly my age, was dressed impeccably and held a phone in her hand. It was recording.

Oh, shit.

'Jessy,' Patrick repeated, his smile making me a little weak in the knees. 'Are we running late?'

'I'm sorry, I hadn't really noticed the time,' the woman said, shooting daggers at me like I'd interrupted something important.

Which I probably had, from the looks of it.

'Wait.' The woman's gaze sharpened as she took in my still-soggy raincoat and surely messy hair. 'Jessy? Jessy Donovan?'

I looked instinctively to Patrick, unsure of what to do.

'Our readers will love this,' the woman continued, gushing.

'An intimate conversation with the lead singer of These Exiles . . . and his new girlfriend.'

My stomach was desperately attempting to leave my body, and the trouble was, I wanted to leave with it.

This was not part of the plan. This had never been part of the plan.

Fake dating, sure. Pretend to be into each other, not hard. Attend industry events, I was hardly going to say no. Not if it meant more time with Patrick.

But this?

No one had ever said anything about having to talk to journalists. Interviews, sound bites, all that shit – that was something Patrick had to do.

'I-I –' I swallowed. 'I can come back later, I didn't realize you – sorry.'

'No! No.' Patrick rose to his feet, and I took the chance to take him in. Dressed all smartly in dark trousers and a crisply ironed shirt, but with the sleeves rolled up to show those delicious forearms – he was a vision.

Patrick stepped closer, looking intently at me.

'No, stay,' the woman was saying behind him.

'Come and sit by me.' Patrick's voice was low, and it ran through me, warming me up from the inside.

Hearing it there, in front of the journalist, did something strange to my legs.

Without thinking, I moved towards the sofa, Patrick's hand resting on the small of my back.

'We won't be long, just a few more minutes.' He slipped his arm fully around me as I sank into the plump cushions. 'You don't have to say anything. This interview is about me, not us.'

Out of the corner of my eye, I saw the journalist wilt.

Well, hey – if all he wanted was for me to sit beside him, that I could do.

The warmth of his arm around me was enough to calm the nerves I had thought were going to send me into a panic. I breathed him in, his scent calming like nothing else, and felt my heart rate slow.

'This is Gina Heart. She's interviewing me ahead of our Southeast Asia tour,' Patrick said politely, all smooth and professional.

I tried to smile, even as my spirits sank.

The Southeast Asia tour. Somehow, I had completely managed to forget that after the Songwriter Awards, after our contract had come to an end, Patrick wouldn't be able to keep seeing me. He wouldn't even be staying in the country.

The reminder of the hard, and fast approaching, end to our agreement made me nauseous.

Patrick would be gone, and I'd be left here, left to my real life. It was going to feel so empty without him.

In that moment, I realized I wanted him all to myself. Why should I have to share him when I had such little time with him already?

Unaware of my racing thoughts, Gina picked up the interview where they'd left off.

'So, Patrick, we were talking about the lyrics on your latest album,' Gina said, effortlessly shifting back into interview mode. 'I know our readers will be fascinated to learn about the lyrics of 'Adventure'. It's a song that I think is quite close to your heart, isn't it?'

'Yeah, that was a song that came together in just one day,' Patrick said, his voice level and warm, just enough to be professional, and just distant enough to ensure that this Gina woman wouldn't get any ideas –

Not that I was paying attention.

'I think the central message of that song is the realization that, actually, to live is itself the greatest adventure,' Patrick continued. 'The choices you make; the decisions that take you down different roads . . . I am the greatest adventure that I will ever take.'

It was so . . . so lyrical. So thoughtful.

Here was another part of Patrick I had never known – had guessed at, sure, but to hear him speak about it so eloquently, so calmly, and without any preparation, without knowing what questions he would be faced with . . .

My admiration of him, if possible, grew. I couldn't imagine being able to pull words together so beautifully.

'And I know our time is over, but I just wanted to ask one more question, if I may,' Gina said, making sure her phone was angled towards him. Towards us.

Patrick nodded. 'Sure.'

'It hasn't escaped your numerous fans that you're in a new romantic relationship,' the journalist said brightly, gaze flickering curiously at me. 'Butterflies, wasn't it?'

'Yes. It's a great app,' Patrick said easily, no hint of embarrassment on his face. 'Jessy's sister, Laura, created it, and it's really impressive stuff. Everyone should check it out.'

Laura was going to go nuts when I told her about this.

'I know Ms Donovan won't be answering questions –'

'She won't,' Patrick interjected quietly.

It felt addictive, to be so protected.

'I just wondered if you could give us something, Patrick,

anything about Jessy and your new relationship,' Gina said determinedly.

I mean, it was her job.

Before I could stop and think how this would look, I placed a hand on Patrick's thigh and gave him a small smile.

His smile was bigger, warmer, and it made my cheeks burn, my eyes dropping at the intensity of his gaze.

'Jessy is . . . Jessy is someone that I am enjoying spending a lot of time with,' Patrick said softly, looking at me all the while. 'And I'm enjoying that time. That's all I'll say.'

Is that it? I was aware of a haze of movement around me as Gina finished her recording and said something about sending for approval in a week. But I didn't hear any of it.

'I'm enjoying that time. That's all I'll say.'

I wanted him to say more. Mean more, feel more – but I couldn't ask that of him.

I was just someone who was convenient. Someone he had to spend time with, contractually. So why not indulge and blur the lines?

The snap of a door. I blinked.

Gina had gone.

Patrick exhaled slowly as he leaned back on the sofa. 'Well, that's done. The whole world will be reading it soon enough.'

It was a weird thought. 'Seriously, the whole world?'

'Yeah, that stuff gets everywhere. Cassie once said –' Patrick bit himself off before he could finish.

Curiosity welled within me, and though I knew full well he wouldn't want to talk about it, I found myself asking, 'You don't miss her at all?'

'Miss her?' Patrick shrugged, and I could see the pain

in the supposed nonchalance. 'I miss what she should have been. The mother she couldn't bring herself to be.'

For a moment, Patrick somehow became younger, more open.

He cleared his throat. 'That was then. This is now. And right now, I am just relieved that the interview is over.'

'You were amazing,' I found myself saying with far more warmth than he was clearly expecting.

The disbelief was written large across his face as he laughed. 'Yeah, sure.'

'No, really. That whole "adventure is the journey you go on with yourself" bit?' I placed my hand on his. 'It was amazing. How could I not be impressed?'

He was flushing, those gorgeous cheekbones brushed with soft pink. 'It's just music. Not rocket science.'

I laughed for real at that. 'Erm, yeah, sure. You're just creating the soundtrack to the lives of millions. No big deal.'

His eyes widened at my words. What, he seriously didn't know?

'Patrick, you . . .' I swallowed, conscious of the way his fingers curled around my waist as I said his name. 'Patrick,' I repeated, and almost moaned as he did it again. 'You're creating a . . . a legacy, I guess. Something left on this planet long after you're gone.'

'We're hardly the Beatles,' he protested, but this time with a light smile on his face.

'You don't know that! You don't know what you'll create, you – we're both so young,' I said enthusiastically. 'There's so much of your life ahead of you, so much you'll come up with. What better way to spend a life?'

Silence fell between us for a moment. A warm, cosy silence I'd only ever known with Patrick.

'It's a pretty cool thing to spend a lifetime doing,' I said softly.

Patrick shrugged. 'What else is there?'

Well, that was the question, wasn't it? If I knew the answer to that, I wouldn't be stuck colour-coding Karun's spreadsheets and listening to Cathy gossip about her neighbours.

'I . . . I thought working in finance was the thing I'd spend my life doing. I know it sounds boring,' I added, giggling at the expression on Patrick's face. 'But numbers . . . they're all organized and sorted and balanced, and it gives me such a kick to see them like that. But working at GSR – I don't know. It's not what I thought.'

And it scared me. Thinking about feeling that unfulfilled for the rest of my life.

'Honestly, though, I don't think I'm good at much else,' I said with a shrug of my own. 'I don't think I've found my place in the world. Not yet.'

'You'll find something,' he said quietly. 'You're too brilliant not to find something.'

'Charmer.'

'Maybe.' Patrick grinned. 'Maybe I should write a song about you.'

My giggles filled the hotel suite. 'Don't you dare.'

'Why not? You might like –'

'Absolutely not!' Laura and Anna would love it, but the thought had me mildly horrified. Besides, what would he even write about? Our fake-but-kind-of-not relationship? Yeah, that wouldn't go down well.

'You wouldn't like one?' Patrick's face was teasing, his eyes sparkling with danger. 'You don't want to be immortalized as one of my conquests?'

'I think you'll find that's "many conquests",' I shot back with a laugh. 'And I do not want to be included in that list.'

'Why not?'

Crap, why couldn't I explain this? Becoming part of a These Exiles album, written out there for the whole world to see? 'You don't owe me a song. I'll never need one.'

Patrick's smile softened his expression. 'You are quite something, you know.'

Before I could reply, the door opened.

'Sorry, Mr Tetlow, but another journalist has arrived,' said the receptionist with an apologetic expression. 'I said you were done for the day, but –'

'But Derek left instructions, I bet,' Patrick said throwing me an exasperated look. 'Send them on in.'

When the door shut, he turned to me. 'I'm sorry, Jessy. Lunch will have to wait.'

'That's OK,' I said, rising and hating the distance I'd created between us. 'I'll just –'

'Where do you think you're going?' Patrick's face held a look of genuine confusion. 'I need you to stay.'

I sank bank on to the sofa and into Patrick's arms. 'Are you sure? I don't have to –'

'I'm sure,' Patrick said with a soft smile. 'I need you here, with me.'

'AND THIS IS ME,' I said with a smile, turning to gaze up at the man who had suddenly come over all chivalrous. Not that Patrick wasn't usually every part the gentleman, but this was a little excessive. 'You didn't have to walk me all the way to my door, you know.'

'I was instructed to make sure you got home safely.' Patrick shrugged, a strange sort of mischievous smile on his face. 'And I wouldn't dare upset the very scary lady who asked.'

We'd stopped outside my hotel room door, the long corridor empty, and I let out a soft laugh, the moment too fragile for anything louder. *Scary lady?* There was only one person that could be. 'Anna?'

Patrick didn't answer. He stepped forward instead, a look in his eye that had me pressing up against the door behind me for support. That heat, that need –

'Patrick –'

'She and your sister made me swear I wasn't going to hurt you,' Patrick murmured, his gaze sweeping down my body before returning to my eyes. 'And I'm not.'

Breathing. Breathing, I remembered, breathing. I should do some of that. 'You're not?'

He shook his head slowly. 'No. But I am going to kiss you.'

There was no time to argue – not that I was going to. Patrick's kiss was swift, sharp and demanding, and my hands were already curling in his hair, pulling him closer.

All higher thinking fled my mind as Patrick's hips pressed up into mine, pinning me to the door, his hands first cupping my face but swiftly moving to cup –

'Patrick,' I breathed, arching my breasts into him.

His lips had travelled down to my neck as he murmured something into the hollow there, his voice jagged, but I couldn't hear him over the pounding in my ears. His lips returned to press against mine, teasing them open, his tongue plunging into my mouth just as his hand somehow found its way under my top, under my bra, my whole body roaring with need as his thumb brushed my nipple.

I needed this. I needed him. We'd held back so long, but we weren't holding back now – somehow my fingers had crept under his shirt, and I felt wiry hair that only made the need burn brighter in me. Patrick's tongue had pleasure roaring through me and I whimpered in his arms, legs weak, willing to give him anything, anything he asked for –

'And what time do you call this?' came a far too familiar voice.

I froze. Patrick froze. Kissing me, which was rather delightful . . . but considering his hand was quite literally in my bra, my cheeks couldn't help but burn as I pulled my hand from his shirt and turned to see . . . Laura.

My sister, standing in my hotel room doorway. With her arms crossed.

'Laura,' I said weakly as Patrick removed his hand and tried to smile. 'I – I completely forgot. Pizza night.'

'Pizza and *Temptation Hotel* night, yeah.' My twin grinned, her gaze ping-ponging between the two of us through her smudged glasses. 'Now scram, Patrick, this is a "no boys allowed" kind of party.'

I looked at Patrick. 'Sorry, I –' Regret laced my voice. I was getting really sick and tired of being interrupted.

'No, it's fine. I'll see you Wednesday.'

Patrick stepped back towards me quickly and brushed a slow, delectable kiss to my lips before turning to walk down the corridor. It was all I could do to hold on to the wall for support and try to ignore my sister's hysterical laugh.

SEVENTEEN

Did I ever tell you that I'm destroying the world today?
I was watered down so I fired up, the earth is gone
and the air between us is all I can breathe . . .
– from 'Elemental', by These Exiles

'PATRICK . . .'

God, I would do anything to keep Jessy moaning my name like that.

It was outrageous, really. Here we stood, in the middle of a pavement, kissing and being a general nuisance to those around us.

And I didn't care.

'We're supposed to be – Derek said –'

'Fuck Derek,' I whispered, desire quickly setting everything in me alight.

God, if I didn't let off steam soon –

'Patrick!' Jessy pulled back this time, cheeks pink, as some passer-by tutted at us. 'We – we really should go. Otherwise we're going to be late, right?'

'Fine, fine. We're not far, the venue is around here,' I said, trying to pull myself together.

No woman had ever made me feel like this, made me

cast all my cares to the wind and kiss like that. No one but Jessy.

But she was right. Derek and half the music industry were waiting for us.

We continued making our way down the street, though at a much slower pace than before. Every step that brought us closer to our latest outing would mean less time for just the two of us.

'OK, so this is the main pre-awards show for the Songwriter Awards,' I explained. 'The actual ceremony is streamed live, that's far more public, but this one – it's more intimate, only for the nominated musical artists. And their extremely hot dates, of course.' I winked. 'It's essentially another form of glorified networking.'

Jessy made a face that spoke, in no uncertain terms, to what she thought of that.

'Networking? I get enough of that at GSR Financials,' she said darkly.

'I know, it sounds lame – but it's mostly about being seen,' I said as we halted at a pair of traffic lights. 'See and be seen, you know?'

'It sounds exhausting,' Jessy said with a shiver. 'Do we have to go?' The hesitation in her voice was clear.

Not go?

I'd always gone. I'd always done what Derek had said – he was our PR guy. He was the one who made sure that when These Exiles toured the world there were people there to play to.

Without Derek and his master manipulations, was there even a band?

We were making music long before we ever met Derek, I reminded myself. Still, Derek was behind a huge part of our success. I figured the least I owed him was doing as he asked.

'I mean,' Jessy added, smiling nervously, 'I'm never going to say no to spending another evening with you at someplace fancy, but . . . but do I have to share you?'

Two more weeks.

That was all we had together.

Five weeks had seemed like such a long time when we'd sat down in that meeting room and gone over the contract.

Now I was beginning to realize that a month with Jessy Donovan was never going to be enough.

Just fake date the girl. Just pretend you're into her.

How wrong I'd been.

When had the pretending stopped and real, red-hot emotions entered the chat?

I breathed in slowly, trying to find some equilibrium. It'd gone so far beyond that.

'You don't have to share me,' I said, surprised at how level my voice sounded. 'But I promise we're going to have a fantastic time.'

Jessy rolled her eyes. 'All right, come on then. I mean, how bad can it be?'

It was bad.

For a start, the place was packed. I'd forgotten just how many people had been shortlisted for awards, and of course each of them had brought a date, so as Jessy and I walked from room to room it was a struggle to push our way through. Conversations bubbled up from all directions, snippets about investors and contracts and conversion rising above the hubbub. A folky sort of group was playing music in one corner, making it almost impossible to hear anyone properly, the lights were low, the drinks were flowing –

'This is insane.'

I shivered; Jessy's breath on my neck could end me, and she didn't even know it.

Well. As I looked at her and saw her grin, perhaps she did.

'Is your whole life like this?' she asked lightly, pulling me by the hand over to one of the photo booths that lined one wall of the room we'd just entered. Flashes of light under the curtain suggested it was already occupied. 'Just going from one highbrow shindig to another?'

'Only during awards season,' I said darkly. 'And, honestly, they're not all that much fun.'

Not any more. It was all so fake and performative.

And then there was Jessy. Jessy – smiling as a trio of women left the booth, yanking me in –

'Jessy, what –'

The photo booth was narrow, probably only a few feet wide. The low lighting barely made it in here, casting us in near darkness. Almost all I could do was feel her – not exactly a hardship – and hear her.

Hear her ragged breathing.

'What are we doing in here, Jessy?' I couldn't help but ask, my hand still entwined with hers.

I could almost hear her grin. I could definitely hear her giggle.

'Well, I don't know about you. But me?' Jessy's voice was light, playful. 'I'm just proving that I can make this party far more fun.'

In the next moment, I had arms full of Jessy. This kind of

thing did not happen in real life – but this wasn't a dream. Jessy really was pinning me against the wall of the photo booth, and she really was kissing me, her hips pressing into mine.

A moment not kissing Jessy was a moment wasted.

We'd kissed before, but this was different. This was private, but still so public, risking interruption with every frantic second. The Jessy kissing me now was unrestrained, the heat in her pouring into me, as her hands made their way under my shirt.

'Patrick,' she whimpered, and fuck, I needed to hear more of that desperately.

And I knew exactly how.

'Patrick!' Jessy's eyes were wide as my hand skimmed along her thigh and up under her sundress, my thumb brushing the fabric of her pants.

Gritting my jaw with aching self-control, I tried not to moan as we continued to kiss – the music pounding just on the other side of the curtain, Jessy nibbling my lip, my right hand stroking, slowly slipping past the fabric to –

Fuck. I wasn't going to last long.

Jessy's legs began to quiver either side of me. As she ground down on to my fingers, I realized I hadn't been the only one holding back.

'I've wanted to do this for weeks,' I murmured as I trailed kisses down her neck, forcing myself not to lose it, all while my two fingers slowly slid into her. 'God, Jessy, you feel amazing.'

She did. Trying not to think about just how fucking good it would be to sink myself into her, I carefully stroked and teased, trying to build a rhythm to give her pleasure.

And that was when I discovered that Jessy was a vocal girl.

'Yes – yes, there,' she moaned, tipping her head back and leaning almost all her weight on to my other arm, which had snaked around her waist. 'Yeah – harder – harder – yes . . .'

It was exhilarating, hearing the effect I had on her as I kept stroking and I quickened my pace, my thumb circling intently as her whimpers increased.

'Oh – oh – oh God I'm so close,' she groaned, and it was all I could to do concentrate, to keep the rhythm. 'Patrick – Patrick –'

Her moans of pleasure swiftly became a cry of ecstasy. I could feel her coming around my fingers and I captured her mouth with mine to keep anyone from hearing.

And then it was over.

Jessy leaned on me, collapsing with exhaustion.

'That,' she managed, 'was . . . great. But now I really don't want to go back into that party.'

She wasn't the only one.

Giving a woman pleasure like that – seeing her lose herself . . .

There was nothing like it.

And after sharing that with *Jessy*, feeling her breathing quicken, sinking my fingers into her . . .

I needed more. Instead of ebbing, my hunger for her had only grown stronger – but as the music from outside the booth started to encroach back into our peaceful corner, I knew I would have to wait.

'We can't stay here,' I muttered regretfully. 'Even if I want to.'

As her breathing slowed, Jessy gently leaned away. 'I'd rather stay here.'

I laughed at the sight of her pout. I knew how she felt.

Here in this dark photo booth there were no expectations, no fame or fortune. We were just Jessy and Patrick, two people who wanted each other. Who liked each other.

When we finally stumbled out of the booth, I was almost certain everyone could see on our faces just what we'd been doing – but I didn't care.

I glanced at Jessy and saw her flushed cheeks, mussed hair, that languid smile.

I wanted to do something else wild – something I could look back on, when Jessy had disappeared from my life, and know that what we had was special, even if it could never last.

And it can't, can it?

Our lives were so totally different. I travelled the world making music – hell, after the Songwriter Awards, I'd be heading back out on tour, and God knew when I'd have the chance to fly back home. And Jessy? Jessy had friends here, a community, a job she would have to go back to eventually.

It wasn't like I could ask her to give all that up just to follow me around the world like a groupie. While I was gone, she was going to move on with her life. I would be relegated to nothing more than a fun story told at future birthday dinners.

So that left me a choice.

As our impending end date loomed, I committed to making the most of the little time I had left with Jessy. Whatever the future held, she'd never forget me.

'Let's make sure to get a bunch of photos with some of these guys, keep Derek happy,' I said, swinging a hand over her shoulders and trying not to think about just how close we'd been only minutes ago – how close I wanted to be again. 'And then let's escape.'

*

'YOU KNOW,' JESSY SAID as we slipped out of the back door, nodding our thanks to the security who'd seen to the mass of photographers out front. 'The night doesn't have to end here. We could go . . . there.'

'There?' I repeated vaguely, looking in the direction she was pointing. 'Oh.'

It was a tattoo parlour, one of those bougie ones that offered local anaesthetic while you waited and you usually had to have an original design already prepared.

I wasn't really a tattoo kind of guy. Not for any particular reason – but I had never felt compelled by anything enough to have it immortalized on my body.

One glance at Jessy, though, and I was all for it.

What better way to make sure I had a part of her forever?

'Want to go in?' I asked, already knowing the answer.

Her smile broadened. 'You read my mind.'

'Yeah, right. Come on then.' I took her hand and led us across the street.

The tattoo parlour's interior was everything I had expected from the outside. It felt more like a beauty boutique, all clean marble and spot lighting. There was some incense burning somewhere that was a little too sweet for my liking, but the woman at the desk smiled warmly as her gaze flickered over us.

'Good evening,' she said brightly. 'Please, have a look around.'

The designs were impressively laid out in lightboxes all over the walls. Honestly, if there wasn't a medical-looking chair and the word 'tattooist' emblazoned over the door, I would have guessed that this was a fancy art gallery, not a place where someone got ink layered under their skin.

'You want to get one?' Jessy asked quietly, squeezing my hand.

This was mad.

Seriously, people did not just wander into tattoo places and get a tattoo. This was something you thought about for ages, considering the pros and cons, thinking about –

My gaze met Jessy's, warm and trusting and . . . something else. Something that left me feeling breathless.

'Yeah, I think so,' I said back just as quietly, and found to my surprise that I really meant it.

A tattoo with Jessy . . . Well, if I couldn't keep the woman herself . . .

'You could always get matching tattoos. Very popular,' suggested the woman by the desk.

I turned back to Jessy. She was leaning up on her tiptoes to examine a few of the designs.

'They're all so gorgeous,' she murmured, almost to herself. 'Look at the detail.'

My heart swelled with affection. She was so . . . so thoughtful. So observant. Always seeing the beauty in the smallest of things.

'I want to get a tattoo with you,' I heard myself saying.

Jessy stiffened, just for a moment, then turned to me slowly. 'You do?'

'Yeah. Something small,' I added hastily. 'Something to remember this by.'

Jessy's smile was wistful. 'Something to remember this by.'

My gut twisted.

Something to remember *us*. Because soon, there wouldn't be an us any more.

Contract complete. Reputation improved. App successful. On to the next tour.

And she knew that – Jessy knew all that, just like I did.

But still, she wanted something to remember me.

'What about one of these?' Jessy grabbed my fingers and pulled me over, and all I could think was that, twenty minutes ago, those fingers were inside her.

Bringing her to climax –

Fuck. Patrick, do not get turned on here, do not –

'I like the idea of a musical note,' I said aloud, mostly as a distraction from my own unheeding dick.

Jessy's nose crinkled. 'Isn't that a bit clichéd?'

I couldn't help but laugh. 'I guess so. What do you have in mind, then?'

I'd meant for herself, but instead she turned and gave me a careful examination, her gaze tripping up and down. It felt . . . good.

'What about an anchor?' Her voice was soft, lilting, as she made her suggestion. 'Something that keeps you grounded. Centred.'

'I love that,' I said simply, and meant it. It was hard to feel grounded among all the chaos in my life, always had. I took my own chance to run my eyes down the length of Jessy's body, before suggesting with a cheeky smile, 'And a seagull for you.'

It had its intended effect. Her laughter rang loudly through the parlour. 'A seagull? A bird that eats literal trash?'

'That isn't why I chose it!' I protested, laughing with her and spotting the woman by the desk smiling at our antics. 'I thought – well, a seagull flies wherever it wants, doesn't it? It's happy on land, in the air, on the sea . . . it's a survivor. It can go anywhere. Do anything. That's how I think of you.'

If Jessy was going to look at me like that much longer, I was going to do something that would get us locked up for public indecency. And Derek really would kill me then.

Jessy had no such qualms. She threw her arms around my shoulders and kissed me. It was passionate, eager and over way too quickly. 'That's perfect. Thank you,' she said as she leaned back.

'So – so are we doing this?'

Jessy's smile was almost surprised. 'I think we are.'

I went first.

'Just here,' I said, placing my forefinger just behind my right ear. 'I don't want it too obvious – it's for me, not for anyone else.'

And for Jessy.

But I didn't say that last part.

'You are very brave,' Jessy said, holding my hand on my other side as the woman carefully sterilized her hands.

'Oh, I don't know about that,' the tattooist said as she laughed. 'Behind the ear there's almost no nerve endings. It won't hurt a bit.'

And it didn't. Honestly, it was over before I could really think about it, and when she held up the mirror to show me her work, I couldn't help but be impressed.

'Oh, wow.'

There it was, through my hair, behind my ear, somewhere that almost no one would look . . . a tangible reminder that Jessy and I had been together.

When I looked over at her, there was a flush of excitement on her cheeks. 'My turn!'

I had assumed that Jessy would pick a similar place for her tattoo – but apparently not.

Stifling the urge to swear, and forcing myself not to stare, I swallowed hard as Jessy pulled down the strap of her sundress and slipped off her bra.

'Just here – my ribs under my arm,' she told the tattooist.

I was doing everything I could not to stare at the swell of her breast. The way her curves became even more perfect with every breath rising and falling.

It was weird, to envy a tattooist, but in that moment as she smoothed an antiseptic wipe over Jessy's side –

'Hold my hand,' Jessy said as she lay back, reaching out a hand.

I responded instinctively, immediately. Her fingers were warm, only a slight tension in them suggesting her nerves.

'Now this one is going to hurt,' the tattooist said quietly. 'This is a painful part of the body.'

'It's OK,' Jessy said quietly, gaze flicking over to me. 'I've got Patrick.'

I lifted her hand to my lips. 'And I've got you. I promise, I've got you.'

Her smile burst something in my chest that had been held back for a while – and that was when I realized the obvious truth.

I want to be with Jessy.

Not just now, but after the contract was up.

I wanted to be with her. In the hard moments, in the good moments. When no one else was there and when the world pulled us in different directions. I wanted her by my side, and I wanted to be her person.

And I had no idea what to do about it.

EIGHTEEN

*... and when I look back, hand in hand with you, we'll
see what we did with our lives, and it was
beautiful, beautiful, beautiful ...*
– from 'Beautiful', by These Exiles

THERE WAS A PARTICULAR name for the sort of exhilaration someone felt after getting a tattoo, right?

I was almost sure there had to be. The rush of pain, the corresponding delight from knowing you'd conquered another few seconds of agony to get to the beauty of the design.

It still buzzed through me, even though we'd been inked two days ago.

'I still can't believe we did that,' Patrick said with a grin as he took a bite of chicken.

I tried not to laugh too loudly in the already overcrowded chicken shop. 'Me neither.'

This place was perfect – the best sort of spot to end the night after another of Derek's events.

Seriously. Is this my life now? Sneaking in as many moments with Patrick as I can?

Apparently. Patrick's gaze rarely moved far from my own for long, and each time his warm hazel eyes rested on any part of me I could almost feel the heat tingling across my skin.

'Does it hurt?'

'Nah, not since the first day,' I said with a shrug as I glanced down at my side.

The seagull tattoo was absolutely tiny, only about an inch, hidden under my arm and my sundress. My bra still couldn't be put back on – too tight – and I was more than a little aware that when the evening started to get nippy, so would I.

But that was the least of my problems.

The real trouble?

I was falling head over heels for Patrick Tetlow, and I was almost certainly going to have my heart broken.

'Laura's mad at me, of course.'

Patrick frowned. 'Laura? Why?'

'We always said we'd get matching tattoos – I told her that hasn't changed,' I said, rolling my eyes. 'But you'd think I'd betrayed her!'

'You two are very close, aren't you?'

It was impossible not to grin at that. 'Aren't all twins?'

'I guess so.' Patrick's gaze was soft. 'I like that she's got your back. That you have someone in your corner, always. You want the last bit?' He held up the piece of chicken.

I shook my head. 'Nah, you have it.'

The thirty-piece box had disappeared criminally quickly as we shared it between us.

'Seriously, glowing yellow curry sauce?' I'd wrinkled my nose as Patrick had leaned past me to place his order, the scent of him almost enough to distract me from his weird condiment choices.

'Do not knock it until you've tried it.'

I'd tried it. Once I'd downed more lemonade than I thought was even possible and stopped glaring at Patrick, who was clutching his sides with laughter, I dipped my own chips in mayo and swore never to eat anything off his plate again. Moments later, I had begun to tease him about the way his fingers kept meandering to his ear, just about managing to stop himself from touching his anchor.

God, it suited him. How was it that getting tattoos together was one of the sexiest and most intimate things I had ever done with a guy?

'Do you think Derek will be impressed that we stayed right until the end of his precious event?' Patrick said offhandedly, snagging a chip from my portion.

I batted his hands away as discomfort swirled within me. 'I hope so. We managed to last longer at this one than the one before.' It was getting harder and harder to remember to care about what Derek wanted from us. What Patrick's label wanted from us. Now I thought about it, I hadn't asked Laura in ages how this whole fake relationship was going for Butterflies. I hadn't heard how the app downloads had been going for days now – almost a week?

I unlocked my phone, fully intending to drop Laura a message – but got distracted by an email that popped up. Karun. Oh, hell.

> Hi Jessy,
>
> Great work with Owen yesterday – really appreciate you meeting our high value clients. Looking forward to seeing you back in the office when your sabbatical is over. There are a few things we should discuss.
>
> Karun

Ugh. Work. I placed my phone down and tried not to think about how much I was dreading going back.

'First kiss,' Patrick said, returning to the game that we'd been playing since we sat down.

This was not a topic I wanted to linger on. 'Ross,' I said, putting away my phone and picking up a chip and dangling it in the air as I tried to smile. 'Well, first grown-up kiss anyway. And, honestly, it was not great.'

'Sloppy?'

I threw a chip at him. 'Yep, and not the good kind. You?'

'Katie . . . Katie someone. How have I forgotten her surname? She was my school crush.' Patrick shook his head fondly. 'OK, next. Earliest memory?'

'Oooh, toughie. I think most of my memories are of Laura,' I said with a shrug. 'I guess that's normal, with twins?'

'Nothing about the two of you is normal.'

I threw another chip at him.

'Your loss,' he quipped, dunking it in his curry sauce and slurping it up. 'So just you and Laura, nothing concrete?'

'I can remember being on swings with her. Our mum was trying to push both of us, and both of us felt hard done by. I was crying, I think.' I grinned at the memory, at the innocence of it – at how only now I could see how tough my mum had it, having to raise two children all on her own. 'What about you?'

'Oh, nothing good. Cassie making me butter pasta,' Patrick said with a shrug, leaning back in his seat.

He always did that when he didn't want to talk about something. Shrug, and lean back – as though he could put physical distance between him and the topic he didn't want to touch.

Still, I was curious. 'Butter pasta?'

'Exactly what it sounds like. Pasta cooked to the point of disintegration, with butter.' Patrick shrugged again, that little movement telling me everything I needed to know.

He must have noticed my look, because he smiled awkwardly. 'You don't have to feel sorry for me.'

Heat flared in my cheeks. 'I wasn't –'

'I don't tell you these things for sympathy,' he continued, a quiet calm in his voice that was far too soothing. 'I can talk to you about anything, Jessy.'

My name sounded so good on his lips.

'Last orders!'

I jumped, glancing over at the counter and the clock above it.

Midnight. Fuck.

'Come on,' Patrick added, rising to his feet and grabbing a handful of chips from my portion. 'Let's get you home.'

It was the comfortable way he said it that made my heart warm. Everything was so . . . so easy with Patrick.

I mean, obviously it wasn't. He was a millionaire pop star and I was a broke nobody.

But still, everything between us felt easy.

The night air was freezing after the cosy warmth of the chicken shop, but I'd grab a decaf coffee on the way back to the hotel, and thankfully it was only two streets over from –

'Ah,' said Patrick.

'Yeah,' I said quietly, reaching up and touching the grill that had been pulled across the gates to the station. 'I guess it closed early. Must be issues with the trains.'

Whatever it was, it meant a very long walk or a criminally expensive taxi back to my hotel.

Well, that was what you got, I suppose, for staying out all night with a guy you literally couldn't leave alone.

Precisely what we were going to do after the Songwriter Awards next week . . .

Easier not to think about it.

'Well, I guess I better start walking,' I said cheerfully, pulling my light summer jacket closer around me.

'You're not going to walk all the way from here, are you?' Even in the darkness, I could see Patrick's concern.

It was stupid how happy it made me, seeing him worried. 'Yeah, it's OK. I'll probably just speedwalk.'

'You still like staying in the hotel?' Patrick asked.

'I mean, it's nice . . . but weird. I thought living in a fancy hotel would be dreamy, but I just get so –' Perhaps a shrug was easier. I didn't want to admit how alone I felt in that huge room sometimes.

'Lonely,' Patrick finished for me with a rueful smile. 'I get it – it's one of the reasons I hate going on tour. I mean, it's amazing, playing for fans all over the world . . . but hotels are so empty.'

Empty. Yeah, he was right. Even though it was full of guests, I'd never been somewhere that felt more hollow.

'I've had Anna and Laura crashing with me most nights, to be honest,' I admitted, trying not to sound like a toddler who needed babysitting. 'But Anna went out on a date tonight and Laura has a big investor meeting in the morning.'

A twinge of guilt; an investor meeting I hadn't had time to help her prepare for. Before Patrick – and this whole relationship – I would help Laura prep for all her meetings. Big or small.

'Must be nice to have them with you,' Patrick said with a shrug. 'I can't wait for the guys to get back from their penance tours.'

'Yeah, it's nice. It isn't home, though,' I said with a wry smile. 'But then home is a houseshare with a bunch of guys who don't know how to put milk back in the fridge, so . . .'

I trailed off, trying not to sound ungrateful. This last month had been a whirlwind beyond anything I could ever have imagined.

Patrick looked at me in quiet contemplation before he opened his mouth again. 'You could crash at my place. For the night, I mean.'

For a second, I was speechless.

Not once, in all our weeks of dating, had Patrick invited me back to his place.

I understood his need for privacy. Respected it even.

So why had he invited me over now?

I was suddenly grateful for the cover the darkness of night provided. My cheeks were surely scarlet from the heat emanating from them.

Did that mean *crash at my place* . . . in my spare bedroom? Or was he looking for a continuation of our photo-booth activities?

I swallowed. *I want a part two of that night, so badly.*

Try as I might, I couldn't tell what Patrick was thinking just by looking at him. As I stared into his eyes, a calm sea reflected back at me. Not expecting, not pushing. Simply offering.

'If . . . if you wouldn't mind,' I said quietly, testing the water by dipping a toe in.

It didn't seem to make any ripples. Patrick just smiled. 'I wouldn't have offered if I wasn't fine with it.'

Fine. What did *fine* mean?

I had a short walk to think about it, which wasn't nearly enough time. Over the last few weeks, this whole fake relationship thing . . . it had to be in public. Derek had been clear about that – our dates had to be seen, be visible.

There'd never been any reason to go back to my place. Or his. And even as we began to spend time with each other outside of the scheduled events, even after the photo booth, we had never crossed that line.

I shivered with something like anticipation as we stepped up to a tall building that looked, honestly, pretty normal. Not massively different from where I lived, only the street was a bit greener.

'Cold?' Patrick put his arm around my shoulders.

'Yeah,' I lied.

I didn't want to give him a reason to remove his arm. Even if the physical contact between us had my stomach twisting with nerves, and my heart racing and my nipples tightening –

Chill the fuck out, Jessy!

Patrick wasn't calm either. I could sense the coiled tension running through him. His hands shook lightly as he fumbled his key at the door. His nerves told me everything I needed to know.

He hadn't brought another girl back to his place. At least not recently.

Which made me feel good. And then like an idiot. I had no right to feel possessive over him.

I had no claim to Patrick Tetlow – not even as his fake girlfriend. Sure, we both knew there was something more here. But Patrick had never brought up being exclusive or taking this beyond its written end date.

And why would he? The whole world was his oyster.

'Here we go,' Patrick said quietly after we'd walked up two flights of stairs and he'd unlocked a door with a large 23 on it. 'Home sweet home.'

He might call it home sweet home, but it certainly didn't feel very homely. Honestly, the hallway had hotel lobby vibes more than anything else. There were no pictures on the walls, no knickknacks, no half-mangled umbrella by the door or myriad coats hanging up. It almost felt like no one lived here.

It also wasn't the palatial cavern that I had kind of assumed it would be.

From where I was standing, as Patrick closed the door behind us, the hallway opened up into a kitchen–lounge thing, there was a bathroom just to my right, and then two other doors. Bedrooms, right?

That was it. No walk-in wardrobe, plunge pool or snooker table, like I always assumed a pop star's home would have.

No cinema. No bar.

Just . . . a flat.

I mean, obviously not just a flat. The lights came on automatically and music started playing in the sitting room; there was definitely a sword – a sword? – mounted on the wall that I could see through the open doorway, and the furnishings were so high-end that I was a little worried about staining the upholstery with the lingering grease from the fried chicken we'd been eating earlier. I wiped my hands discreetly on my sundress.

'So, I guess this is the bachelor pad,' I said lightly as Patrick dropped his keys into a bowl that sat on the carpet by the door.

'Yeah.'

'Where's the cinema, and the pool table, and the built-in bar?' I raised one solitary eyebrow.

Patrick's laughter filled the space and, instantly, the room felt more alive. 'What, not meeting your high standards?' he asked.

I grinned back. 'Well, you just keep surprising me. I was expecting your place to be more of a –' I gesticulated, looking for the right word. Patrick continued laughing. 'I thought it would be more bachelor pad-like, I guess.'

But I shouldn't have been surprised. All this time I'd spent with Patrick had proven he wasn't the playboy, 'pop star gone wild' type. At least, not any more. Not for a long time.

He shrugged, half-self-deprecating and half-pleased. 'Well, sorry to disappoint. If I'd known you had such high expectations, I would've made sure to get a hot tub built into the living room. Or maybe I should have gone full Vegas and found a tiger?'

I chuckled before letting a peaceful silence settle over us.

Here, the two of us . . . It was the first time we'd actually been alone. Properly alone. Somewhere we couldn't be interrupted.

I swallowed as we stood, unmoving, in the hallway.

Two doors. Two bedrooms.

Which one was Patrick going to suggest that I sleep in?

'I guess –'

'Should we –'

Our laughter felt muffled in the hallway. 'Sorry.'

'Nah, it's OK.' Patrick shrugged his coat off and held out his hand for mine. 'What were you going to say?'

What was *I going to say?* I could hardly think. There were quite literally two doors, two options ahead of me, and I wasn't sure, not really, which I wanted.

Well, I knew which I wanted – but I didn't know what Patrick wanted. What he'd wanted when he invited me round.

If he showed me into the spare bedroom, I tried to tell myself, that was nothing – nothing – to do with how he felt about me.

It was the responsible thing to do. The respectful thing to do. After all, I wasn't sure how I felt about him just assuming I would fall into bed with him – though after our photo booth moment, maybe I shouldn't be that surprised.

And it shouldn't matter, should it?

This thing between us might not have been fake any more, but it wasn't real either. We weren't together in any meaningful way.

But it meant something to me. *He* meant something to me. Sometimes Patrick felt like the realest part of my life, the only part in colour, the only part with a soundtrack. The brightest part of my life I really loved.

Patrick stepped forward as I handed him my jacket. 'You know,' he said, 'I could never have imagined this – you – happening all because of Butterflies and a stupid dating contract.'

I grinned. 'You know, I think we're a bit beyond the contract.'

'Oh, Jessy. We are way beyond it now.' Patrick's voice was low, and he couldn't know how he was making my whole body thrum. 'And it doesn't matter what the internet thinks, or the paps, or any of them. We know the truth. We know that this is real,' he whispered, his eyes darkening as they flickered over my face. 'That we do care about each other.'

My lungs struggled to take a breath. 'I thought – when –'

My stomach fluttered. I couldn't believe I was hearing the words I'd been longing for.

'Since the tattoos.' Patrick smiled ruefully. 'Or maybe before that. But that was when I really knew, for definite, that I didn't want to lose you. Not for anything.'

Overwhelming joy burst though me as I laughed, reaching out for his hand, hating even the tiny distance between us. 'I thought – I thought maybe the way you felt about it it was all in my head! But the way you look at me sometimes –'

'Can you blame me? Damn, Jessy, you're beautiful.' Patrick's voice sizzled through me, lifting my spirits, burning my affection for him into my heart like a tattoo. 'And you're clever. And you're kind.'

I couldn't bear it any more, not being in his arms. I stepped into his embrace and pressed a swift kiss on his lips. 'I'm not the only one. Clever fingers.'

His groan was enough to propel me to kiss him again, the heat flowing through us one that I recognized and so desperately wanted to experience again.

Who wouldn't?

The kiss deepened. I needed his hands on me, everywhere. And I needed us naked, like, yesterday.

'Come on,' Patrick muttered against my lips, pulling me towards the nearest door.

His bedroom was as sparse as the hall. It had a bed, untidy duvet and three pillows scattered across the top, and a small bedside table with a lamp without a bulb.

But none of that mattered to me.

It had a bed.

'God, Jessy.' Patrick panted, like we'd been doing more than just kissing. 'Do you have any idea how mad you've been driving me?'

He pressed fluttering kisses along my shoulder before

he lifted the hem of my sundress and pulled it over my head.

There I stood, in nothing but my pants. The delicate bandage covering my tattoo was so small I could barely feel it –

But then I couldn't feel anything, save heat and longing and need as I stood before Patrick Tetlow, my celeb-crush-turned-fake-boyfriend, almost completely naked.

Almost.

'You know, I barely kept control of myself, when you were getting that done,' Patrick said nonchalantly as he pulled his T-shirt over his head.

And I barely managed to keep control of myself as those perfectly sculpted abs were revealed. 'What?'

'When you were getting your tattoo – I wanted to drop to my knees there and then. Audience and all,' he breathed, stepping closer to me and dipping his head to bring one of my nipples into his mouth.

Oh, fuck. The way his tongue swirled before biting –

The cry of need that escaped my lips was a strangled one, but it only seemed to spur Patrick on.

'Fuck, Jessy, I need to be inside you,' he muttered, kissing my lips hard as his fingers fumbled at his trouser belt.

Before long the offending items were off, and there we stood, naked save for our underwear.

'I need you,' I whispered, stepping forward and slipping my thumbs into the waistband of his boxers. 'Right now.'

The way he groaned made me feel so fucking powerful – so powerful I didn't hesitate to pull off the last of our clothes.

Holy fuck.

My mouth watered as I took him in, in full. I had never wanted anyone this badly.

Patrick stood there, all chiselled and almost glowing in the night. We hadn't bothered putting a light on, or closing the curtains, and the amber streetlight poured through and lit him up like a piece of art.

And then there was the way he was looking at me.

'You are gorgeous,' Patrick breathed, his gaze raking over my curves and dimples. 'I don't know how I've managed to go this long without –'

'I don't know how you're going this long without it now,' I said teasingly, grabbing his hand and pulling us on to the bed. 'I was promised sex, so what are you going to do about it?'

Excitement drummed through me as I laid myself down on Patrick's bed and looked up at him.

This was it. This was the moment that I lost myself to him.

I could try to tell myself that this wouldn't matter. That sleeping with Patrick wasn't going to change things.

But it would.

It would change me. Irrevocably.

'I'll do anything you want, Jessy,' Patrick said, voice low, his tone full of something close to worship. He descended on to the bed.

Except not quite with me. Not where I expected him to be, at least.

'Patrick!'

'You weren't specific!' he said delightedly as he knelt between my legs and pushed my knees apart.

I squirmed against his hold, his words enough to make me ache. 'Patrick –'

'Just lie back for me,' he murmured. 'If you want me to stop, just say.'

Stop him? I wanted him to hurry up; the ache inside of me was starting to border on painful, I wanted him so damn –

'Ohhh!' My back arched of its own volition as Patrick slowly lowered his head between my thighs.

Oh, yeah.

Patrick might not have brought a girl back to his place recently, but he clearly knew what to do. He knew what I wanted, what I needed, without a single word from me. His tongue speared deep as my fingers entangled themselves in his hair, trying not to thrust my hips deeper.

God, this was incredible. The spasms of pleasure pouring through my body, pulsing as his tongue picked up a riotous rhythm that I could barely follow, were hurtling me towards my peak.

Building, building, and even as Patrick's fingers held my knees down, I squirmed under his expert ministrations.

'Fuck, Patrick, yes, yes!' I couldn't help but cry.

And then I fell apart.

Body exploding, ears ringing, my voice cracked as I cried out his name and ground down impossibly harder on to his face.

As my climax subsided, slowly, slowly, Patrick lifted his head and grinned. 'I could do that every day.'

The flirtatious wink was undermined by just how wrecked his voice sounded. Hearing him – seeing him after he'd brought me to such pleasure – made a shudder run through my body.

'Careful,' I whispered, shocked at how weak my voice was. 'Or I'll start demanding it.'

God, the thought of spending every day with Patrick – it was intoxicating.

Not, however, as intoxicating as the man himself.

He leaned across me to the bedside table, and when he straightened up I could see him rolling on a condom. The excitement that I'd thought would calm down now the edge had been taken off roared to life again.

'Ready?' the man I was slowly realizing I was probably in love with asked in a soft whisper, holding himself above me – as if there was any chance I would want him to stop now.

I nodded. 'Yes. Yes, please – please, Patrick.'

I wasn't usually the sort of woman to beg, but I needed him – needed everything he could give me.

Patrick's eyes widened and his lips parted in an unspoken moan as he slowly slid into me.

I couldn't help but let out my own audible sound as he pushed in. The intimacy, the intensity, the scent of him, the feeling of being known and fully adored by him – sex had never felt like this before.

By the time Patrick had sunk himself hips deep into me, I knew I would never want anyone else.

Not ever again.

'I'll try to go slowly,' he said, his jaw tight.

'Don't,' I murmured, lifting my head to kiss him and tasting myself on his lips. 'Don't go slowly. I don't need that right now. I need everything you can give me.'

It was true. I was too pent up for anything else. We could try it slow another time.

Patrick hissed as he almost withdrew entirely before sinking back in. 'I want this to be special.'

'It will be. It's you,' I whispered, rocking my hips to match his rhythm, revelling in the unspoken understanding we shared.

There was no one in the world who understood me like Patrick – and he had never let anyone in like me. This was new, for both of us, a sharing and an exploring that was unique.

He was mine. And I was his.

With each thrust, Patrick pushed me closer and closer to the peak I had only just climbed down from, and it was all I could do to hang on to his shoulders and accept the kisses, the murmurs of affection, the praise that made my whole body tremble.

Before long I was close, so close, but I knew I couldn't be pushed over the edge like this –

'I'm close,' Patrick panted, his eyes brilliant as they stared down at me. 'You?'

'I can't – I won't be able to –' Frustration boiled through me.

How exactly I thought I was going to explain it in that moment, lungs panting and body tingling, I didn't know – but still, he understood.

Without slowing his thrusts, Patrick shifted his right arm so that he was leaning on his left, and gently brought his free hand to the place where our bodies met.

'Oh fuck – yes, Patrick, yes – yes!' Without warning, I tumbled over that edge I'd been teetering on.

'Jessy,' he groaned, sinking his face into my neck and pressing a kiss there. 'Jessy.'

His pleasure came and fired through him, I could feel it

as he thrust his hips deeper, deeper, and his groan of ecstasy was music to my ears.

When he collapsed into my arms, there were only two things I was sure of.

That this was exactly where I belonged.

And that I was definitely in love with Patrick.

NINETEEN

So when I say take my hand I mean take a chance, take off fears, take off expectations and leave them at your door as you step out, step out of banality and into the wild . . .
– from 'Risk It, Baby', by These Exiles

SOMETHING WAS PULLING ME out of sleep, and I hated it.

'Ughhh.'

That was all I could manage. Sleep was so good, so precious, and now I was waking up?

Waking up with a smile on my face. A smile I didn't understand. What was so good that I –

My eyes snapped open as memories poured through me.

Jessy. Jessy, laughing as we walked in the park. Jessy, listening to me at that dim sum place. Jessy, grinning as she got a seagull tattooed on her. Jessy, panting and quivering under me –

I looked over.

The bed was empty.

The sudden swell of disappointment was so tangible I could almost taste it. My bed was empty, my bedroom too as I glanced about in the hope that she had just got up.

I tried to quieten my breathing, tried to listen to see if she'd just popped to the loo or hopped in the shower.

My flat was completely quiet – the kind of silence that only came from emptiness.

Sagging back on to a bed that now felt lonely, I tugged a hand through my hair as I tried to think why.

Despite the fact that it could only be, what, eight, nine in the morning, Jessy was already gone.

She had fucked me and then left me? It didn't make sense.

I glanced down and noticed I'd pulled on my PJ bottoms at some point, which made me feel a little less physically exposed, but still so emotionally vulnerable that nausea roiled in my stomach.

Where was she? Why had she just . . . gone?

I looked around. She hadn't even left a note.

I tried not to panic. I thought we had spoken truthfully last night when we'd shared about our feelings. I'd told her, hadn't I, that this was more than the contract, more than a fake relationship?

It was hard not to feel a little taken advantage of. I mean, was that all it had been about? Now she'd slept with me, she was out of here?

I shook my head. Jessy wasn't like that. She wasn't Celine.

Still bleary-eyed, and wishing we'd bothered to close the curtains so I hadn't woken up so early, I groaned as I reached out and grabbed my phone.

07:23. Fuck.

I blinked. And a message from Jessy.

After staring at my phone a long, hard minute, I tapped in my passcode and read her message.

> **Jessy**
> Sorry about leaving while you were asleep. Had to run – desperately in need of new clothes – but last night was perfect. Same again tonight? Minus the curry sauce x

I released a breath I hadn't realized I was holding, tension leaking out of my body with it. My smile was bright and I kind of wished she could have seen it. *Same again?*

There was very little I wouldn't be up for when it came to Jessy.

Warm tingles were travelling up my spine as I pulled my duvet down and propped myself up in bed. It was one thing to completely worship a woman I was swiftly falling in love with, but it was quite something else to fall asleep with her in my arms. The intimacy had been beyond anything I had ever known, or could have ever expected. Sex, yes, but closeness. Vulnerability. That was something else.

It was hard to believe she'd managed to slip out without waking me.

This was . . . this was so much more than I had expected. More than I had hoped for when I first admitted I was tired of pretending. Certainly more than I'd ever known before – I mean, Celine?

It had been nothing like this. Nothing like Jessy. This was so much better.

My phone lit up.

> **One unread message from Derek PR**

I tried to think quickly whether Jessy and I had done anything last night that would have landed us in trouble – with Derek that was – and came up empty.

I opened the message, confident its contents wouldn't be berating, for once.

> **Derek**
> What the hell is Jessy doing?

I blinked. What?

I read the message again, but there didn't seem to be any obvious answer to Derek's weird, cryptic message.

Jessy? What had she done? Nothing that I hadn't done, but Derek didn't seem to be mad at me.

He wouldn't be up this early, he never was, but I tapped out a quick message that he'd see when he finally woke up.

> **Patrick**
> What are you talking about?

I locked my phone and allowed it to drop on to my bed.

Jessy. What could she possibly have done to stir Derek's anger? Maybe there had been some faux pas I'd missed. Maybe she hadn't smiled at the right person, or had smiled at the wrong one. I hadn't seen her make any particular mistakes last night – probably because I was too busy ogling her the whole time.

Jessy was the sort of woman a guy could spend his whole life searching for, hoping for, but never actually meet. She wasn't interested in what I could give her or what my fame could afford her, she was only interested in me, in –

My phone flashed with a new message. I picked it back up from where I'd dropped it.

Derek? This early?

When I opened our chat, there was no actual message from him, just a link. A link to one of the gossip sites he had made us promise never to visit. Apparently, there were all sorts of articles about These Exiles, citing sources that were less than reputable, and it was better we never let that sort of thing get in our heads.

Weird. What had he seen that was worth breaking his own ban?

I tapped on the link and, while waiting for the page to load, I wondered if I had any actual food in the flat – I couldn't remember the last time I had done a food shop. Before I could make any breakfast plans, the page finished loading –

And my stomach dropped.

Yeah, I wasn't going to be wanting any breakfast.

The article was an exposé, with a headline that made me nauseous.

GIRLFRIEND OF THESE EXILES LEAD SINGER CAUGHT CHEATING

I stared, hardly able to take in the words.
It was a lack of sleep. It had to be.
I read the headline again.

GIRLFRIEND OF THESE EXILES LEAD SINGER CAUGHT CHEATING

Was it an old article? I had stayed well away from the internet when Celine and I had come crashing down, but I had known we'd made it into all sorts of headlines – to my horror.

I had a quick look at the date in the byline. The article had gone live in the early morning.

What. The. Fuck

They had to be talking about Jessy – but that made no sense. She wouldn't – she wouldn't cheat. That wasn't the sort of person she was. And when would she have found the time? We spent practically every moment together.

Half-wishing I could just close the tab and stop reading, I scrolled down.

For a second I thought my heart had stopped beating as the first image in the article loaded.

Jessy. Jessy, inside a fancy restaurant ... with Dillon Carmichael, the famous actor who'd just won an Oscar.

What the actual fuck was going on?

I sat up slowly in bed, as though that would change the image I was staring at. The photo wasn't super detailed, but it didn't need to be. I would recognize her features anywhere.

And she was laughing.

Laughing.

Complete unknown Jessica Donovan hurtled to fame last month after being confirmed as These Exiles lead singer Patrick Tetlow's girlfriend. Jessy, who up until recently was an employee at GSR Financials, has been seen with Patrick at numerous events over the past few weeks. But apparently one famous boyfriend wasn't enough to satisfy her.

I was going to be sick.

Knowing I should stop reading, I told myself I should close the tab. I kept scrolling.

Another photo, but this time with a different man. In this photo Jessy was sitting on a bench outside a pub, wearing the sundress I'd begun to think of as my favourite. Even now, my breath grew short seeing her in it. Or maybe that was the shock?

My gaze zeroed in on the caption.

Jessica Donovan seen with Tim Kellersly, famed artist who recently sold a piece for £20m

I tried to swallow, but my throat didn't seem to be working.

'We know the truth. We know that this is real. That we do care about each other.'

Was it all fake, the whole time?

My gaze raked over the article. *Lunches . . . dinners . . . seen in public . . . what must her boyfriend, Patrick Tetlow, think of all this . . .*

What did I think? I was thinking – how could I have been so stupid?

This was Celine all over again. It was like copy and fucking paste. God, I must have doormat tattooed on my –

My hand flew to my ear. It was still tender just behind it.

Shit. I'd got myself tattooed for a woman who hadn't even bothered trying to hide the fact she was cheating on me.

Derek
Have you read it? There's more

I was afraid to tap the second link – scared to see how else Jessy had betrayed me, but I couldn't stop myself. A different article pulled up, with a photo at the very top of Jessy smiling, arm in arm with . . . Cassie.

That was when my heart really did stop beating.

PATRICK TETLOW'S MOTHER AND GIRLFRIEND BEST FRIENDS!

Cassie Fletcher, mother of These Exiles lead singer Patrick Tetlow, has spilled the details from her lunch with Jessy Donovan, girlfriend of her famous son.

'Once I met Jessy, I knew she was the one for my Paddy. She's helping me patch things back up with my boy, you know. I know he loves her dearly. Jessy told me he's been showering her with gifts and jewels,' said Cassie. 'Not that he's ever showered me with jewels, his own mum –'

I was going to be sick. I was actually going to be sick.

I'd trusted her – I'd never told anyone about Cassie. But I had told Jessy. I'd asked her to back off. That things between me and Cassie couldn't be fixed. I had thought she'd listened. Thought she had understood.

All the fucking while she'd been chatting to my own mother behind my back.

I was livid.

Not that he's ever showered me with jewels –

I stumbled out of bed, dropping my phone on to the duvet as I grabbed clean clothes. Where I was going, I didn't know – but I couldn't just lie here when the memory of having Jessy in my arms just hours ago plagued me.

God, how could I have been so stupid? How had I not seen the betrayal coming? I wasn't sure what was worse. The shit with my – with Cassie, or all the fucking men she'd apparently been seeing. I knew we weren't officially dating, but last night had changed things. I thought –

What was it about me that made the women in my life want to betray me? What kind of fucked-up cosmic karma was this? I'd finally let my guard down, after so long keeping people out, and all that happened was that I got hurt. Again.

After tugging a T-shirt over my head, I picked up my phone, rage fuelling me to recklessness.

> **Paddy**
> **Where are you?**

I fired off the message to Jessy. 'Shit,' I muttered under my breath, chest tight and painful.

I needed to talk to her. I never wanted to talk to her again. I didn't know what I wanted.

We had a contract. But I'd be damned if I was going to let a piece of paper force me to be with a woman who didn't even have the integrity to tell me she was seeing other people.

Which, by the way, I thought furiously, *is completely against the contract.*

Fuck. I couldn't wait around for her to reply. I needed answers and I needed them now.

It took me three attempts to find a pair of matching shoes and two minutes to remember how to lock my own front door.

> **Paddy**
> I need to see you

I'd sent the message before I started down the stairs, and by the time I'd reached the bottom of my block of flats I had a reply.

> **Jessy**
> Missed me?

> **Paddy**
> Where are you? At home still?

Had she even gone home, or was that another lie?

> **Jessy**
> Can't stand to be without me, huh?

Before today her casual flirty tone, the speed at which she replied – both of those things would have made a smile spread across my face.

But now I wondered. Was she deflecting? Was she with another guy? Why hadn't she just said where she was?

> **Jessy**
> Ran home to grab some clothes. Why, what's up?

> **Paddy**
> lmk your address

She'd sent it before I reached the Tube, and as I tapped in, I tried to calm my racing heart.

My brain wouldn't stop reminding me of the images from both articles. The photo with Dillon was particularly bad. She knew what Celine did had messed me up. And then, there she was, doing the same shit.

Oscar winner. I wanted to punch something.

Was this going to be the rest of my life? Always desperately trying to be better, to be enough . . . and never managing it? Trying to trust, and having that trust flung back in my face?

It took me less than half an hour to reach Jessy's street.

When I knocked on the door, I could feel the tension thrumming through my body. I was surprised I wasn't shaking with it.

A part of me hoped, prayed, that there was some reasonable explanation for all this. That Jessy hadn't gone behind my back, like the article said. There had to be something.

Jessy wouldn't – she wasn't the type. But if there was one thing life had taught me, it was that no one could ever be fully trusted. Not when it came to me.

Jessy's front door opened and a guy blinked at me. 'Yeah?'

I stared. He was tall, with a scraggly beard and a cup of tea in his hands. He looked so at home I was taken aback for a moment, wondering if I'd got the wrong place. I looked at the door number again.

'Hello?' The guy frowned. 'What do you want?'

'I . . . does Jessy Donovan live here?' I managed.

His gaze was sharpening now, and I had to hope he wouldn't recognize me. 'Yeah, she's one of my housemates. Are you –'

The confusion faded.

That's right – Jessy lives in a houseshare.

'She's in the living room.' The guy gestured to the right with his cup of tea before turning and walking away.

I guess that counted as an invitation.

Stepping gingerly over the threshold, I saw immediately that Jessy's hallway was absolutely nothing like mine. There were about fifty coats of different sizes, shapes and colours, mostly hung up by the door, but some had slid down to the floor. Twenty or so pairs of shoes were piled up underneath them, a vacuum and a mop propped up against them. The place had not so much a lived-in but a worn-down sort of vibe.

And to my right was a door, slightly open.

And through that door came a voice.

'Ross – seriously, we can't –'

I had never walked so quickly as I did to that door, and when I pushed it open, I saw one thing.

Jessy. Jessy, pressed into the embrace of a guy who looked all too comfortable with his arms around her. My brain short-circuited, before starting up again and firing in all directions.

So, this was Ross. The famous ex-boyfriend. Or perhaps less of an ex and more like the current boyfriend. The one who had treated her badly. The one her mother had hated and her sister had warned her about. And she had clearly ignored both of them.

'Jessy.'

Ross turned to look at me as I spoke, her name tugged from my lips before I could stop it. His brow wrinkled as Jessy stepped out of his embrace.

'Patrick, you got here quickly –' Was the surprise in her voice from having been caught?

'Patrick who?' Her ex folded his arms and looked me up and down with a territorial glare that I recognized. It was one I'd seen on my own face.

Possessiveness.

'He's no one,' said Jessy quietly. 'You need to go, Ross.'

'He's no one.'

Fire burned in my chest. 'Yeah, you should go.' I directed all my anger at Ross. I needed to direct it somewhere, why not at him?

'Or what?' he spat, stepping towards me, chest out in a poor imitation of a threat. 'You going to get one of your people to fight for you?'

I laughed in his face as I shoved his shoulders, heat boiling in my veins. 'I don't think I'll need any help getting rid of you, you pathetic shite –'

'Ross!' Jessy screamed as the man lunged at me.

I stepped back, dodging the swing, tempted to hook my right but forcing myself not to.

There would be paps outside before you know it. Best not to get photographed after a brawl.

Jessy was speaking in a low, urgent voice. 'Just leave – go, Ross, get out –'

'Fine.' Ross shrugged and moved to draw Jessy in again, but this time she stepped back, her cheeks pink – with embarrassment or anger I wasn't sure. 'I'll see you later, Jessy,' he threw over his shoulder as he left the room.

He had walked out of the room before I could say anything, but when the door clicked shut, I breathed out slowly.

Silence filled the room. A silence I couldn't let go on any longer.

'I can't believe it,' I said quietly. The adrenaline that had pumped through me not even a minute ago was suddenly gone. The only thing I felt now was empty.

Jessy had wrapped her arms around herself, her gaze far away. 'What?' Even her voice sounded distant.

'I –' My mouth was dry, and I swallowed again before I continued. 'I can't believe you would do this to me.'

I sounded so pathetic. Here I was, standing in a living room with two beat-up sofas, a bookcase with hardly any books, and a TV that looked like it had seen better days, in front of a woman I had thought I was in love with and maybe loved me back.

Where the fuck had it gone so wrong?

'What are you talking about?' Jessy asked, genuine confusion written across her face. 'I . . . I saw your message, but Ross –'

'Yeah, you were busy.' My tone was cold. It had to be. All my hopes of finding some kind of explanation for Jessy's behaviour had disappeared. Now I was in protection mode.

A state I knew all too well.

'Patrick, is there something wrong? Last night –'

'Last night was a mistake.' I cut across her, hardly able to believe she could even refer to it.

Jessy Donovan was not the woman I thought she was.

She stared at me in confused horror. 'A mistake?'

God, she was good. How did she get her voice to wobble like that?

'Yeah. I guess it was just another mistake you made,' I said bitterly, hating how this hurt so much. 'Like meeting all those other guys in public, when you should have brought them back here.'

Jessy stared. 'Other guys? What are you talking about?'

'Did you seriously think I wouldn't find out, Jessy? You think cameras haven't been following you everywhere, just waiting for a chance to catch you slipping up?' My chest was heaving with the effort to keep my anger under control. 'You cheated on me,' I said bluntly. 'In front of the whole fucking world – I'm an idiot,' I said, my voice descending into mumbling. 'Such an idiot, thinking I could trust you.'

'Cheat on you – you're not – what are you talking about?'

'I was taking this seriously!'

'And so was I!' Jessy looked bewildered. Could she really not see how she had hurt me? How she had humiliated me? If the articles weren't enough, seeing her with her ex, inside her house – somewhere she'd never invited me – was the last straw.

I swallowed hard. 'I thought this – I thought we could be something more, but you couldn't wait to cheat –'

'You know what, I'm really getting tired of you accusing me of being unfaithful. Not that there's even anything for me to be faithful to,' Jessy shot back at me, her tone angry now. 'The whole thing was supposed to be fake, remember?'

I took a step away, the pain her words inflicted so tangible I was almost surprised not to see them cut into me physically.

It had been fake. It had felt real to me. But that was it. It had only felt real *to me*. Jessy had just been entertaining me all along.

'Patrick, just talk to me. Please!' She reached for me, but I jerked away quickly. I didn't think I could continue standing if she had taken my hand.

Pain bloomed in her eyes at my rejection, and she dropped her arm.

Good. Let her see she isn't going to worm her way out of this one.

I should have felt satisfaction, but all I felt was hollowed out. How could this have gone so wrong so quickly? Hell, I'd been burned before, but this had been a flame I'd willingly fanned.

And now I was the one nursing another burn.

'And my mother? Seriously?' I muttered, lost in the memory of the articles that had shattered my morning. Shattered my heart. 'You know how I feel about her – how she and I . . . Did you really think I wasn't going to find out?'

When I managed to lift my gaze, my gut twisted. She was so beautiful, and I had really thought –

'Patrick,' Jessy said slowly, reaching for my hand. 'I have no idea what you are talking about.'

TWENTY

*There aren't words, no words in the world for
what you've done to me . . .*
– from 'Wounded', by These Exiles

'PATRICK.' I SPOKE SLOWLY, truly confused at how the day I had so been looking forward to had morphed so quickly into this. 'I have no idea what you are talking about.'

It was, considering everything that had happened, a relatively calm approach. I mean, he had assumed the absolute worst of me and was accusing me of things that were outright lies.

Cheating on him? And what was this about Cassie? I'd never even met his mother.

What a shitshow this last hour had been. First Ross had just turned up, like we hadn't been broken up for ages. I hadn't wanted him here, or anywhere near me, but my housemates had let him in – I was going to be having a word or two with them about letting random men into the flat. And now . . .

'No idea? Seriously? First off, your fucking ex just tried to punch me,' Patrick said quietly. 'Were you actually going to just watch as your ex punched your current boyfriend –'

'Current boyfriend?' My heart skipped a beat as I stared in shock.

He considered himself – I mean, I'd hoped, but I hadn't wanted to assume –

But for some reason Patrick's face was twisting into a grimace. 'Right. Yeah, my bad. You don't want to tie yourself down.'

'No, I –' My brain was whirring too slowly to keep up with the twists and turns of this conversation. 'Ross just turned up here, I didn't ask him to – I would never invite him round, Patrick,' I told him, like it was obvious. It should have been. He knew how much Ross had hurt me. How that relationship had left me unmoored. How could he think I would willingly let Ross back into my life?

'So, what? He just turned up?' Patrick's tone was unbelieving.

'Yes!' I exclaimed. 'He's been trying to get through to me these last few weeks, but I have him blocked. I wasn't expecting him to turn up like this.'

I could see Patrick weighing my words, his expression softening – but only for a moment.

When his gaze met mine again, his eyes were flint. 'Couldn't fit him into your packed timetable? Too busy seeing other people?'

Too busy – 'Other people?'

'Yeah, other people,' Patrick shot back at me, pacing across the room to the window as though he couldn't even bring himself to look at me any more. 'You thought I wouldn't find out?'

'I have no idea what you're –'

'Don't lie. It's all over the internet, Jessy! I thought you of all people would be the last person to lie to me.' Patrick was leaning against the windowsill with a strange look in his eye. 'I shouldn't have expected anything less from someone who was pretty much paid to date me.'

Heat burned across my cheeks. It must have looked like an admission of guilt, because horror broke out on Patrick's face.

'Fuck, that was a shot in the dark – you were paid to date me? What, by Derek?'

'No!' I should have told him this at the very beginning. 'No, I mean – Derek offered me money, but –'

Patrick swore under his breath.

'– I told him no!' Why was he so quick to believe the worst of me? 'He put it into Laura's app, I never saw a penny –'

'Right, and I'm just supposed to believe that, am I? Just like I'm supposed to believe you haven't been secretly dating other people when I've seen the photos?'

All I could do was stare. 'Photos?' The only pictures I'd taken recently had been with the random celebrities we met at the industry events we'd attended. And Patrick had been in all of those with me.

'Yeah, the photos of all those guys you've been meeting– and the one you took with Cassie,' Patrick snarled.

I blinked. 'Cassie? What, your mum?'

The glare in his eyes sparked and did not fade. 'Don't even bother lying – you've been feeding her stories, taking photos with her.'

What the hell was he talking about? 'Patrick, I haven't –' I had never even seen a picture of Cassie.

'It's all over the internet!' His voice was sharp, pained, angry, and I couldn't understand why. Patrick – he was looking at me like I'd stabbed him in the back. 'You know, I actually fell for you.' His voice was low, level, but there was a sort of dull finality in it I didn't like. 'I can't believe that I made myself vulnerable with you. That I shared – It's all online, Jessy. You and my mum, cosy little chats about me – you know how I feel about her!'

'Patrick, you know ninety per cent of what you read online is absolute crap –' He had told me that himself.

'Chatting with my mother? I can't deal with this. I just can't, Jessy. Just because your mum is dead, that doesn't mean you can fix mine. Consider our contract terminated.'

There was no time to say anything, no opportunity to grab him as he passed me. Patrick stormed by at a pace that I couldn't have matched, even if I had wanted to – and I wasn't sure I did. He slammed the door behind him, and within a few seconds, I heard the front door slam too.

He'd gone.

Slowly, very slowly, I lowered myself on to the sagging sofa.

'Just because your mum is dead, that doesn't mean you can fix mine.'

The words cut me deeper than anything else Patrick had thrown at me.

I dropped my head into my hands.

Yeah, I could go after Patrick.

But I'd done this before, hadn't I? Chased a guy that hadn't deserved me. Hadn't deserved my forgiveness, or a second chance.

I'd promised myself – I'd promised Laura, and Anna – that I wasn't going to make the same mistake again.

'I can't deal with this. I just can't, Jessy . . . Consider our contract terminated.'

A tear, hot and unwelcome, trickled down my cheek.

TWENTY-ONE

Do you think in every world we're dancing like this, laughing like this, do you think in every universe I found you like this? Do you think there's a you and a me out there, not speaking, not talking because I broke your heart?
– from 'Hello Alternative You', by These Exiles

'SMILE! SMILE, PATRICK!'

'Over here – no, over here!'

'Back a bit, left a bit, no right, *my* right – yeah, that's great, smile!'

Smile.

They wanted me to smile.

My life was falling apart, I hadn't eaten all day because every time I tried to take a bite of food it just tasted like cardboard . . . and they wanted me to smile.

Thankfully, Derek had been clear with me when he was hovering around as I was being pinned into this damned suit. 'Don't smile, Patrick.'

I'd glared at our publicist as I glanced up from my phone. I'd been typing out a lyric idea.

Call me quick, lest you slip, through my fingers

'I'm not smiling.'

'Not now – I mean tonight,' said Derek, tapping away at his own phone. 'On the red carpet.'

'And I'm not supposed to be smiling, because –'

'Because you are a dark and mysterious singer.' He glanced up and took a long look at me. 'And because we don't want any questions about you and Jessy. If you smile, the journos will think they can get a scoop from you. Channel your best pissed-off energy.'

My snort echoed around the hotel room Derek had booked for me and the stylist. *Channelling my best pissed-off look?* That wouldn't be hard. I'd been in a constant state of being pissed off recently.

'Yes, something like that.' Derek pointed at my face before looking back down at his phone and taking a seat in the armchair behind the mirror I had been instructed to stand by. 'Look, you're all over the news and the socials, and that's good. You know, all PR is good PR.'

Good? The woman I'd thought I loved was cheating on me, and that was good?

'But we don't want to be answering questions about Jessy, not this close to the Songwriter Awards. Everything from here on out has to be about you and the boys.'

'I understand,' I said in a monotone voice. And I really did. It wasn't like I wanted to talk about Jessy, anyway. Not to anyone, but least of all the media.

Derek must have sensed something in my tone, because I looked up to see him staring at me, concern on his face. 'You OK, man?'

'I'm fine,' I tried to reassure him, but I knew I wasn't convincing anyone.

'It's just, you seem –'

'Seriously, Derek. I'm fine. You don't have to worry about me.' I didn't sound fine. Anyone who knew me would be able to tell I wasn't fine.

I'd blocked Jessy after I'd stormed out of her house, and even gone as far as to delete Butterflies as soon as I got back to my flat. I just wanted to forget that she even existed.

Turned out that was easier said than done.

I looked away from Derek's eyes, not wanting to see the truth in them. That I was the furthest thing from being OK.

He finally got the hint. 'All right, if you say so.' And he left it at that.

I stared at my reflection, unable to meet my own eye, and pulled my phone from my pocket to check the group chat with the boys.

> **Matt**
> I never saw it coming – you OK, Patrick?

> **Wes**
> We'll grab drinks when we're all back, you're not alone in this

> **Ben**
> Fuck her

The flicker of a smile flitted across my lips. No matter what happened, I could always count on my friends to be on my side. It would be so good to have them back here.

That was an hour ago. Now I was standing here on the red carpet of a film premiere, hating every second of it, blinded by all the cameras.

'Patrick, have you spoken to Jessy?'

'Has Jessy given you an explanation for what she was doing with –'

'Patrick, is it true you and your mother –'

I couldn't do this. I didn't remember it being this bad when Celine had cheated on me, but maybe that had been because she'd given her own little interviews. I gritted my teeth and focused hard on not smiling, which, unsurprisingly, was pretty easy.

Part of me felt as though I was never going to smile again.

More flashes of light went off and I tried not to blink, eyes watering. Were there seriously people who enjoyed this?

I couldn't think of anything worse.

'Move along now, thank you,' one of the ushers muttered, pulling me aside to stand on another marker, where a whole new set of photographers and journalists was waiting for me.

Great.

'Patrick! Over here!'

'Look here, Patrick – smile!'

I was going to kill Derek. All I had wanted to do was hide away in my flat and wait for the guys to come back. Without them here, I was so damned . . . exposed.

Vulnerable.

Naked.

I couldn't remember the last time I'd had to do a red carpet, or any proper event, without them. Wes, Ben, Matt – they were always beside me, a buffer between me and the paparazzi who were determined to 'get something'.

On my own, this whole thing was a nightmare. My chest felt tight, and I couldn't take anything but quick, shallow breaths. My fingers were tingling as they hung awkwardly by my sides, and there was a lump the size of a fist in my throat that made swallowing difficult.

'Where's Jessy?' yelled a journalist who I recognized. I was pretty sure we'd done an interview with her last year, before our last album dropped. 'Where's your girlfriend, Patrick?'

Great question.

A part of me, and I hated that it even existed, had hoped . . . well, that she'd be here. It was impossible. Derek would never have allowed it. But we'd talked about attending this premiere together what felt like years ago. Back then, I had been looking forward to having her on my arm. Of flaunting her in front of the world.

That was when I'd believed there was something real between us.

Now . . . now I knew what she really was.

I turned my back on the media without a word. If they wanted to know where Jessy was, they should go hound her. Besides, it wasn't like I had a clue.

'And if you'd just wait over here, Mr Tetlow.' The usher was pointing to a covered area just around the corner that was, thankfully, away from the cameras.

I walked away from the yelling photographers, journalists, influencers – the whole bear pit of them – and reached my sanctuary. It appeared to be some sort of waiting zone, and I recognized a few of the faces hanging around.

I nodded politely at the ones I knew and walked past the ones I didn't, before finding myself a solitary spot to stand in.

I had walked the red carpet just like I'd been told. As far as I was concerned, my job here was done.

Slipping my phone out of my pocket, I dialled the last number in my call log.

Derek picked up immediately. 'I was watching you live, you looked great!'

'Thanks,' I replied, half-heartedly.

'No smiling, excellent job.'

'Yeah, thanks.' I took in a deep breath. 'Can I go home now?'

I'd known what the answer would be before I even asked, but there was still a flash of disappointment as I heard our PR manager's answer.

'Absolutely not – they're going to want your reaction after the film,' he said resolutely.

I groaned, loud enough for some of the models standing near me to look over. I turned away quickly.

Fuck. I don't want to be here. 'I'm serious, Derek, I'd rather just leave –'

'And I'd rather just have clients who do what they're told.' Even through the phone, I could hear the acerbic grin on his face. 'Look, this is important. Until Wes finishes at the UN and Ben . . . well, the less said about Ben, the better. Until the gang is back together for the Songwriter Awards, this is the last public appearance for These Exiles.'

I looked down at the ridiculous green suit the stylist had put me in. 'I'm only one quarter of These Exiles.'

'So perhaps I should make you stay four times the –'

'Yeah, good luck with that.' There was no chance I was going to stay a second longer than I needed to.

'Look, Patrick,' Derek said, 'it's the last public event before the awards show, and I just need you to put your best foot forward. It's only for one more night. You'll have the boys back soon.' He paused. 'Have you spoken to Jessy yet?'

That familiar pain lanced through me.

'You know I haven't. I told you I'd blocked her. Besides, why do you even want me to speak to her?'

Derek sighed down the phone. 'Look, I'm not saying you should trust her blindly, or even that what was reported wasn't true. But I'm not convinced *everything* in that article was accurate. You know these gossip sites like to make things more ... salacious.' He took a breath before he continued. 'I didn't send those links to you because I thought Jessy was actually cheating on you. I sent them because the optics were bad, and I wanted you to know what had happened before you were ambushed by it. I ... I never expected it to spiral into this.'

The *this* in question was the Cold War approach I had adopted. I hadn't had any contact with Jessy since our argument. I'd had Derek's assistant deliver Jessy's things to her apartment. I had done everything humanly possible to avoid her.

Since her betrayal.

'It doesn't matter, Derek, because it's over.' Too much had happened. Cassie, Ross, the other men. It was all too much. 'It's over.' I repeated, voice unsteady. If nothing else, I had learnt Jessy couldn't handle fame. Couldn't handle the pressure and the expectations that came with it. That came with being in a relationship with me.

'Your call, Patrick. Let me know when you're out of the premiere and we can talk strategy for –'

'Yeah, fine,' I muttered.

As I wrapped up the phone call with Derek, I saw someone approach me from the corner of my eye. I hoped that if I kept my head down they would get the message. But a moment later, I felt a tap on my shoulder.

'Hey, Patrick! It's Patrick, right?'

I grimaced and replied without looking up. 'Yeah, that's me.'

I slipped my phone into my pocket and turned to smile at the guy – only to freeze when I got a proper look at him.

It was Dillon. The actor Jessy had been photographed with. *Why must I suffer like this?*

'Look, Patrick, I just wanted to say, no hard feelings,' Dillon said with a grin.

I didn't move. I didn't even think I was breathing. I was completely frozen. The sound of the chaos outside, in the media pen, broke me from my trance. 'No hard feelings?' Who the hell did this guy think he was?

'Yeah. I mean, I know it's made the internet go wild,' Dillon said with a shrug, that million-dollar smile far too relaxed. 'But they'll jump on anything that even looks like a story, right?'

The balls on the man. 'Right.' What was I even doing still talking to him? It must've been morbid curiosity.

'I mean, she's fantastic, Jessy, isn't she?'

I couldn't believe it. Did this guy have no tact? No care in the world? Or had he just seen what I'd so spectacularly missed – that Jessy and I had been fake, from beginning to end?

Clearly Dillon didn't care, because he barely paused for breath. 'She was honestly brilliant. I hadn't known what to expect when I agreed to meet with her about GSR, but she really convinced me to –'

'Wait, what?' Were my ears ringing? I couldn't have heard that properly. 'GSR. As in, GSR Financials?' What did Jessy's company have to do with him?

Dillon nodded, completely unfazed. 'Yeah. I mean, that's how we met. They're my accountants, part of their "high net-worth" department or whatever, and we were talking about future investments, and she told me about Butterflies and her sister's vision. She had some fascinating ideas about long-term portfolios –'

'You met her . . . for work?' I repeated slowly.

Dillon looked at me like I was slow, which, in fairness, even I was starting to question. Nothing the guy had said since he'd approached me was making sense. 'Yeah, of course. And I think I'm going to invest in Butterflies. It's really taken off. Obviously, most of that is since you two started dating. But still, I think there could be some real longevity with it. But, hey, I just came over to say sorry about the shit with the press. You know how they can be.'

I did. I knew better than anyone.

And I'd believed them over Jessy.

'I'm sure Jessy must have explained, but I thought, man to man, you deserved an apology from me too. I should've thought about it.'

'Jessy must have explained.' My whole body stiffened. Except I hadn't let her.

I had asked her about it, sure – but I hadn't actually stuck around to hear her answer. I'd been so busy expecting the worst that I hadn't bothered to listen to her speak.

It didn't justify the absolute betrayal of her chatting with Cassie . . . but it at least explained why she was so damned confused about the dating thing.

Oh, fuck. I've really messed up.

'Right, everyone, we are going to start making our way in.' An usher smiled brightly, the double doors opening and murmurs of excitement rippling through the crowd. 'If you would all make your way to the –'

Completely unmoored by Dillon's revelations, I allowed myself to be swept along with the current, hardly thinking, and definitely not noticing when I'd taken a seat and the film had started. The next three hours went by without me taking much notice of my surroundings. I couldn't have told anyone what the film was about, occupied as I was with my own tumultuous thoughts.

I had been wrong. I had been wrong about the men Jessy had supposedly been dating.

And if I was wrong about that, I could have been wrong about . . . about Cassie.

I knew how much my mother loved attention. That she couldn't stop herself trying to make a story out of nothing.

But the photo. The photo of Cassie and Jessy was real. There was no faking that. That wasn't a long-lens pap situation, that was a personal photo that Jessy had happily taken.

I turned it over in my head, every which way. Was there a way to –

Sudden blinding light. I was broken out of my bubble, and the person sitting beside me turned to me. 'So, what did you think of the film?'

'Film?' I repeated vaguely. *Right. The premiere.* 'Uh, I thought it was great. Really good . . . uh . . . cinematography.'

I didn't wait around to hear their thoughts.

I needed to see Jessy.

What felt like only seconds later, I had made it past the waiting press – whom I'd ignored, even as they snapped photos they'd surely spin into some new story – and reached my driver.

'Ah, Mr Tetlow, did you enjoy the –'

'We need to get going,' I said, wrenching open the door and giving him the address.

It took a lot longer than I thought to get there, and I should have spent that time figuring out what I wanted to say, but as I staggered out of the car and ran up the stairs to Jessy's hotel door, I still didn't have a plan. I knocked and waited for someone to answer. The door opened and, suddenly, Jessy was standing right in front of me.

She was wearing that favourite sundress of mine, her eyes bright but fading in brilliance as she saw me.

'Hi,' I said, unsure of how to start. 'Jessy, I need to talk to you. Can I –'

But Jessy was already shaking her head. Not a good sign.

'I don't want to talk to you.' Her tone brooked no room for argument.

'Please,' I tried again. 'I really want to –'

'No,' Jessy said resolutely.

Fuck. I had to convince her to hear me out. 'Can I just come in? There's a lot I have to say –'

'Anything you want to say to me, you can say right here,' said Jessy, leaning against the door frame, arms crossed in front of her.

I swallowed. This would have been a whole lot easier if I could think clearly while in her presence, but then that had been the problem all along. I hadn't thought clearly.

And now I had to put this right.

'I met Dillon tonight,' I said simply.

Jessy raised an eyebrow. 'OK. And what has that got to do with me?'

Shit. Was she honestly going to make it this hard? 'He told me –'

'Wait, let me guess.' She held her hand up, a look of fake contemplation on her face. 'I'm guessing he told you what I tried to tell you myself,' Jessy said, and her voice was level, quiet, as though she'd already cried all the tears she was going to over me.

I was scared to think about what that meant.

'I . . . it didn't . . . I mean, I should have –' God, I was doing a terrible job of trying to explain myself to her.

'I tried to tell you I was meeting him for work,' Jessy interrupted me, as though she had been preparing for this moment and wasn't going to be shaken from her script. 'Karun asked me to meet a bunch of rich clients to talk to them about GSR and protentional investment opportunities. I was talking to Dillon and Tim about portfolios and long-term investments. It's a huge deal for me – and for Laura. I used the opportunity to talk to them both about Butterflies, trying to convince them to invest in it.'

I swallowed hard, thoroughly chastised. 'I'm sorry –' I could barely look at her.

'This was big for me. For my career,' added Jessy, her voice matter-of-fact. 'I met with – oh, I don't know, five high net-worth clients. Two of them were guys. I notice that the meetings I had with women didn't make it into the headlines.'

Heat seared across my chest. 'I know. I know I shouldn't have jumped to conclusions.' And I'd be kicking myself for a long time afterwards for it. 'But you were meeting them at restaurants and pubs. You can see why I thought –'

'Yeah, that's how loads of business is done,' Jessy said with a shrug, like she was unfazed. By me, by this conversation, by the excuses that clearly had no effect on her. 'If you'd just asked me – if you'd just listened, Patrick, you would have got it. I wasn't dating anyone else, I would never – the idea that I would betray you like that, it's just . . .'

Her voice trailed away as she shrugged again, her attention not wavering from my face.

It was just a business thing. I mean, how many times had I been taken out by a company for lunch or dinner? Not all business was conducted in an office. I knew that.

And . . . and that was all Jessy had been doing.

'So, now you get it,' Jessy said ruefully, folding her arms across her chest and wincing slightly. 'Kinda sucks that it took Dillon – a guy – speaking to you for you to believe me, instead of just listening when I asked you to. I tried messaging you, but you blocked me. I thought you knew me better than that.'

The horror of what I'd done – of how quickly I'd assumed the worst, and not given Jessy even half a chance to explain – was still trickling through to me.

I took a deep breath before saying what I should have started with. 'Jessy, I'm sorry. If I had known –'

'Yeah, I'm sure you are, now.' She brushed off my apology as though it didn't matter. 'Are you going to apologize for that shit you chatted about me and your mum?'

Cassie. 'No.' The pictures with the other men might have been misconstrued, but there was nothing that justified Jessy meeting with my mother behind my back. And there never would be.

Her eyes were cold. 'Then I think you were right.'

I blinked, unable to follow. 'Right?'

Jessy's nod was brief, perfunctory. 'Yeah, this contract is over. No more fake dating. No more anything. I'm so done with you – with this. It's over.'

I had said the same thing to Derek only hours ago, yet hearing my own words repeated back at me still cut deep.

'Laura's app has got all the good publicity it's going to get,' Jessy continued, her words coming from a long way away, 'and, from what I can see, your record label won't be too upset this whole thing didn't work out. I mean, people date and break up all the time, right? Nothing newsworthy about this coming to an end.' She said it like it was so simple. Like we hadn't spent weeks in each other's pockets.

Am I ready to give that up?

'And you . . . you hurt me.' Jessy's lips lifted, but it wasn't a smile. 'Shit, Patrick, you immediately believed the absolute worst of me. If that had been you, I would never –'

I forced myself to speak. 'I know. The pictures were just so convincing. You looked like you were having fun with them and it . . . it made my blood boil.' I had never had a problem with jealousy, but the anger that had spread through me at the thought of Jessy out on dates with those men, it had truly surprised me. I'd put it down to her betrayal at first, but the longer I interrogated my feelings, the more I realized I'd been equal parts angry and jealous.

Jessy was mine. I didn't want to share her.

'And what about the way you spoke about my mum? What possible excuse could you have for that?'

I winced. I'd been out of line there. 'I should never have said those things, Jessy. You didn't deserve that, no matter how upset I was.'

'I don't want to date a guy who doesn't trust me,' Jessy said after a pause, her voice layered with more emotion now. 'I refuse to, actually. I don't want someone who thinks I'd be capable of being unfaithful to them.'

'Jessy –'

'Or to be with a guy who doesn't trust me to be seen with other men in public. That's the kind of shit Ross used to –' Jessy halted herself, covering her mouth just for a moment before letting it drop. 'And I deserve better than that.'

'I know. I know you do.' How had my fears managed to twist what was already so good? 'But it just felt so close to what Celine had done to me. It was like it was happening all over again.' Surely she could see how I'd been triggered.

'I am not Celine.' Jessy stepped forward, her eyes full of hurt. 'You should have trusted me!'

Her outrage felt so misplaced, I couldn't help but fire back, 'What, like I trusted you about Cassie? Only for you to go and meet with her!'

Anger sparked in her eyes, and she looked me dead on as she said, 'And where exactly do you think I would have found your mother? Seeing as I've never even seen a picture of her?'

'I don't know.' I hadn't given much thought to how the two had met, too enraged every time I thought about them to interrogate it. What did it matter how it started? 'I figured she must have found you on socials –'

'She approached me on the street and asked for a photo. I didn't even know who she was!' Jessy snapped, her temper finally getting the better of her. 'Laura was with me, she can tell you – the woman didn't give me her name, how the fuck was I supposed to know who she was? What, you want me to ask for proof of name and address for everyone who approaches me? I thought she was a fan.' Her voice broke. 'She said she was a fan of yours.'

Oh . . . oh shit.

That sounded exactly like my mother. It was exactly the kind of underhand thing Cassie would do.

Guilt flooded through me. I had really screwed this up. Probably beyond repair.

'Fuck,' I whispered.

Jessy held my gaze. 'Yeah. You're an idiot, and I want nothing more to do with you.'

I winced, but I could hardly argue with her.

'I should never have agreed to this – this, all of this,' Jessy said, picking at the fabric of her dress. 'I should have known I'd have my heart broken. But, like you said, it doesn't matter because it was never real. Obviously.' She took a step back and pulled the door almost to a close. 'Bye, Patrick.'

'Jessy –' This couldn't be it.

I needed more time. Time to wrap my head around everything. Time to convince her we were worth another shot. But time was the one thing I had run out of.

'This is over. Whatever this is – whatever this *was* –' Jessy broke off, tears in her eyes now. 'I just can't do it, Patrick. I can't. I won't.'

And she turned away and shut the door in my face.

TWENTY-TWO

Is this what you pictured? In your fantasies, in your wildest dreams, is this what you pictured? Was this the goal – are you happy now? Was this the treasure – are you happy now?
– from 'The Treasure We Buried',
by These Exiles

'IT'S ME,' A VOICE called, with a noise that sounded like a bag being dropped by the hotel door. 'Jessy?'

'She's got to be up by now, right?' Anna's stage whisper was loud, even from the small kitchenette in the suite Derek had said I could stay in until, and I quote, 'the storm has blown over'. 'God, I'd forgotten how gorgeous this place was.'

A prickle of uncertainty crept up my spine as I leaned against the cabinet, bottle in hand. 'Laura?'

I hadn't left the hotel room in three days. Calling in sick on day one had made Karun huff down the phone, but honestly, I couldn't even bear thinking about going to work.

What – sit at my desk while my heart was breaking and colour-code spreadsheets that someone else would take credit for?

No thank you.

And of course, that didn't matter any more.

It had only been the speed of Laura's response to my SOS earlier that got me out of bed in the first place.

> **Jessy**
> Emergency

> **Laura**
> I'll be there in an hour

It was weird.

The text reminded me of the very one that had dragged me into this mess, all those weeks ago.

Another thump. 'Laura?' I called out from the kitchen. 'Anna? I was wondering why it took you so long to – hey.'

My heart plummeted as I saw their faces freeze.

Freeze at the sight of me – which wasn't super flattering. I was sitting – not lying, thank God – on the kitchen floor. I was wearing an oversized hoodie I'd grabbed at a charity shop last year when my heating had gone out. In my left hand was a bottle of wine, half drunk and with a lipstick ring around the neck. In the other hand was an ice cream tub. It was nearly empty.

'Oh, Jessy,' Laura said quietly, stepping through the doorway towards me, glasses slipping down her nose before she pushed them back up with her thumb. 'You look . . . shit. Respectfully.'

I grinned through the haze of sugar and cheap booze. 'Well, that can't be true. Not if this wine and the ice cream are anything to go by.'

'I'd half-expected your emergency message to be nothing more than a brilliant and tactical excuse to get me out of bed,' Anna muttered, stepping around to my other side and dropping on to the floor beside me.

But this wasn't an act. 'It's over,' I said quietly. 'It's all over.'

Laura's face dropped. 'You haven't – fuck, please tell me you haven't done anything –'

'No! No, I don't mean – my job. It's over,' I said with a helpless shrug.

Anna stared as though she hadn't heard me. 'No.'

'Yup.'

'No –'

'If you're just going to sit on the floor and disagree with me,' I said darkly, lifting the bottle of wine for another swig, 'then fuck off.'

My sister's glare was severe. 'If you're not going to tell me what's happened, I'll just leave.' She waited. 'Jessy?'

I just sat there. How had my whole world fallen apart in a matter of days?

'I can't help you if I don't know what's wrong!' Anna said sharply, eyeing me with that lawyer look of hers.

And yeah, I was well aware of the accuracy of the statement, considering that I had told Laura and Anna practically nothing about why Patrick and I . . . about why he and I weren't . . .

They didn't need to know.

Just that it was over.

'And it really is over with Patrick,' I said quietly, still not sure which hurt more – the loss of the man I really cared about, or the implosion of the only proper job I'd ever had. 'It's over,' I mumbled, lifting the bottle.

'Over – with Patrick?' I'd never seen Laura look so outraged. 'Like, actually over? I thought all that break-up stuff was Derek wanting bigger headlines –'

'Yeah, he accused me of lying and messing with his . . . his private life.'

Just because your mum is dead, that doesn't mean you can fix mine!

Those were words that my sister absolutely did not need to hear.

Anna swore under her breath. 'I'm going to kill him. I warned him, I'm going to kill –'

'First things first,' Laura muttered, jerking her head towards me.

Me? What did I do?

Delicately, making sure she didn't spill a drop – not in this economy – Anna pulled the bottle of wine from my mostly unresisting hands. 'There we go.'

'Oh, come on –'

'Not at ten in the morning, thank you,' Laura said severely, though with a wry smile. 'All this time, and I'm still looking after you.'

I'm not saying I was always the one to fall apart, because I wasn't. We were tough, Laura and I. We'd had to be.

But she was my older sister, even if only by minutes, and sometimes I was perfectly happy letting her take care of me. She always knew what to do, always resisted the urge to despair – an urge I embraced whenever I could, especially if it meant I could justify having pizza in bed.

'I guess I should be glad you're not dating him any more,' Laura said lightly, slowly lowering herself so that she was sitting on the floor with us. 'He gave this big interview. In preparation for the awards thingy this Saturday.'

A shiver of tension rippled down my spine. 'An interview.'

See, this was the trouble when you blocked certain keywords from your social media. You missed out on things. Like the fact that your ex – fake ex? Whoever – had done a public interview in which he'd likely had to talk about you.

Fun.

'What did he say?'

Laura sighed heavily as she took off her glasses. 'He was being asked again and again, far as I can make out, what had happened with the two of you. If you were together or not, and if you'd broken up, whether he was back on the dating apps.'

I pulled my knees up to hug them. 'Great.' Exactly what I wanted to hear.

'The prick should have kept his damned mouth shut,' Anna said darkly, shifting over to sit next to me, her arm slung around my shoulder.

'Again – what did he say?'

My sister's dejected look worried me. She took a breath before saying, 'He said he wasn't on any of the dating apps. Not even Butterflies.'

Ah. I winced.

Yeah, that was definitely bad. The whole point of me doing this thing was to promote Butterflies.

'Users have started to delete their accounts,' Laura said, dropping a finger into the ice cream tub, swooping it around and bringing it to her mouth. 'Now there's absolutely no chance of matching with their favourite pop star. Not that they would have been able to, with the two of you dating. But in their minds they must have thought they were in with a chance. Especially after everything in the press.'

'But what are you going to do, Laura –'

My sister's snort halted me in my tracks. 'Oh, don't worry about me – your little chat with Dillon has proven that I can get funding from a wider group of people. But, yeah. Not super helpful.'

We fell into silence, sitting there on the kitchenette floor of a hotel suite that I could absolutely not afford and would most definitely have to move out of soon.

I felt awful. Butterflies was everything Laura had worked for, everything she'd sacrificed for. This had been her dream: to start apps and make money, make millions – change the world with a foundation, invest in our local communities, open a centre where we'd grown up.

Be one of those people who did something.

'Talk to me about your job,' my twin said quietly. 'You said it's over?'

I slipped my phone out of my hoodie pocket. 'Yeah, I got a call yesterday. Karun very kindly recorded it as per GSR Financials policy and sent it to me. As an audio record. To, and I quote, "prevent any later misunderstandings".'

Anna swore under her breath and handed me back the wine she'd so recently confiscated.

'Wow, big corporates are really something, aren't they?' Laura screwed up her nose. 'Let's give it a listen, then.'

I pressed play and my little recorded voice started up. Oh, it was even worse hearing it the second time around.

'I really wanted to have this conversation in person, Ms Donovan, but as we're nearing the end of the month and the paperwork has to go through today –'

'Paperwork? I sent you the deck on Monday for the –'

'I am afraid we are terminating your position at GSR Financials, Ms Donovan.'

Yep, listening to it a second time was so much worse. I still couldn't believe it. Seriously, did I break a mirror or upset the heavens or something?

Laura spoke over the end of the recording. 'But you'd done everything they wanted!'

'I mean, I did take like a five-week break from my grad job,' I pointed out, not quite sure why I was defending Karun or GSR Financials. 'I'm just relieved I recorded it so I couldn't trick myself into thinking I'd dreamt it. All I could hear was a buzzing as my pulse grew in volume and *thump, thump, thumped* in my head.'

'You poor thing,' Laura said sympathetically, her face a picture of concern. 'But you don't look . . . devastated.'

'I just got fired,' I said, taking another swig of the insanely sweet wine. 'But, you know, I'm strangely OK about it.'

Because the panic . . . still hadn't come.

Weird. I'd sat there, preparing myself to fight it off as soon as it arrived, and it just *hadn't*. Even the dread from first receiving the call was disappearing.

Weird as fuck.

Laura looked over at me with a spoon in her mouth. She was still eating what was left of my ice cream.

'Please tell me you didn't go in and sign a bunch of stuff?' Anna said, like she hadn't taught me better.

'Nah, I knew not to go in without my legal representative.' I grinned, nudging her and enjoying the warmth of having my sister and bestie around me. God, I loved them. 'I told you, I'm fine.'

'Says the girl who just downed the equivalent of a large glass of wine in one pull,' Laura said pointedly. 'Shouldn't you be panicking? Freaking out or something? How much have you got saved?'

'A bit. But they're giving me six months' pay.'

It was bizarre. Everyone our age I knew lived in fear of exactly this: losing their job and finding themselves back on the market.

Hell, it's not like I loved my work at GSR Financials. But it paid me a wage. Enough to live. To support myself.

And now . . .

'You know, I think . . . I think,' I said slowly, lifting my gaze to my clearly concerned sister, 'I'm going to use this as a reset.'

Anna blinked. 'A reset.'

My shrug was perhaps a little too nonchalant. 'Yeah. I mean, I was chasing after finance because I thought that was what you were supposed to want. If you're even halfway decent at maths, work in finance, right?'

'That is what everyone does,' Anna agreed.

Half my uni group were working at banks or investment firms or stuff like that, and it was just . . . what we did. What I'd always assumed I would do.

'Perhaps it's time to think about what I actually want out of my career,' I said slowly. 'Out of my life.'

When had I stopped dreaming and started settling?

'You've got that faraway look in your eyes you used to get as a kid,' Laura pointed out, sticking her spoon back into the ice-cream tub and scraping out the last bits. Her dedication to leaving nothing behind was impressive. 'What are you thinking?'

'I just . . . my whole life has been about the next thing,'

I said. 'Got to pass my exams at school to get to uni, got to get into the best uni, got to get the best marks to get the best grad job . . . it's like I've been running a marathon with no finishing line.'

Anna picked up the wine bottle and took a swig herself. 'Fuck me, do you want to be more cheerful?'

'No, I mean – well. I can stop the marathon now, can't I?' I glanced about myself and tried to take a deep breath. 'I've barely spent any money but rent these last few weeks, Derek's been covering pretty much all my expenses. And Karun will get me six months' pay. I can just . . . stop. Work out what I actually want. At least for a little bit.'

I wasn't so lost in my thoughts that I didn't notice Anna and Laura exchange a look.

'Don't worry, I'm not about to join a commune or backpack around the world with a guy called Gerald I barely know.' I grinned, grabbing the wine from Anna. 'I just . . . yeah. Freedom from real life for a bit would be rather nice.'

Although, of course, the last few weeks with Patrick had been the best escape from real life I'd ever find. A different world. A world of glitz and glamour . . . and late-night talks in chicken shops, and throwing myself off buildings.

But that was all over now. And I needed to move on.

'The first thing we need is a better bottle of wine,' Anna said briskly.

'No, the first thing we need,' Laura countered, 'is more ice cream.' She looked at the empty tub forlornly.

I grinned. They were both wrong. I knew exactly what I was going to do. 'The first thing we need . . . is coffee.'

TWENTY-THREE

Can you hear me? If I shout a little louder, grovel a little deeper, will you hear me?
– from 'The Mistakes I Own', by These Exiles

THE ECHO REBOUNDED AROUND the studio as I allowed the door to shut behind me.

It was an echo I knew well, but it had been weeks since I'd been in here. The box of cables we'd left half-sorted had been cleared away – a flash of guilt went through me at the thought of the poor intern who'd been forced to do it – and there was a fresh smell in the air that suggested the place had been cleaned recently.

I stepped slowly over to the electric keyboard. I plonked a few keys. It wasn't plugged in.

Why did it feel so strange to be back? It hadn't been that long; the studio was the place I was supposed to feel most at home.

The most centred.

'There you are, Patrick.'

I turned and grinned at Wes, who was striding in with two coffees. 'Please tell me one of those is for me.'

'Sorry, I need the extra caffeine boost,' Wes said breezily, setting them down and lifting one out of the tray to his lips. 'You know I've recently discovered this new place, Maria's?'

I hadn't expected the visceral reaction, the shooting through my spine, the tearing in my chest –

'She does this incredible –' Thankfully, his voice got cut off.

'There he is!' The door opened and in stepped Matt, a wide grin on his face. 'Taking one for the team there, catching all the headlines!'

My full-body wince must have been visible, because Wes said curiously, 'What have you done now?'

'The man's done nothing,' Wes began. 'It's that Jessy –'

'I don't want to talk about it,' I snapped.

Matt shifted on his feet. 'My bad, man. Didn't mean anything by it.'

Trying to force my hackles down, I gave my friend a brief nod. 'It's fine.'

It was not fine. Sleep eluded me, I still had absolutely no desire to eat, and every time I picked up my phone I half-expected to see a message from Jessy.

Then I remembered that I wouldn't ever receive a message from Jessy again.

The boys moved on, catching each other up on their activities across the globe.

'The reality show wasn't all that bad,' Matt was saying, stretching out on a chair as he swiped Wes's spare coffee. 'I could have done without the cameras in my face all the time, but after a while you start to forget about them.'

'Yeah, well, I still think I got the sweet end of the deal,' Wes replied, dropping down on to the piano stool and casting me another curious glance before continuing. 'It was incredible.

Some of the programmes they're doing out there are truly life-changing.'

My bandmates' chatter continued, though I couldn't bring myself to pay much attention.

It all felt so . . . so far away. I could smile, nod at regular intervals, brave through it and pretend as though I was perfectly fine.

Because I should have been. Fine, that was.

Jessy was just a woman.

A woman I met almost accidentally on a dating app.

I hadn't expected it to be anything – the contract had forced us to spend time together . . . and I hadn't even noticed that I was falling for her until it was too late.

Until I had royally fucked it up.

And now? Now, it felt like there was a huge gaping hole in my chest. Something had been scooped out, and I felt irrevocably changed.

Without Jessy in my life, everything felt . . . empty.

I'd never been like this before. It was horrendous, discovering my happiness could be so dependent on another person.

But it had been my own actions that had pushed her away.

I had no one to blame but myself.

'What's up, gang!'

I turned and forced a smile as Ben walked in, all smile and sunglasses.

Wes and Matt grinned and welcomed him in, while I sat back in the chair I'd somehow found myself on.

'– great to see you –'

'– how was that charity event, huh? I didn't spot –'

'Yeah, it was OK,' Ben said brightly, pulling away from the two of them to approach me, his smile slightly fading.

I stiffened. A serious Ben was never normally a good thing –

'Thanks,' said Ben, dropping on to the chair beside me.

My suspicion must have been written all over my face, because he laughed.

'No, I mean it. Thanks, dude.' He clapped me on my shoulder.

'What for?' I asked, genuinely confused.

Ben gave a nonchalant shrug, but I could see the tension in his eyes. 'For covering for me. Taking the blame. Dealing with all this shit because of it and never giving me up.'

I couldn't remember seeing Ben this . . . this serious. Not ever.

He continued, his tone sombre. 'You know that charity stuff Derek made me do?'

I shrugged. 'Yeah, how did you find it?'

'It was pretty transformative, I can't lie. I went into schools with a group that educates kids on the dangers of drink-driving.' A shiver rustled through him. 'Fuck me. They wanted me to talk about watching a friend make bad choices, and the whole time it was my bad choices that could have really hurt . . . just . . . thanks, man.'

He didn't need to thank me, but I was glad he'd learnt something from the work he'd been doing. 'No worries. Just try not to dick about any more, yeah?'

'Well, no promises.' The twinkle in Ben's eye was back, but there was a seriousness in his expression that reassured me he wouldn't be making that mistake again.

'Hey, Patrick!'

We looked up. Wes had finished his coffee, had apparently wrestled his second coffee back off Matt and was looking over at us curiously. 'I thought you said Derek wanted us here at eleven?'

Ah. Yeah. Right.

'He didn't,' I said quietly. 'But I did.'

The confusion on my bandmates' faces was expected – but I hadn't been able to think of a way to convince them to come in this early without the spectre of Derek looming above the request.

'You?' Matt frowned. 'Why, what's up, man?'

Taking a deep breath, I said softly, 'I have a new song.'

Matt's frown disappeared. 'Your writer's block, it's gone?'

Ben's groan was painfully predictable. 'Shit, man, do we really have to start on the next album right now? Seriously?'

'We're meant to be playing at the Songwriter Awards tomorrow,' Wes pointed out. 'Don't you think we'd spend our time better practising the song we've picked to perform?'

'I was thinking we could perform this new one instead,' I replied steadily.

Ben swore under his breath.

'We do not,' Matt said firmly, 'have time to write and learn a new song in just –'

'It's already written,' I interjected, hating how desperately I wanted this, needed this. 'All you'd have to do is learn –'

'And then perform it on a stage before hundreds of people in the audience and millions streaming live?' Ben snorted. 'With less than twenty-four hours to practise. Bro, have you lost your mind?'

'I think we should do it.'

Three heads turned towards Wes. His quiet way of speaking had always cut through the noisiness of Ben and Matt.

For the second time, Ben swore under his breath.

Wes shrugged. 'I can't think of a better way to get people's attention. We've been hounded with questions about a new album for weeks.'

'Yeah, but a completely new –'

'Let's hear it,' Wes said, leaning back against the electric keyboard.

My stomach lurched as I picked up one of the session guitars from the rack. Despite my hopes, part of me hadn't expected them to even want to hear it, and now it came to it . . . well. I wasn't sure I felt prepared.

'Need a key?' Matt shot over.

I shook my head. 'Nah, not for this.'

The last thing I needed was another instrument as a distraction. It was going to be hard enough getting this out at all.

Unlocking my phone and opening the finalized lyrics, I blew out a long breath.

There was nothing, almost nothing, more vulnerable than sharing a song for the first time. Even with my best friends.

'OK, here we go,' I muttered, mostly to myself.

The chords felt like home as I strummed the opening. Glancing at my phone was hardly necessary as I sang about the woman I'd managed to let get away.

Jessy Donovan.

Butterflies, it was butterflies the moment I first saw you
Coffee cup, looking up, seeing the world change in your eyes

The lyrics had poured out of me. That was, the linking lyrics had – most of the imagery I'd jotted down as our fake dates had turned into something so much more.

Ink my soul upon your heart if you love me too
Call me quick, lest you slip, through my fingers

It was one of the few songs I'd written with almost no edits. It hadn't needed them.

And when we take over the world, and we will
Carve your joy, fuck the ploy, contract over

I should have felt self-conscious, playing the first song I'd ever written about an actual woman to my bandmates – but I couldn't feel anything. Just the lyrics. Just the ache in me. Just the need for her.

And it should never have been me
But it should have been you
It was never supposed to be us
But it could have been true
And if all I have to do is put away my fears
I need you to know your name is music to my ears.

As the chords faded in the studio, I forced myself to swallow the knot that had emerged in my throat. How on earth I'd managed to sing the whole thing, I didn't know. Emotions churned in my chest, hope and pain and regret all warring within me.

I looked up.

Wes was staring, his brow slightly furrowed. Ben exhaled slowly, shaking his head without saying a word.

Tension gripped me. If the boys didn't like it, then I wouldn't know what to do.

'Well,' Matt said, breaking the silence. 'That was bloody brilliant.'

I breathed a quiet sigh of relief.

'Understatement of the year!' a familiar voice called from the doorway. 'Lead single for the next album, is it?'

I winced as Derek stepped into the studio, though it didn't last long. The man was holding coffee.

'Right, you guys, I think it's about time that you broke for an early lunch,' our publicist said smoothly as he handed them out. 'Yes, Wes, it's oat milk – off you go.'

'It's not even half eleven,' Ben pointed out with a grin.

'And yet here I am, telling you very politely that you need to go,' Derek said smartly, pushing the final coffee into my free hand. 'Not you, though.'

I blinked up at him as I carefully put the guitar down. 'What?'

'Out, out, out,' sang Derek, prodding my bandmates in the arms. 'Come on, I got you coffee, the least you can do is give me ten minutes with –'

'What has he done now?' Matt called out, chuckling as he made his way to the door.

'Whatever it is, it can't be that bad. Derek doesn't even look mad,' Wes quipped.

Only Ben lingered. 'You want us to hang around, Patrick?'

Before, I could say anything, Derek replied. 'I will not say it a third time, Ben, get out of here,' he ordered severely. 'Come back in an hour, OK?'

Part of me wished I could ask them to stay. Despite what Wes thought, whatever Derek wanted to talk about, it wasn't going to be good.

The door had closed behind them before I could marshal my thoughts into any sort of order, and Derek pulled Ben's chair around to face me before he sat on it.

'So,' he started. 'I heard from Jessy's lawyer.'

This time it was my stomach that twisted. 'Lawyer?' Did he mean Anna?

Oh God, she was actually going to murder me.

'They wanted to formally terminate the contract. Which they can't do, not without paying a huge amount of money,' Derek said, looking closely at me.

Did he want a reaction out of me?

I hardly knew what to say. Just hearing Jessy's name sent me into a tailspin. Hearing she wanted out of the contract was . . . not surprising. But it hurt, nevertheless.

'But I gave her the out,' Derek said after a pause, looking at me with something like pity. 'So she won't be there. At the awards, I mean.'

My shoulders slumped and disappointment overwhelmed me. 'She won't?'

Our PR manager shook his head. 'Look, Patrick. I don't want to pry into your personal life. Despite what you might think, I don't want to control every little thing you boys do.' He took a breath before continuing. 'But it sounds to me like you and Jessy have unfinished business. Any chance you could make it right with her?'

I hesitated, unsure what Derek's angle was. 'Why? Wouldn't it be better if I just moved on from her? Better for my reputation – for the band?'

'Because it would make you happy, idiot,' Derek shot back, relaxing into his seat. 'It might surprise you, Patrick, but I actually care about your feelings, and your wellbeing. All of you are great assets for the record label, sure, but if you're going to be making music well into your fifties and not marrying women young enough to be your daughters, you've got to stay grounded now.'

Well. When he put it like that.

'So, it's definitely over with you and her?' he asked again.

'Yeah.' I sighed, dropping my head into my hands.

'And there's no way you would take her back?'

I glanced up at him. 'That's not the problem.'

'Ah.'

'Yeah. It was my fault,' I said, defeated. When I continued, I kept my voice low. 'The articles, they weren't – it wasn't true what they wrote. But I reacted badly. By the time I found out the truth . . . it was too late. The damage was done.'

The two of us sat in silence as my mind turned over all the opportunities I'd had to slow down, to stop and think about whether Jessy would really do what I'd accused her of.

All the opportunities I'd missed.

'Well, then I guess we'll just have to do this awards show and try to forget about her.' Derek rose to his feet. 'Now, you think you and the boys will be ready to debut this new song tomorrow?'

TUNING THE GUITAR BACKSTAGE was a lot easier when I could tune Matt and Ben out. Their bickering put old married couples to shame.

'I'm just saying, it's so uncomfortable –'

'This isn't about whether you're comfortable or not –'

'But surely I'd play better if –'

'This is the Songwriter Awards, you seriously don't want to wear a suit?'

My fingers moved slowly along the E string. *Just focus on the guitar. Don't think about the song. Don't think about Jessy, or how you woke up reaching for her last night.*

'Ready?'

I looked up to see Wes smiling, a look of soft concern in his eyes. 'Yeah.'

'It's a great song,' he said gently. 'I'm sure everyone's going to love it.'

He grasped my shoulder as I nodded, unable to find the words.

I'd lost Jessy but gained a song. I wasn't sure I was happy with the trade, but I would have to learn to be.

'Two minutes to go,' hissed a woman wearing a headset and looking down at a time sheet on a tablet. 'Two minutes!'

Two minutes until These Exiles stepped on to the stage and debuted a completely new song to the world.

We'd done this before. Not actually at an awards show, but we were a band: we played new music live all the time. This wasn't any different.

At least, that's what I told myself.

So why was my stomach twisting – my pulse pounding a thousand times a minute?

Maybe this was a mistake. Perhaps we should have just gone with 'Adventure', or 'Clifftop Ode', both crowd pleasers we knew how to perform without really thinking.

But deep down, I knew we had to play this song.

Jessy wasn't here, but perhaps she would watch the stream. Perhaps she would hear it. Perhaps she would know, understand, that I was still thinking about her.

'And we're a go!' hissed the person with the headset.

I blinked. It couldn't have been two minutes already.

'Big smiles, lyrics are on the prompter, you'll smash it!' whispered Derek with two big thumbs up. 'Go get 'em!'

Ben snorted, but he pasted on a smile and stepped around the corner as a huge cheer erupted from the audience.

This is it.

I followed him, the familiar routine sinking in with each step I took on to the stage. For a moment, all thoughts fled my mind. The crowd was huge – not stadium big, but sizeable enough to still feel daunting. The microphone was waiting for me, there in the middle of the stage, and there was a comfort in slipping into the old habit of stepping towards it and smiling.

Even if the smile wasn't for them.

'This is a song,' I said quietly, my voice echoing into the large space as Matt moved his mic closer to where he stood by the electric keyboard, 'for a woman who never asked for a song . . . but inspired one anyway.'

Ben gave us the beat and we launched into what I had called 'Butterflies' in my head.

The chords progressed, the music swelled, and I opened my mouth, the words pouring out as effortlessly as breathing.

'Butterflies, it was butterflies the moment I first saw you –'

And that was when I looked down at the crowd and saw Jessy seated in the front row.

TWENTY-FOUR

All I ask is the world, and I would give it to you if I could hold in my hand everything you give me . . .
– from 'The World', by These Exiles

THIS WAS A MISTAKE.

I knew it was.

But then, I had known this was a mistake right from the start.

I should never have signed that contract. I should never have joined Butterflies when Laura asked.

But I had, and I did . . . and now I was front row at the Songwriter Awards, staring up at the most handsome man I had ever known, listening to a song I was almost certain had been written about me.

'*Coffee cup, looking up, seeing the world change in your eyes . . .*'

Oh, this was a mistake.

And it was all Laura's fault.

'Just this one teeny tiny favour!' she had wheedled, turning up at my hotel suite with Anna, a look of steely determination and a dress that was far too short.

'It was *just one favour* last time,' I'd pointed out hotly, 'and look where it got me!'

Absolutely not.

It was never that simple.

'Look, I spoke with Derek –'

'Why?' I groaned. 'Come on, Laura, like I need –'

'And he says that Patrick is moping.'

Anna was grinning, lounging elegantly, as she always managed to do, on the sofa.

I blinked. 'Moping?'

Laura didn't need to say any more. I could see it in the twinkle in her eyes through her glasses, the brightness of her smile, the way she wouldn't lean back in the armchair. 'Moping.'

I groaned.

It shouldn't mean anything. I had sworn I was going to move on from it – that I wouldn't look back. But that was harder said than done. Everywhere I went, every time I closed my eyes, I was reminded of Patrick. Of us.

I missed him. I could admit it, at least in the privacy of my own mind.

And the longer I went without seeing him, the more my anger faded. Sure, I had been less than impressed with the way he had handled things. But deep down, I understood why he'd reacted like that. His words had hurt, but I could only imagine the hurt he had felt, seeing those articles for the first time. I had finally taken a look at them myself and could admit they painted a damning picture.

I looked back at the pleading faces of my best friend and my twin.

'Jessy, it's just one night –' Laura started.

I knew exactly what she was talking about: the Songwriter Awards.

'He probably doesn't even want me there!' I tried to argue. Surely he'd moved on by now. An actress, a singer, someone who knew how his world worked.

'It's just one night.' Anna picked up the refrain. 'And I don't want to get serious about it, but you kind of have to go. Like, contractually.'

They were up to something. I could tell by the guilty glances Laura kept sneaking Anna. 'But you said –'

'I said I'd look at the contract, and I said I'd speak to Derek,' Anna said firmly. 'And I did. And he pointed out that the break clause holds a significant financial penalty –'

I groaned and dropped on to the sofa. 'So, I don't have a choice. I have to go to this damned awards show?'

Anna's smile had been a little too sly. 'Yep.'

And that was how I'd ended up here, wearing another one of Anna's dresses – which was again way, way too short – sitting in the front row of an awards show where I absolutely did not belong, looking up at the guy I was still pretty sure I was in love with.

Perhaps he won't see me.

There were loads of people in the crowd. Surely, he couldn't see all our faces.

A stupid thought. The instant it flashed across my mind, Patrick's gaze dropped and met mine.

'And as you let me into your world, I realized it was you . . .'

I had hoped I'd feel . . . nothing, when I saw him again. Relief, maybe, that I was free of him. Delight, perhaps, that there was a new These Exiles song. Maybe a little bittersweetness about what could have been . . . But not this.

Not this overwhelming urge to be close to him.

Not this painful, searing hope that he was happy to see me.

Not this aching affection that didn't have anywhere to go. I loved him.

And I hated that.

'Central sun, letting none into your orbit – until me . . .'

This was completely insane – the song was about me. Wasn't it? How could it be about anyone else?

The widescreens to the right and left of the stage showed the camera carefully pan over to Patrick, his face literally feet high so that those at the back could see him.

Suddenly the shot changed and now the camera was focused on me, and there was *my* face, ten feet tall, being livestreamed to millions –

Great.

'And I'd rather argue with you than receive anyone's smiles, caffeine high, you're my sky, flying with you . . .'

My stomach jolted. This was insane. At this point, there were too many coincidences for this song not to be about me. As my thoughts raced, I had to focus all my efforts on keeping my face calm.

What was I supposed to do? *Should I smile? Is that weird?*

No, no smiling. We were no longer together and my heart hurt. Any attempt at a smile would surely be a pale imitation of the real thing. But the song was good, it was so good, lyrics that poured into my heart and awakened the feelings I'd tried to kill off every day that we'd been apart.

'Oh my God, it's you!'

I smiled awkwardly at the woman seated beside me. 'Hi.'

'You're Jessy Donovan!' she whispered over the music as Patrick continued to sing. 'Did you see the article?'

Really? Was she seriously asking me that? 'Yeah, I –'

'I was so glad to hear that you weren't cheating on

Patrick,' she said warmly, as though we knew each other. 'It was great of your company to come out and state that you were meeting all those guys for work! Such nasty things, those gossip sites, I don't know where they get off.'

They . . . they what?

'You've got to go up there!'

I grasped the arms of my seat. 'Oh, no, I don't think –'

'Yeah, you've got to go up there!' The man seated on my other side pushed my shoulder forward as he hissed, 'He's singing about you, isn't he?'

I turned my head slowly and met Patrick's gaze. His eyes were warm and still trained on me. I was starting to feel like this whole performance was for me.

'Ink my soul upon your heart if you love me too . . .'

'I'm not saying it's love, but I can't call it anything else, calm my fears, love my tears, my body burning for yours . . .'

This was a dream. It had to be.

'And when we take over the world, and we will, carve your joy, fuck the ploy, contract over . . .'

This was not the sort of thing that happened to me.

There he was.

Patrick.

'You're my anchor, and yet I'll let you fly high, little bird . . .'

I smiled at the memory of our recklessness. Getting those tattoos was absolutely wild – every time I looked at my seagull, I saw Patrick's smile as he held my hand.

'– and if you take this leap of faith as I abseil down your heart –'

I couldn't help but laugh at that.

'And if all I have to do is put away my fears –' Patrick sang, looking deep into my eyes, as though the whole world had stopped existing – *'I need you to know your name is music to my ears.'*

Oh my God.

The song came to an end with cheers and celebrations, and I couldn't tell if the pounding in my ears was from the crowd or from the sound of my racing heart.

He had actually done it. He'd written a song for me.

'Ms Donovan?'

I blinked. I hadn't noticed the woman all in black and wearing a headset approach me, but she glanced down at her tablet then back to me with a sharp nod.

'You are Ms Donovan, correct?'

'Yeah – yes, I'm –'

'This way, please,' she said, gesturing to the left.

Before I knew what I was doing I was on my feet, and the crowd was muttering, my face still being blasted on to the screens. For a second, I panicked, thinking I was being pulled on to stage. But that didn't make sense. The band had already gone backstage.

'I was told to bring you this way,' the stagehand said, gesturing to our left. 'Come on, we don't have much left of the ad break!'

So it was in a kind of daze that I allowed myself to be pulled forward, my ears almost ready to burst at the screams of the crowd. I could hardly think as I staggered forward, head spinning, the gazes of a thousand people staring –

I stepped to the left and halted at a door that the stagehand had just opened. Inside was some sort of dressing room, though it was mostly empty. There was also a screen. A screen showing a replay of Patrick singing– or maybe it was one of those delayed livestreamed things, so they could cut out the swearing?

Whatever it was, my ex-boyfriend-not-boyfriend, famed celebrity and musician, had sung a song all about me to the world.

This could not be happening.

'I'll leave you here,' said the stagehand, closing the door behind her before I could say anything.

And so I did the only thing I could. I turned to look at the images of Patrick and the rest of the band bowing on the screen.

It was impossible to stay away from him; the draw that pulled me towards him was magnetic. The crowd was going wild, and still all I could do was stare at Patrick.

'And that was These Exiles,' said the awards host as she stepped dazzlingly back on to the stage, the camera immediately panning away from Patrick. 'Now, the next award was hotly contested last year and has proven to be just as competitive today. The nominees for the –'

'Jessy.'

I gasped.

The door had opened and there stood Patrick.

And the rest of These Exiles behind him.

'Great song, mate,' Matt said, clapping Patrick on the back as I tried not to be overwhelmed by being this close to the entire band.

I mean, I knew Patrick. And the rest of them . . . were just people.

People who were world famous.

'We're heading backstage to the green room,' Wes was yelling into Patrick's ear in the doorway as a singer started to croon back on stage, their voice carrying all the way out to us. 'Derek said to take your time.'

'Great, thanks,' Patrick said, as he stepped fully through the door and took me in for the first time.

I could have tried to leave, but what was the point? I was

done attempting to resist this man. Done pretending I didn't miss him terribly.

'I am so sorry,' Patrick said quietly, closing the door and leaning against it. 'I didn't know you were going to be here tonight.'

My heart sank, but only a little. What I'd seen out there, in his eyes, was enough to convince me Patrick still cared for me. 'And did that make it . . . what you sang . . . would me not being here have made it less true?'

Patrick shook his head slowly, a flicker of vulnerability in his eyes. 'No. No, it was all true. It's all true, Jessy. God, I am so, so sorry for how I behaved. For how I spoke about your mum . . .'

I swallowed. 'I won't lie, you hurt me. Like, really bad.'

'I'm sorry.'

I could tell he was – that hurting me had hurt him just as keenly. 'Laura and Anna are really pissed at you.'

Patrick winced. 'Fair. They did warn me never to hurt you. Look, there's – there's no excuse for what I said.'

God, there was nothing I wanted more than to launch myself into his arms – but I couldn't do it. Not yet. I needed to know he was more than just sorry. I needed to be sure he would never treat me like that again.

I was worth that.

Patrick took a deep, steadying breath. 'I totally understand if you don't want to – I mean, if this is over. If you've moved on. You do deserve better, and if you choose to end this for good . . . I mean, I get it. But you should know, if there's even a tiny part of you that wants to try again . . . to make this work, make this real –'

My heart was thundering, my fingertips pressed into my palms, and I was so desperate for him to keep going.

I wanted him. But I had to protect myself.

Patrick's smile was steady, his voice certain. 'I'll never behave like that again. I'll never turn on you like that. I'll always ask for your side of the story – because I trust you, Jessy.'

And that was all I needed to hear.

I closed the distance between us in seconds, kissing him and almost whimpering in relief.

This was where I belonged: in Patrick's arms. I never wanted to be parted from him again.

Patrick clung on to me just as tightly, as though he was scared I would disappear if he wasn't holding me.

The kiss deepened: pleasure poured through me, sparks of bliss tingling across my body, and I had the vague thought that – if we weren't careful – Anna's borrowed outfit was going to live up to its name as 'the fuck-me dress'.

Patrick broke the kiss. 'I'm so sorry, I'm such a dick –'

'You are a dick,' I said with a nod. His face was an absolute picture, and I had to laugh. 'What, you think I was going to disagree? Nope, you've still got some making up to do before I let you forget it.'

I wouldn't really hold it over him. But he didn't need to know that.

Patrick let out a breathy laugh. 'I was a complete jerk,' he said fiercely, not letting go of me as he stared deep into my eyes. 'Just because I've been messed about in the past, that doesn't mean – you are *you*. You're Jessy. You're not anyone else.'

A smile slid across my face. 'Yeah, I know.'

'But it took me too long to get it, and I'm sorry,' Patrick said earnestly, his eyes bright.

I knew that. He'd told me numerous times already. But more importantly, I could see it in his face, the genuine regret.

'I know.' I smiled simply.

Patrick kissed me hard, and I moaned. My fingers itched to pull his hair and take the kiss deeper, but I tried to remember we were in public – in a room anyone could walk into at any moment.

'And I won't interfere,' Patrick said quietly, nuzzling at my collarbone with his nose. 'With your job – your work, I mean – you can meet a thousand guys, or girls, for whatever –'

'You don't need to worry about that,' I interrupted, trying not to laugh. 'Patrick –'

'I mean it, I trust you. I won't get in the way of you doing what your boss needs you to do,' he said resolutely, his hands gently sliding down my waist to cup my bum.

My grin was wide as I said, 'I think you'll find that pretty unnecessary. Maria is a relatively easy-going boss.'

There it was – the frown of absolutely adorable confusion. 'I thought – Karun –'

'Yeah, so I got fired from that place,' I said lightly.

The look of horror that tracked across Patrick's face was almost exactly the same one I'd seen on my sister's. 'What? Are you OK?'

Warmth suffused me.

Not 'What did you do?' or 'What are you going to do?' or even 'How much money do you have saved?'

Nothing practical.

Just a check to see if I was OK.

I love this man.

'I'm fine. Like, weirdly fine,' I said with another laugh that eased the concern on his face. 'I thought I'd be devastated, but . . . yeah. It's OK.'

Patrick's hazel eyes still had a tinge of worry to them. 'And you're going to be OK? With rent and everything?'

'I've got a temp job at Maria's,' I said softly. 'All that coffee knowledge is finally coming in handy.'

He smiled then, a true smile that warmed me up, inside and out. But when Patrick spoke again, his voice was ... not nervous, but something like it. 'Look ... neither of us expected to meet this way, or date this way –'

'We certainly did not.' I grinned, my stomach lurching. '*Famous celebrity meets failed finance girly.* Not a romance you'd expect, am I right?'

'Jessy,' he chided gently.

'Patrick.' I laughed.

He smiled at me indulgently, before continuing. 'The contract is up. We've fulfilled all the requirements.'

A knot twisted in my throat.

It was. I mean, we had.

'And now it's up, I want to take you out. You and me.' Patrick lifted a hand to caress my cheek. 'Just us. Not because of a contract, or an app, or a publicity stunt. I don't want to tell Derek –'

'Or Laura,' I said. 'Or Anna.'

Though how I was going to keep it from them, I didn't know.

'Or anyone.' He nodded. 'Because I'm pretty sure I really, really like you. Like, I'm falling in love with you.'

I laughed, equally shocked and delighted, as I stared up into the handsome face, all chiselled jaw and honesty. 'Yeah?'

'Yep. Before I even knew it, I was in too deep,' Patrick confessed with a rueful look.

I arched an eyebrow. 'You know, that's not a bad lyric.'

'Jessy, I'm pouring my heart out here –'

'Good. Because . . .' I took a deep breath. 'Because I have a horrible feeling that I really, really like you too, Patrick. Maybe even love you too – and I want to date you. For reals.'

His laughter shook through me. 'For reals?'

'You know what I mean!'

Our laughter filled the small dressing room, and I knew I never wanted to leave it. In here, we were just Patrick and Jessy. It was out there, in the outside world, that we always needed to be something else. Something bigger.

'So . . .' Patrick looked at me. 'For two people who have been famously in love, it starts all over again. What are we going to do now?'

I shrugged. 'I'm not sure. I want to find some purpose for myself. Something that means something. And I don't know what that looks like yet,' I admitted, smiling up at the man I loved. 'But I know I want to do it with you.'

His smile warmed every inch of me. 'Well, while you think about working all that out . . . what about a date? Will Maria let you have the time off work?'

Time off work? What on earth was he talking about? 'Why would Maria care what I do in the evenings – the cafe closes at four.'

I should have guessed he had something up his sleeve by the teasing grin.

'Well,' Patrick said coyly, 'the kind of place I had in mind would mean taking a little more than an evening off.' He paused, keeping me in suspense.

I dug my elbow into him and he immediately surrendered.

'OK, OK! I was thinking, if you wanted to . . . you might come with us.'

I blinked, confused. 'Us?'

His nod was slow, his gaze curious. 'On the Southeast Asia tour.'

All the breath was pulled from my body. 'Wh-What?'

No. No, he can't have said that. He doesn't mean –

'Like I said, you might need a little more than an evening off for that,' Patrick teased, kissing me again. 'But if you don't want to –'

'*Don't want to?* Don't want to what, exactly? Travel the world with an internationally famous band? Or travel with my super-hot, talented boyfriend?' I said with one eyebrow raised.

A flash of joy flickered over Patrick's face before he leaned in for another passionate kiss.

Hmm. I could get used to this.

As the kiss got more and more heated, Patrick's hands travelled from my waist down to the hem of my dress, dragging it up.

'Patrick!'

'What? You don't want –'

'I didn't say that,' I said, cheeks burning. 'But what if someone –'

'No one is going to come in here. This is your life now.' Patrick's gorgeous expression was far too wicked. 'Backstage kisses, travelling the world, coffee brought to you in bed – and I'll do anything you want, Jessy. Anything.'

Anything?

I tried not to smile. 'Anything?'

He pressed a kiss on my collarbone. 'Anything.'

'In that case, I would like a – a private rendition of my song,' I gasped, just about managing to speak as his kisses burned across my skin.

Patrick chuckled as he nuzzled my neck. 'Is that all?'

'Oh, and you should be naked while you sing it,' I managed, clinging on to his shoulders as my knees trembled with building need.

'Will you be naked too?' he asked, lifting his head to meet my gaze.

I swallowed a moan and raised a teasing eyebrow instead. 'Maybe.'

Patrick's grin warmed me to my toes. 'Well, what are we waiting for?'

God, I really hope no one walks in on us . . .

ACKNOWLEDGMENTS

This book wouldn't exist without a great number of people. Anyone missed from the list is entirely my error, as are any mistakes that you find in this book (please don't look too hard).

Mary and Gordon Murdoch
My wonderful husband
Awo Ibrahim
Natalia Lucas and the UA Team
Jess Dunne
Hannah Sandford
Debs Warner
Caroline Curtis
Lauren Maxwell
Sofia Miller Salazar
Naomi Green
Jess Mackay
Maya St. Pierre
Six Red Marbles

IF YOU WANT TO CATCH THE VIBE OF
THESE EXILES,
HAVE A LISTEN TO THESE SONGS!

REIN ME IN
BY SAM FENDER

A COUPLE MINUTES
BY OLIVIA DEAN

ABOUT YOU
BY THE 1975

SPRING INTO SUMMER
BY LIZZY MCALPINE

ORDINARY
BY ALEX WARREN

ALL I ASK
BY RACHEL CHINOURIRI

TEXAS SUN
BY KHRUANGBIN AND LEON BRIDGES

CRYING LAUGHING LOVING LYING
BY LABI SIFFRE

IN MY LIFE
BY THE BEATLES

DREAMS
BY FLEETWOOD MAC

LINGER
BY THE CRANBERRIES

FAST CAR
BY TRACY CHAPMAN

DON'T THINK TWICE, IT'S ALL RIGHT
BY BOB DYLAN

RESENTMENT
BY BEYONCÉ

LOOK OUT FOR THE NEXT BOOK IN THE BUTTERFLIES SERIES

COMING SOON!

About the author

Hello! I'm a Brit writing happily ever afters with heart and humour. Under a different pen name, I'm a *USA Today* bestselling author with over 50 books published. I live with my darling and supportive husband, a neighbourhood cat that inexplicably doesn't want to make friends, and more cheese than is good for me.